PRAISE
THE CADDIE WHO WON THE MASTERS

"John Coyne has done it again . . . a riveting golf story at
a world famous venue, with a keen sense of accuracy and
history woven into the details. A must read for anyone who
loves the game of golf."

—Todd D. Bramson, Augusta National c addie

"I am impressed with Coyne's ability to clearly depict the nuances
that make Augusta National such a different shrine. His descrip-
tion of situations—the unique, the weird and the nearly unbelievable—mirrors many I have seen over the years. Some rarely seen."

—John Derr, Award-winning golf journalist and
CBS-TV announcer who covered 62 Masters

"John Coyne has shown us he not only knows golf history and
Augusta National but more importantly he is a Master writer."

—Ron "G-Man" Gerrard, sports broadcaster and
co-host of the webcast, On The Fringe

"John Coyne knows golf and golf history, and he understands
the intricate workings of the human heart. Anyone who loves golf
—and many readers who don't—will appreciate his skill and
be happily drawn into this fine story."

—Roland Merullo, author of *Golfing with God*

"The book was amazing. I as though I was walking down Magnolia Lane and spending the night in the Crows Nest. Reading
the book took me back to my visits to the Augusta National
and the Masters over the last 52 years."

—Fred Daitch, owner of Intl. Uniform, Inc., Augusta

THE CADDIE WHO
WON THE MASTERS

JOHN COYNE

A PEACE CORPS WRITERS BOOK

A PEACE CORPS WRITERS BOOK.
An imprint of Peace Corps Worldwide.

THE CADDIE WHO WON THE MASTERS. Copyright © 2011 by John Coyne.

Library of Congress Control Number: 2011923676

ISBN-13: 978-1-935925-04-0
ISBN-10: 1-935-92504-0

First Peace Corps Writers Edition, March 2011

For John Kerwin

A PLAYER NEVER WINS THE MASTERS on his own, as those of us who follow golf know well enough. But in all honesty, when I look back at my week in Georgia, I don't know which one of those golfing legends helped me the most. Of course, my caddie played a part—that young kid who showed up out of nowhere to carry my bag. And certainly Kerry had more than her share of influence on how it all turned out.

Golf writers pointed to what occurred on the third round at Amen Corner, saying that was the turning point. Yet the truth is, so much more had happened to me before that afternoon out there at the far end of Augusta National that I can't say my eagle on 15 was the decisive moment. Even though it was there—on the back side in the third round—were my game turned around in the fading sunlight of moving day, as Saturdays on tour are called, and I came into contention.

In retrospect I know that what transpired up in the Crow's Nest of the clubhouse before the tournament was more important than any shot I made at Augusta National.

So when I put into place the bits and pieces of my time in Georgia, as if they were some sort of mythological mystery, all I can say for certain is that my life began to subtly shift the moment I stepped off the Washington Avenue bus at the front gate of Augusta National Golf Club on the Sunday afternoon before the opening round. I realize now I wasn't in control of my own destiny that week, but, of course, others who have played the Masters have also said as much.

I do know that on that first day I looked more like a forty-year-old caddie than a player, standing there at the bus stop with a suitcase in one hand and my clubs slung over my shoulder. I was a wrinkled, unshaven mess, wearing baggy pants, beat-up Nikes and a golf cap jerked down on my uncombed, thick, salt-and-pepper hair. Anyone who was watching—though no one was—would've taken me for one of those old-time loopers who travel from club to club hoping to grab a bag and earn a few bucks to buy another bottle of booze. What separated me from the caddie yard were my sticks. One glance in my bag would have told any player that even if I wasn't first class, at least the clubs were.

I stepped across the wide street and said hello to the uniformed Securitas guards standing in front of the white-brick gatehouse. I told them my name—Timothy Jack Alexander—and that I had come to play.

Cars filled with players, officials, reporters, and members of Augusta National were slipping by me at the entrance. The cars slowed, the people inside presented credentials, then they were waved ahead. The sleek automobiles rode smoothly under the speckled sunlight filtering through the canopy of those ancient magnolia trees that stretch from the gates up the famous drive to the white-columned plantation manor house.

I showed the guard my invitation. Every year, the winner of the U.S. Mid-Amateur is offered a chance to play in the Masters, and having won the tournament, this was my year. The letter was signed by Billy Payne himself, the chairman of Augusta National.

Next the guard wanted me to prove that I was really Timothy Jack Alexander. I showed him my Southern Illinois University faculty ID, with the mug shot of me looking as if I had just played thirty-six holes on a hot August afternoon.

"Would you like a lift to the clubhouse, sir?" he offered, comprehending now that I wasn't a crazy old guy trying to crash the gates.

I shook my head, saying I wanted to walk onto the famous Augusta golf course. It was for sentimental reasons, I explained, but still the guard frowned. Who'd ever heard of a Masters qualifier wanting to walk down Magnolia Lane?

I thanked the guard, swung my bag onto my shouder and, on foot, followed the limousines through the iron gates of Augusta National, the citadel of golf in America. I knew it was the home of legends. What I never dreamed was what the legends would mean to me.

Sunday

1

A SLIP OF PAPER moved across the small coffee table in the sitting room of the Crow's Nest, stirred perhaps by a puff of breeze.

I was just settling into one of the cell-like rooms that Augusta reserves for its amateurs. What is called the Crow's Nest and consists of four partially-enclosed sleeping spaces arranged around a sitting room, all tucked into the third-floor attic of the Manor Clubhouse, the first cement house to be constructed in the South. Originally built as a plantation mansion in 1854, it has been the famed clubhouse of Augusta National since 1931.

I had followed one of the club's employees up a narrow steep staircase to the attic rooms. He wanted to carry both my suitcase and my clubs, but he was an older guy and I told him no. I was superstitious about my sticks, I said, and only I could carry them. He nodded knowingly. He had been around golf long enough to understand how ritualistic players can be.

He chatted his way up the stairs, telling me that only amateurs stayed in the Crow's Nest, located under the windowed cupola and originally built so the master of the plantation could overlook the indigo fields and see if his slaves were at work.

Then he added with pride, "Tiger Woods, he stayed here in '95 when he first came to the Masters. He was an amateur then, like yourself, sir, and I showed him to this Crow's Nest."

He pulled himself up straight and asked if there was anything more I might need.

I shook my head, and thanked him for his help.

"My pleasure, sir. My pleasure. If you need anything, you just ask for Lightnin' and I'll be with you." He kept smiling. Then his eye caught the sheet of stationery.

He reached down and picked up the note, saying, "This might be for you, sir."

It was a folded piece of Augusta National Golf Club-crested stationery with my name scribbled on the outside. My immediate guess was that, Billy Payne, had sent a note to welcome me, and also to remind me that I had agreed to speak at the amateur dinner on Wednesday night.

"It looks like I'm first to arrive, Lightnin'," I went on, happy to have any kind of pleasant conversation, if only with a club employee. I had been traveling all day from Carbondale and the little exchange was enough to make me realize how lonely I was, and how far from Illinois, far from Kerry and home.

"Oh, they'll be comin' along soon enough, I'd expect." Lightnin' kept smiling, his weathered, dark-skinned face showing more hard times than years. "All the young ones, we get them up here in the Nest," he remarked.

"Well, I don't qualify there," I answered, grinning. "As being young, that is. I won the U.S. Mid-Amateur, and only old guys are allowed in that tournament."

Lightnin' nodded, as if he understood which championship I meant, and that I wasn't another one of the college champs who camped out in the Crow's Nest during tournament week.

"Well, sir, you may not be the youngest, but you're also not the oldest amateur to tee it up for the Masters," he said companionably.

"That would be George Zahringer," I answered, remembering my Augusta history.

He shook his gray head. "No, sir. That would be our own Mr. Bobby Jones." I could hear the pride in his voice.

"Well, right you are." I let the man have his moment, but the fact was, Jones had stopped playing the Masters in '48, when he was only forty-five. Zahringer was in his fifties when he played. I had looked up the dates, hoping I might be the oldest amateur, but Zahringer had me beat by several years.

"Did you ever meet Bobby Jones?" I asked, guessing he had. I was prepared for every employee at Augusta to have a Jones story, and I wanted to hear them all.

"Mr. Jones and Mr. Roberts, they hired me when I wasn't much more than twelve years young. They put me in the kitchen cleaning pots. It was Mr. Roberts, he's the one who called me Lightnin' because of how fast I could clean a metal pot."

"And you've been at Augusta ever since?" I asked, knowing the answer. The stories of the black employees at Augusta National were legendary. They came as poor kids to caddie or to work the grounds and ended up in the big clubhouse as waiters and cooks and locker room attendants.

"Yes, sir, sixty-seven years come this September. Only job I had but in the army. And I cleaned pots in the army, too," he added, chuckling.

"That's some career, Lightnin'," I said. "Something to be proud of."

I tapped the note against my fingers, anxious to read it, but

I didn't want to be rude. If it had been from Kerry, I knew the front office would have told me when I registered.

"It's the Lord who has shined his light on me," Lightnin' replied. Then, back to business, he gestured towards the narrow partitions and said that as the first to arrive, I could take any bed I wished.

I opened one of the half-louvered doors and glanced in. There was nothing more than a single bed and, beside it, a table with a small lamp. I felt a swift pang of recognition. It was like my bed in Carbondale, the little cot where I'd been sleeping since Kerry had come home the last time from the hospital in St. Louis.

I had assumed I would be skipping the tournament. It was Kerry who had insisted I go. She had had another operation for her cancer and while we were both worried about what was next, she told me I had to play. I owed myself this trip to the Masters, she said. I owed her.

Not able to wait any longer, I glanced down at the note in my hands. My name had been hastily scribbled in pencil by someone with poor penmanship. I flipped it open. The message was one line: "Meet me at Amen Corner this afternoon." No signature.

Amen Corner is famous at Augusta National, and famous to anyone who follows golf. A stretch of three holes-11,12,13-on the back side, far away from the clubhouse, it was named by a New Yorker sportswriter, Herbert Warren Wind. He took it from the spiritual "Shouting at Amen Corner" to sum up what golfers felt like when they managed to play safely through that long par 4, tight par 3, and short dogleg-left par 5, made especially dangerous by Rae's Creek, which crossed the fairway twice,

I looked at Lightnin' and asked if he knew who had left me the note.

He shook his head. "Don't know who could've done it, sir. No one's been up to the Crow's Nest all morning."

"Where is it?" I asked.

"Where's what, sir?"

"Amen Corner."

He smiled, amused perhaps by my ignorance. "Why, everyone knows where Amen Corner is, sir." He spoke nicely, as if dealing with a slightly dim-witted stranger.

"Point me in the right direction and I'll find it," I answered. "I'll just walk the fairway until I reach the back side."

"Ain't nobody out there now, sir," he said, puzzled by my determination to find the spot.

"Well, whoever left me this told me to meet him there." I handed Lightnin' the creamy, embossed slip of paper and nodded that he should read the note.

Lightnin' held the paper out at arm's length, staring at the spidery penciled script. Perhaps it was my imagination—perhaps it was because I had been traveling all day—but I thought I saw his hand tremble. He thrust the note back at me, shaking his head, moving quickly toward the dormitory door. "If there's nothing else, sir," he said, and then, without waiting for an answer, he was out of the Crow's Nest and down the steps, moving like lightning.

2

I GLANCED AGAIN at the one-line note. "Meet me at Amen Corner this afternoon."

The way Lightnin' had taken off, something had obviously frightened him. I could only guess he'd recognized the scribbled handwriting. It had to be a member or employee of Augusta National. No one else could have gotten into the Crow's Nest. But who would care that I had arrived? And why would he or she want to see me out on the course? Who?

I chose one of the cubicles and tossed the note on the narrow bed, too tired to worry about it now. I'd take a shower and a nap, and after that, if it was still light enough, I'd walk out to Amen Corner. But before I did anything, I needed to call home and tell Kerry I had arrived safely. More important, I needed to hear her voice.

I sat down on the bed and took out my phone. Augusta National didn't permit cell phones anywhere on the grounds. The club was for golf, nothing else, but I hoped I was okay using one inside the clubhouse.

I hit the redial button and listened as the tiny gadget entered our home phone number. What an amazing age of miniature marvels, yet even with all this new technology they still couldn't cure Kerry.

"Hello, darling!"

Even from six hundred miles away her voice was strong and sharp and eager to speak.

"Hi, honey, I've arrived!" I smiled and exclaimed, "In the Crow's Nest!" I sounded, I guessed, like a kid at camp, happy to be calling home.

I swung around and stretched out on the bed. Hearing Kerry's voice made me feel immensely better. I kept grinning into the tiny cell phone.

"Tell me everything," she said at once. "What's it like? Have you seen anyone famous? Is Tiger there?"

I kept smiling, enjoying her enthusiasm. Now I just wanted to please her with stories about Augusta. I told her about Lightnin' and the note, and how it had frightened the old man.

"Oh, dear," she said. "What was that about?"

"I haven't the foggiest. I need to take a shower, clean myself up. Then I might walk out to Amen Corner."

"Be careful, okay?"

"Kerry, it's Augusta National. Nothing is going to happen to me. Ike came here when he was president."

"Ike had the Secret Service."

"I'll be careful," I agreed. "Did you have it done?" I asked next, talking around the topic.

"Yep, no big deal. I was in and out of Dr. Kestin's office in minutes. Very routine."

"Great." I sighed into the phone.

"Now go see who wants you," she said at once, changing the topic.

"I love you," I whispered.

"I love you, too, and I don't want you to worry about me. Peggy is here," she said, mentioning our youngest child. "Remember, this is your week. Play your heart out and don't think about me. It's the Masters," she added, as she had been saying since the invitation arrived.

"I wish you were with me, that's all."

"I wish I were too, honey. Now go play your heart out."

That was her mantra. She had been saying it since I qualified. She wasn't going to let her cancer stop me from teeing it up at Augusta National.

"Okay," I whispered. "I'll play my heart out."

"And call me later."

"Of course."

"And work on your putting."

"Always."

"You win the Masters on the greens," she added, as if she had been playing Augusta National all her life, as if she even played the game.

"I'm not going to win, Kerry. I'm lucky to be here."

"You will win. Call me later." On those instructions, she hung off.

I didn't move. I placed the phone carefully on my chest and closed my eyes, overwhelmingly exhausted from the trip, from the weight of Kerry's illness, from my own worries about making a fool of myself playing in the Masters. I was totally out of my league. My winning the Mid-Amateur had been a fluke. It was match play and I was better at match than medal. Playing medal you can't overcome bad shots or hide your bad holes.

I glanced at my watch. It was already close to five o'clock.

Time to shower if I wanted to walk out to Amen Corner before dark. I'd take a couple of balls and my putter and see what the greens were like. Kerry was right—winning the Masters was all about putting.

3

IN THE PRO SHOP, an assistant was worried about me. The players were finished for the day, the course was empty, and he wanted to send a caddie with me to make sure I didn't get lost among the dogwoods. After all, he said, Amen Corner was as far away from the clubhouse as anyone could get and still be on Augusta National. I told him I'd be fine, all I needed were directions, which he provided. I thanked him, hooked my Ping putter under my arm, and headed off, stepping for the first time onto Augusta's rye-green fairway.

There is nothing more magical for any golfer than to be on a course at twilight, alone with the strange geography of holes cut through groves of pines and dogwoods, among azaleas and redbuds, jasmine and camellias, and the evening mist. I've never met anyone who didn't feel at peace on a golf course, walking from fairway to fairway.

It's a place in many ways more sacred than a church. And if

any golf course could be a church, then Augusta National was a cathedral.

Augusta National Golf Club was originally a 365-acre indigo plantation. By 1857 it had become a plant nursery. At the height of the Depression the property was purchased by Bobby Jones, the brilliant amateur, and a friend of his named Clifford Roberts. Together they hired a Scottish golf architect, Alister MacKenzie, to design a course. There were American architects they could have hired, but Bobby Jones didn't want an American course—he felt they were too prescriptive. He wanted MacKenzie to design a golf course where every hole presented a problem or a puzzle for players.

Bobby Jones also wanted a course like St. Andrews in Scotland, with wide fairways, undulating greens, and bunkers that came into play only if a shot was mishit. He wanted each hole to look wide-open from the tee, and playable for any high handicapper, a hole that was a hard par and a difficult birdie.

Jones also borrowed ideas from Sara Bay in Sarasota, Florida, a course built by the American golf architect, Donald Ross, with elevated greens that required-pinpoint approach shots on the slopes and crowns.

Together, Jones and MacKenzie created what today is called the Doctrine of Deception. Rather than holes where it seems clear what a player needs to do, they built holes where golfers think they have two or three chances, and therefore try a shot that is above their ability. And that's why the Masters Tournament is so thrilling. The winner is always the player who can pull off the impossible shot. And playing the impossible shot is the only way to win a green jacket at the Masters.

I walked out to the par-5 13 hole on the back side. Then, reaching the green, I crossed over a tributary of Rae's Creek and headed up the fairway, following the dogleg that boomeranged around an avenue of azaleas stretching to the tee five hundred yards away. Walking a golf course in reverse was how I prepared for a tournament. Instead of looking over a hole from the vantage point of the tee, I liked to see it the other way, from the green back to the tee. It took away my fear of playing a new course. Arnold Palmer, I had read somewhere, also believed that the best way to understand a golf hole was to mentally play it backwards. If the pin is cut on the left side, a player would want to come into the hole from the right side, so back on the tee, he'd set up on the left side and hit across the fairway to have a better angle at the green for the second shot.

When I reached the tee box at 13, I glanced around, looking for whoever had written the note. But seeing no one, I studied the tee. In 2002 the club had bought a wedge of land from the neighboring Augusta Country Club, just so they could add thirty yards of length to the par 5. It was Augusta National's first attempt to make their course Tiger-proof. It failed.

I stood in the shade of the pines and looked across Rae's Creek at 12, then up to the stretch of empty viewing stands behind the tee. I walked down the slope to the twelfth green and dropped the three balls I was carrying. If nothing else, I could practice my putting on this dangerous par 3.

The 12 is the heart and soul of Augusta National, shaded all day by dogwoods and pines. In the winter and early spring there is always an early-morning frost at that low corner of the course. A dozen years ago an underground heating system of steam pipes was installed by the club to keep the green at a constant seventy degrees, warm enough to kill the frost and save the green from damage.

Once the Masters began, I knew, the pin would be cut in the front half, nearer Rae's Creek. As I practiced putting, I reminded myself that I wouldn't get my ball close to the flag during the tournament. It was the rare player who could hit it stiff. I needed to learn how to make lag putts just to give myself a chance to save par.

The problem with this green, and all greens at Augusta National, was finding the level spot on the sloping, fast-running surfaces. When Tiger Woods was preparing to play in the Masters for the first time, while still an amateur and a college student, he practiced putting on the Stanford University basketball court to learn how to handle Augusta's slick greens.

I also knew from watching endless Masters Tournaments on television that on the last day the pin was always cut in the back third. I picked a spot on the lower half and hit my three Titleists across the green to gauge the speed, then followed my balls and toed them together to putt uphill, this time to where the pin would be placed for the weekend, if I made the cut. When I looked up, contemplating my shot, I saw him for the first time. He was standing on the top ridge of the green.

He was an elderly man wearing a brown cap and the signature three-brass-button, single-breasted green jacket of Augusta National members. The blazer had the famous Augusta National logo on the left breast pocket, an outline of the United States inside an embroidered circle. In the center of the crest, a yellow flagstick was jammed into the heart of Georgia.

The old man was small and fragile and his fancy Augusta National jacket hung on his thin shoulder. He stood on the back fringe of the hole with his hands in his pockets looking like death warmed over. His wide mouth was turned down as if he disapproved of what I was doing, but I went ahead and putted anyway. It wasn't until I walked up the slope to retrieve my three balls that he spoke.

Speaking slowly, and with just a slight hint of annoyance, he said, "Uh-huh. You know, Frank Stranahan got his invitation taken away in '48 for hitting too many balls in a practice round. He got into a spat with our superintendent."

I toed the balls together, then flipped them up with the back of my putter and grabbed them out of the air, as the pros always do on television. Stepping closer, I answered with a smile, wanting to show the old guy that I, too, knew my Masters history   .

"There's another version of that incident, sir. It seems Stranahan had taken a liking to Clifford Roberts's secretary, which was interfering with Roberts's own interest in the woman, so the club employees made sure Frank wouldn't be around for the tournament."

"Hello," I added nicely and held out my hand. "Tim Alexander."

The man didn't bother to shake my hand. Instead he replied very softly and slowly, as if pulling his words from a long way off, "I've been waiting for you."

"Really?" I kept smiling. "Sorry to have kept you waiting." I had read enough about Augusta National members to know how prickly they were when it came to their own importance at their private club.

He disregarded my apology with a wave, suggesting it had long been his fate to be disappointed by lesser men. He had taken out a leather cigar case and was now fumbling with it. I resisted an urge to reach over and help the old guy. Opening the small box, he retrieved a cigar, then remarked, in the same deliberate manner, "These cigars might kill me, if that were an issue."

But it wasn't cigars that were on his mind, I realized, as he continued with his pronouncements.

"I want an amateur to win this year's Masters," he stated. "In fact, it's imperative. I have made all the necessary arrangements." He stared coldly at me, and added, "I presume you know about Bobby Jones's wish—that an amateur would someday win his tournament?" When I nodded, he went on in his deliberate way, "I presume you're willing to be the first amateur in the history of Augusta National to finally do it?"

"Well, that would be very nice indeed, wouldn't it?" I slipped the three balls into my pocket and started to ease away. Time to leave, I realized. All I needed was to get tangled up with some loony member.

"Uh-huh…. One moment, young man!" Walking carefully on the uneven turf he stepped off the collar of the green and approached me. As he came close, I watched him, thinking, member or not, I should be on guard.

With that, as if reading my thoughts, he pulled a handgun from the inside pocket of the green jacket.

He did not take aim, just cradled the pistol carefully in both of his hands, presenting it as if it were a work of art.

"Do you know what kind of pistol this is?"

I told him I wasn't familiar with handguns, or firearms of any kind, for that matter.

"It's a .38-caliber Smith and Wesson. It's the pistol Clifford Roberts used to kill himself over at Ike's Pond. You know who Clifford Roberts was?" he asked, and before I could reply, he continued, "He founded Augusta with Bob Jones and ran it for over thirty years…until he shot himself in the temple with this pistol back in '77."

It was dark now. I was having some trouble seeing the old man's face. His voice was weak and his diction slow. Each one of his words came out slowly from deep inside him.

Across the pond, a grounds-crew truck came over the rise and around the observation stands behind the twelfth tee. The headlights picked us out standing on the green. I waved to the driver, seizing on his arrival to extricate myself from this weird situation. I said quickly, "It looks like they've sent security to find me."

But when I turned to say goodbye, I saw I was alone on the green. The old man with the Augusta National member's jacket, and the .38-aliber Smith and Wesson, had vanished in the night.

4

THE GROUNDS CREWMAN, a middle-aged guy, gave me a lift to the clubhouse, going back up the rought of 11 and along the edge of the fairway at 10. We tracked through the piney darkness to the building brightly lit up like a southern mansion left over from another age.

As we came up ten fairway I saw there were lights on in the Crow's Nest. I hoped that meant one of the other amateurs had arrived so I could have dinner with someone. The encounter with the old man had creeped me out, as one of my kids might say. I didn't want to eat alone.

The groundsman swung to a stop by the big oak in front of the clubhouse and pointed to where I might enter through a side door. I slipped out of the truck, thanking him for the lift, then turned and asked which one of the cabins to the right of the clubhouse had been Eisenhower's.

"The one with the presidential crest over the front door."

"Were you around when Ike was a member?" I asked.

"Oh, no, sir. I didn't start working here until '75." He was a large man with big hands and a big head, but despite his size he spoke softly, his southern accent spilling over with warmth.

I stared over at Ike's cabin, surprised at how small it actually was, not much larger than our home back in Illinois.

"There's a pond named after him?"

"Yes, sir. On the other side of the clubhouse; it's part of the par-three course. They say Ike went out for a walk one evening and when he returned he told Mr. Roberts he had found a spot where the club could build a fishing pond. Ike liked to fish."

"Is that the same pond where Clifford Roberts committed suicide?"

The big man turned in the truck and pointed toward the end of the clubhouse, explaining, "Mr. Roberts lived in the clubhouse and had just gotten back from seeing doctors in Texas. He was a real sick man. They say that sometime during the night he walked down to the lower end of the pond and shot himself."

"Is he buried here?"

"His ashes are scattered out there." He nodded toward the course, then turned the truck's engine back on and said he had to get back to work. He was done telling the secrets of Augusta to a stranger.

On my way into the clubhouse I spotted Lightnin'. He was leading a young blond kid up the stairs to the Crow's Nest. I stopped on the second floor landing and waited for Lightnin' to come back downstairs. I wanted to speak to him alone.

When he appeared he told me Zack Trout had arrived. I nodded okay, and asked him about Clifford Roberts.

"You knew him?"

"Oh, yessir," he nodded nervously. "Everyone, we all knew Mr. Roberts."

"And he's dead?"

"Oh, yessir, he's passed now. Mr. Roberts, he died over thirty years ago, sir."

"What did he die of?"

"They say he committed suicide, but some of the boys from the caddie yard, they said it wasn't so; they say someone got to him. But you know those boys—they all come out of the Terry, and you had a knifin' over in that ghetto most every night."

"What do the boys say?" I pressed.

"They say, Mr. Roberts, he couldn't have walked from his room to the dam. That's a steep, slick hill down to the pond, and Mr. Roberts, when they found him, he was wearing slippers. And early that evening he had called the front office and said he heard noises outside his room. He had the night watchman load his pistol. He always had himself a pistol in his room."

"A .38 Smith and Wesson."

"That's right!" Lightnin's eyes flashed in his dark face.

"Was he robbed?"

"Fred Bennett, he was our caddie master back then, he said Mr. Roberts had three, four hundred new bills on him, but there wasn't no money in his pockets when they found the body."

"Who left that note for me, Lightnin'?" I asked again.

"I don't know, sir. I swear I don't. I swear on Jesus himself."

"Why did it upset you then?"

We were standing on the landing at the top of the stairs and I'm sure that if I hadn't been blocking the man's escape he would have bolted past me.

"That note you got, that Meet Me at Amen Corner, well it's a handwritin' I recognized from way back."

"From way back?"

"Yessir." He nodded slowly. "From the old days."

I waited. I knew he would tell me, but I had to let him find the courage.

"I seen that handwritin'," he said again. He glanced around once more to make sure we were safely alone, then he leaned closer and whispered, "That's Mr. Roberts' handwritin'."

"That's not possible."

Lightnin' didn't argue.

The two of us stood on the landing, staring at each other, Lightnin' with his watery white eye and his ancient face, the sad countenance of a man who had spent his life in service to others. And me, an over-forty public-course hacker, a college professor unentitled, by income or pedigree, to be inside this citadel of wealth, quizzing an old man about a mysterious death three long decades past.

I thanked Lightnin' and let him go. He shouldn't have to be bothered with someone like me, who, if history was any guide, would miss the cut and be out of Augusta National Golf Club and the Masters after two rounds.

I took the narrow stairs to the Crow's Nest to meet the new arrival, Zack Trout from the University of North Alabama, who had qualified for the Masters by winning the United States Amateur title. He was tall, thin, and blond and looked more like a point-guard for the basketball team than a scratch golfer. He was talking to his mother on his cell phone when I stepped into the cupola. He was telling her that he did remember to bring his blue blazer and school tie for the amateur dinner on Wednesday night.

I nodded hello and went into my bedroom, slipped my putter into the bag, and stood, debating whether to take another shower before dinner. And then I saw the note on the bed. It was written on the same heavy club stationery, in the same spider-script. "Pleasure to meet you, Mr. Alexander."

I stepped back into the sitting room. Zack Trout was off

the phone. I said "hello" and we shook hands and I gestured to the note and asked him if he had seen anyone bring it.

He shook his head. He told me what I already knew, that Lightnin' had just shown him to the dormitory. He looked worried, as if he had somehow let me down by not having an answer. I waved away his concern and congratulated him on winning the U.S. Amateur. He broke into a grin, thrilled that I knew his record. But like a good college professor I had done my research and checked out all the amateurs who had qualified for the Masters, and whom I would be playing against.

I asked if he had dinner plans, and when he shook his head, I asked, "Well, how about having dinner with me?"

5

BY THE TIME WE HAD CHANGED, our other two roommates had arrived. One was the current British Amateur champ, Ron Gulaskey, an undergraduate at Penn State and looked like the farm boy that he was. The other was a junior from San Diego State, Charles Jacob Smith. He was short and blond with a round face and an old-fashioned crewcut. He had won the U.S. Public Links tournament at Torrey Pines. He asked us all to call him Chuck.

The boys wore linen slacks and school ties with their blue blazers. I told them they looked like the Chad Mitchell Trio and they smiled politely, having no idea what I meant. I wore the seersucker suit I reserved for summer events on campus and, not to be outdone by the college kids, my own school tie.

Our dinner would be in the Trophy Room, named for its glass-enclosed cabinets filled with memorabilia of Masters past. We took a good look, checking out the ball that Gene Sarazen knocked into the hole for a double eagle in 1935. With it was the 4-wood he used to make the shot. There was Bobby Jones's Calamity Jane putter. We all revered it as a relic of the man who'd been the greatest putter in the history of golf.

It was almost eight when we decided to sit down and eat. Lightnin' was there, dressed in the butterscotch-colored jacket and black bow tie that waiters wore when serving meals.

I knew from Augusta's history that Clifford Roberts had a rule about not keeping the staff serving meals after eight o'clock. He didn't want the members to take advantage of the employees, but Lightnin' waved off my concerns about ordering late and showed us to a table.

The room gradually emptied and the four of us sat in the far corner talking golf and finishing our meal. None of the students was in a hurry for the evening to end. It was a special night for them, something that they could share with their teammates and girlfriends back on campus. Plus, they were students and used to being up late. The room, with muted colors and heavy dark furniture, was lit with indirect lights and small lamps, and had the look of any wealthy men's club in America, or the faculty lounges of the Ivy League colleges where most of these Augusta members had been students. It was in surroundings like this that they felt most at home, men alone and safely away from women.

I sat back and enjoyed the boys, listened as they traded stories of tournaments played, of pros they had met, of great shots they had made, of matches won and lost.

Then they turned to talking about the Masters and the dark course just beyond the clubhouse windows. I listened, hoping to pick up a lesson about one hole or another. Here I was, the college professor learning from guys young enough to be my students, or my own kids.

When they came around to me, they asked what I thought, how had I played Augusta? I shrugged and said that all I knew about Augusta was what I had seen on television. They laughed, thinking I was putting them on. Lowering my voice, I asked a question of my own.

I asked them why they played golf. And before they could give me some fumbling replies to a question they hadn't anticipated, I gave them my own answer. Why I was at Augusta National when I was pushing fifty, old enough to be their father, and hadn't God's chance in hell of making the cut.

"Golf was the only thing I was ever really good at when I was a kid," I told them. "Everything else I've done in life, from earning degrees to writing books to staying married and having a family, I had to work hard at, but swinging a club was the only natural thing I had ever done.

"My old man worked on Wall Street when I was a kid, and making money was what drove his whole life. We lived in a big house in a rich suburb, and every few years he'd buy a new house in the same town just because it was bigger or on a better street. I didn't know it then, but I was embarrassed by my old man.

"To spite him, I guess, I started caddying at the country club where only black men worked. I wanted my own money so I didn't have to depend on his allowance. I'm not sure what drove me to golf—maybe that he was a member at the club and I got this perverse satisfaction from working there as a lowly looper.

"He wasn't much of a player, maybe a 20 handicapper, but I was good at the game from the moment I picked up a club. Pretty soon I was living and breathing golf, winning every tournament in Westchester County, beating the kids from the best country clubs in New York. Golf was one thing my old man couldn't master. But because it was a game he couldn't win, it was also of no value to him. He said I was wasting my time. Maybe that was the real reason I wanted to play well and win. Every time I won, I was beating my old man."

I leaned forward as if I were about to share a great truth, a long-held secret, which, I realized then, was exactly what I was doing. I knew, too, from years in front of a classroom that I had to move my narrative in a straight line; I had to marshal it by examples, one detail upon another like building blocks in a children's set.

"I won a golf scholarship to Wake Forest, Arnold Palmer's college. That meant I didn't need my old man's money to go to school. I went south thinking I was the greatest gift to golf since graphite shafts.

"Then at Wake I met a bunch of hotshots like myself who could whack a ball a country mile, get it up and down from anywhere, and drill every putt dead center from on or off the green. These guys were all good and cocky and were convinced they were the next Palmer."

The amateurs were grinning, glancing and smiling at each other, recognizing in my story some truths about themselves. The only difference was that instead of wanting to be Arnie, they believed they were the next Tiger Woods.

"A funny thing happened at Wake," I went on. "In my junior year I started to lose matches, which had almost never happened when I was growing up. I would go out with the guys on my team for a practice round and shoot the lights out. I'd be two, three shots better than any of them. But the next day, in a college tournament, I'd drop a match six and five to the same guys."

The three amateurs nodded and frowned, not knowing where I was going with my story. Chuck Smith's quick eyes shifted back and forth, as if trying to catch my drift. He was a kid, I could see, who did not take anything at face value.

"I quit playing," I told them next. "I walked away from my full scholarship, from Wake Forest. I went home to Westchester and enrolled in a small college in the town next to where I lived. I changed my major from business administration to

English literature. I wouldn't be a country club professional. I didn't need to know bookkeeping to run a pro shop. I stayed in school and got a Ph.D. so I could teach for the rest of my life. I paid for my schooling by going back and caddying at Pelham Country Club, where my old man had been a member."

"But you just won the U.S. Mid-Amateur!" Chuck Smith exclaimed. "What do you mean, you can't play?" He glanced at the others as if to solicit their agreement that I was trying to run a number on all of them.

"Remember how I said golf was the most natural thing I have ever done? What I didn't tell you was that in the fall of my junior year, before the golf season, my old man died of a heart attack in a Metro-North railroad car.

"They didn't know he had died until they got to Grand Central Station. They thought he was just sleeping, slumped in the window seat, his head against the glass, his eyes closed. The conductor nudged him on the shoulder when they reached the end of the line. He keeled over onto the floor. My dad had been dead for over an hour."

"Jesus," Zack whispered, his eyes widening at the shock of my story.

"When my dad died, I stopped winning," I said, continuing to speak calmly. "Since I was no longer fighting him, I no longer had a reason to play. He was gone, and so was my need to win. I never got to the next level with golf. I had nothing left to prove. I had no one to beat. I peaked at nineteen, the year my dad died."

I stopped speaking. It was not so much a dramatic pause as a moment to pull myself together.

"Then a couple springs ago," I continued, "I was driving home to Carbondale, Illinois, from a conference at St. Louis University in Missouri. It was a warm afternoon and I drove into an empty parking lot to rest a few minutes and saw that I had pulled into a driving range. Sitting there, watching a couple of hackers bang out balls, I decided to hit a bucket. I hadn't swung a golf club in twenty, twenty-five years. I didn't have shoes. I didn't have a glove. I was wearing a suit and a tie.

"I bought five dollars worth of clunkers and went onto those green rubber mats and started banging out balls with a beat-up driving range metal wood in a converted cow pasture.

"With my first swing, it felt good. I could hit the ball again. Even though I was only hitting lumpy golf balls into an empty Illinois farm field."

I stopped talking and stared for a moment into the darkness of Augusta National. The college kids were watching me, wondering, I'm sure, just what the hell was going on with this old guy. Then I explained. "You see, I had quit playing when I was your age because I didn't have to escape into golf to find a safe place in my father's world. I picked up the game again when I needed golf to get me through what is happening in my life today."

I paused, realizing I couldn't unburden myself to these kids, couldn't tell them the real reason I had come back to the game was because my wife had cancer and we had both rallied around my game. As if with my playing and winning, we were showing each other we weren't giving up, either one of us.

I smiled, embarrassed at having said too much. To change the subject, I said quickly, "An odd thing happened to me today, just before you guys arrived. I had a message waiting for me." I looked at Zack, "Like the one I mentioned. It said, 'Meet Me at Amen Corner.'"

"Waiting for me out there at the edge of the course was this old guy—and I mean an old guy, older than me. I had taken my putter with me and I was checking out the twelfth green when this guy came out of the woods and told me that this year an amateur was going to win the Masters."

That got their attention. In their bright eyes I could see them judging me, trying to decide whether I was running a number on them, or whether I had somehow stumbled on a piece of valuable information. The Masters, they knew, was famous for heroics, going back to Sarazen's double eagle at fifteen, the "shot heard round the world," as it came to be called.

"Who?" Smith blurted out, cutting off my ramblings. He was a stocky kid with a round, red face and small eyes that darted like horseflies. "Which one of us is going to win?"

I let a moment pass as I glanced from face to face. They were holding their breath. I could tell them anything now and they would believe me—the mark of a good teacher.

I went on, speaking as slowly as if I were reading Yeats to them. "The old man didn't say which amateur would win. All he said was that he was determined to fulfill Bobby Jones's dream of having an amateur win this tournament."

"What dream?" Smith demanded next.

"Bobby Jones was the greatest amateur who ever played the game, and he always hoped that someday an amateur would win his tournament. No one ever has until—until, of course, this year." I smiled wryly at the boys, adding, "At least that's the story this old guy told me tonight out at Amen Corner."

Ron Gulaskey was grinning. "Shee-it," he said, laughing. He leaned back in his chair. "You're playing with our heads, Tim. Now run your story past Tiger or Phil or McDowell. Tell them. They're the ones who'll win this."

Smith kept staring at me. His puffy face was squirreled up. "Whoever is on his game will win this week." He nodded in the direction of the dark course. "Those pros can all play tee to green, but maneuvering on those roller-coaster greens is what counts. It doesn't matter what some old fart—member or not—tells you." He tossed his green napkin on the dining room table.

It wasn't me that was annoying him; I could see that. Just being at Augusta, getting set to tee it up, was unnerving him. I shrugged. Some golfers, I knew, built their game on hostility. I let his rudeness pass and told the others that I was turning in. "This geezer needs his sleep," I said. Zack laughed and said good night, like the well- brought-up young man that he was. Once I was gone, I knew, they'd talk about me, wonder how I had even gotten into the tournament in the first place; they'd take bets at how far over par I'd be after thirty-six holes.

At the door I paused and called back to them, "Remember, our number to beat is 66."

They stared at me.

"Back in 1956 when Ken Venturi played here for the second time as an amateur he shot 66 the opening day," I told them. "It's still the lowest score that any amateur—even Tiger—has ever shot at the Masters."

"Piece of cake," Zack said, grinning.

"The next day Venturi shot 69," I went on. "It was windy that day and even Ben Hogan only managed a 78."

How did that happen? They listened as silently and attentively as players always get when discussing rounds of golf.

"On Saturday, Ken shot 75. The weather was terrible, but he still had a four-shot lead on the field by the end of the day. It looked as if an amateur was finally going to win the Masters.

"Then on Sunday the wind was up again, blowing fifty miles an hour. The greens got real fast. The pros were scoring in the 80s. Still, all Venturi had to do was shoot 40 on the back side, but he bogeyed six holes coming in and lost by one shot to Jackie Burke.

"When he walked off the course, Venturi went up on the lawn, under that big oak right over there, and he sat down and burst into tears as if he were a little kid who'd just lost a junior event."

I paused for a moment and then asked what the moral of the story was.

"Don't burst into tears," said Ron.

I smiled and shook my head, "No," I said, "Don't shoot eighty!"

I left them laughing and headed up to the Crow's Nest.

The clubhouse was quiet. The crowd who'd filled the place earlier was gone, and there was just the four of us, rooming together at the top of the old mansion, left in the building, and a few security guards in the main office.

I walked upstairs and stepped into the sitting room of the Crow's Nest to find the old man with the green blazer jacket sitting alone in one of the upholstered clubhouse wing chairs.

"Uh-huh, and did you enjoy your dinner, Mr. Alexander?" he asked. "I trust you had the peach cobbler. We do peach cobbler quite well here, if I do say so myself." His slight smile faded quickly. He seemed very much at home in the Crow's Nest, sitting casually in the chair with his legs crossed and holding a thick cigar in his right hand.

"Who are you?" I asked. Member or not, he had stepped over the line by invading my space.

"I am the man who will win you the Masters, Mr. Alexander." He spoke grandly and pronounced his words carefully, as if English were his second language. At the same time there was a hard edge to his voice, suggesting he did not appreciate my insolence.

"And how will you ensure my victory, Mr. . . . ?"

He waved away my question with his cigar, implying that I would know everything in good time.

I pulled one of the leather chairs out from the card table and turned it around to face him. He, in turn, flicked a length of ash into the porcelain tray on the end table.

"You have no idea who I am?" he asked.

"No, sir, I do not. Thank you for your generous offer to help, but I think it would be more appropriate, not to mention more sporting, for me to rely on my clubs and my swing and the gods of golf."

The sardonic smile crossed his face. Then the man declared, "My name is Charles DeClifford Roberts, Jr. Around here I'm known as Mr. Roberts. Does that name mean anything to you, young man?"

I nodded but didn't engage him. There wasn't much I didn't know about Augusta National, and I knew this guy was not Clifford Roberts. In the morning I would have to say something to the club's security.   .

I heard voices and, then, almost immediately, the footsteps of my roommates coming up from the Trophy Room. If they'd been home, or back on their campuses, they would just be heading out for the evening at this hour, hitting the bars and meeting girls. But this was the Masters and they had practice rounds to play in the morning.

I looked at my uninvited guest and politely suggested that he leave, that the other amateurs were returning and the Crow's Nest wouldn't accommodate all five of us.

"Don't tell me about this dormitory," he replied. "I slept in this room before you were even born."

I would have to throw him out, I realized. Security would handle the situation once I got him downstairs.

I stood and asked gently, "How 'bout going for a little walk?"

Behind me the Crow's Nest door burst open and the gang came rushing in, still excited and full of talk. They halted at the doorway. Taking a sniff of the air, Zack Trout declared, "So that's why you left us! You came up to smoke a cigar. Hey, Tim, you could have offered one to your roommates."

I started to protest that I wasn't the one who was smoking—

couldn't they see it was the stranger in the wing chair? But when I glanced around, the chair was empty. The man who called himself Mr. Roberts had disappeared.

I stared at the chair. The cushion seat still had the impression of a body. I swept my hand across it, but there was nothing.

Making a feeble excuse about them being too young to smoke, I escaped into my monk-like room and closed the partition door. I dropped down onto the narrow bed before my legs gave out and took a deep breath. My hands were shaking; my heart pounded. If this kept up, I'd have a heart attack before I reached the first tee. My fear of playing in the Masters was causing panic attacks.

I leaned forward and pressed the palms of my hands to my forehead. I concentrated on taking deep breaths to pull oxygen into my system. It was what I always did when I was nervous; I filled my lungs with air.

God, I was a wreck.

Zack tapped on the door to my room and I jerked up.

"You okay?" he asked. He looked worried, the way young people will when adults behave oddly.

I managed a smile and nodded. "I'm okay. Thanks, Zack."

He stood at the doorway watching me. His blond hair was spiked in the bedhead style kids favor. I wanted to stand up and pat him on the back and reassure him that I was okay, but I didn't think I was steady enough.

"Can I get you anything?" he asked. "A glass of water or something?"

He was a good boy. He wanted to help.

I shook my head and explained that I had been traveling all day and my lack of sleep had caught up with me. I made it sound as if it were my age that was doing me in, not my nerves.

Zack grinned. God had given him a million-dollar smile and I assumed that, back on campus in Alabama, he could get any girl he wanted. Behind him, the others were asking if Zack was playing or not. They were gathering around the table in the sitting room, settling in for a poker game. I waved Zack away, told him to play cards. I was fine, I said again, but he appeared not to believe me. In the other room, I heard Smith telling Gulaskey about a poker game he had been in back in Vegas.

Now I had the confidence to stand. My legs felt stronger. My panic was over. I told Zack I was going to hit the sack.

Zack grinned again and looked relieved.

"I'll try and keep them quiet," he offered.

"Don't worry. I'm afraid my snoring will keep you all awake. Just ask my wife."

"Is your wife coming to watch you play?" he asked politely.

"I'm not sure," I replied vaguely. "Maybe, if I make the cut."

"Yeah! Just like that old guy told you out at Amen Corner. Maybe you're the amateur who'll win the Masters." He smiled, making light of my story at dinner, turning it into a joke that we could all share up in the Crow's Nest.

"Right you are!" I pulled my suitcase from under the bed and grabbed my toiletries. It really was time for bed. I could feel my weariness in all my bones and I hadn't yet played one hole at Augusta.

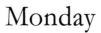

Monday

6

ON MONDAY MORNING before 7 a.m. I woke and dressed, grabbed my clubs and, carrying my golf shoes, walked barefoot through our shared space to the door so as not to wake the young amateurs. The playing cards were scattered on the table, as were empty glasses and candy-bar wrappers. It was oddly satisfying to see that they were behaving like kids.

Looking around to make sure I hadn't forgotten anything, my glance caught the empty armchair, and then the large porcelain ashtray, and then the evidence of Clifford Roberts's visit: an inch of cigar ash.

I stared at the brown ash. Its existence proved I wasn't totally out of my mind. Whoever, or whatever, he was, he'd really been there. I closed the door of the Crow's Nest gently behind me and moved down the steep steps. I was heading for the first tee of Augusta National. It was time to play golf.

Down the first hole, I spotted two men crisscrossing the green with mowers, trimming the putting surface and wiping clean the milky-white overnight dew. There were players and green-jacketed officials standing on the tee box, and a cluster of spectators by the massive scoring board to the right of the first fairway. Slowly, Augusta National was coming to life on the Monday of Masters week.

I was near the first tee when I heard my name being called. I spun around, thinking it might be someone from the front office saying I had a phone call. I had turned my cell phone off over night and always I carried the nagging expectation that Kerry might need me immediately at home.

But it wasn't anyone from the office. It was a tall, lanky kid jogging toward me from the far end of the clubhouse. As he came closer, I could see he was wearing white Foot-Joy sneakers and the famous and familiar white Masters caddie uniform, the long-sleeved jumpsuit that made all the caddies look like house painters. The uniform was clean and bright white, with an all-green Augusta National logo on one breast pocket and a caddie number on the other. His player's name would be Velcroed across the back.

He arrived breathless, saying that he had been waiting for me.

"Why's that?" I asked.

"Because I'm your caddie, sir." He reached out to take my clubs.

"You are? But I haven't checked in at the pro shop."

"Ray Harper, the caddie master. He told me."

"What's your name, son?"

"Clay. Clay Weaver." He smiled. With a mouthful of bright teeth in his tanned face.

"You're an Augusta caddie?"

"Yes, sir. I just qualified. It took me five weeks to pass all the caddie master's tests and get references. Then he added, as if to show he had done his homework, "You won the Mid-Am."

I nodded and smiled, but what I felt was disappointment.

Rather than this nice-enough kid, I had been hoping to grab one of the sons or grandsons of Augusta's legendary caddies, men like "Iron Man" Avery, who had looped for Arnold Palmer, or Willie "Pete" Peterson, Nicklaus's caddie. It wasn't for sentimental reasons that I wanted one of them on my bag. I needed their local knowledge: how to play the wind down at Amen Corner, where to place my drive on the par 4s. Now I'd be teeing off with a kid who was as new to Augusta as I was.

"What do you do in real life, Clay?" I asked, kneeling down to pull out my glove and tees from the small pocket of the barrel bag.

"I'm a caddie," he said, puzzled by my question.

"But you said you just qualified." Standing, I slipped on my white glove.

"I caddie over at Augusta Country Club." He nodded in the direction of Amen Corner. "I only applied here last month."

"You're in college," I asked, watching him.

Clay shook his head. He looked worried now, as if he knew I might disapprove, and said, "I couldn't afford to go." Then he smiled and, nodding toward the course, added, "But I love being around golf; I love to caddie, and in the off-season I work inside, in the men's bar."

"Good for you," I said. "You know what you want out of life. Anyone who knows that is lucky." And I meant it. I nodded toward the tee. "Okay, Clay. I'll meet you up there. I'm going to check in at the tournament office."

"Aren't you going to hit balls, sir?"

I shook my head. "I'll play a couple balls when I'm on the course. That's where I need to practice."

Clay swung the clubs onto his shoulder and moved toward the tee.

"Are you playing alone, sir?" He glanced up at the tee to see if anyone was waiting for us.

"Yep, I think I will. I need to play more than one shot, get used to the course, practice my putting."

Clay nodded, understanding, then said confidently, "Well, let's go shoot the lights out."

"I'll settle for par," I answered back, and headed for the pro shop.

7

CLAY WAS WAITING on the tee with my driver pulled and three balls in his hands when I came back from talking to the caddie master. What I had told Ray Harper was that Clay Weaver wasn't going to work out for me.

I needed a seasoned caddie on my bag, I told the caddie master. When Fuzzy Zoeller won the Masters as a rookie, he said it was just because he'd had an experienced Augusta National looper on his bag. Ray admitted that he'd given Clay my bag only because his father had gotten killed in Afghanistan. "His Guard unit got called up a couple times, and he was killed a year or so back. Clay told me his old man always wanted to caddie in the Masters, so when Clay asked me if he could, I said okay. But I'll make some calls. I'll find one of the guys from the old days. I know this is your big shot; you need the best we can get for you." He smiled, trying to be nice.

"Clay's okay for today," I answered, feeling guilty that I was dumping the kid. "It's a practice round. Let him have this loop and earn a few bucks. We'll worry about another caddie tomorrow." I thanked Ray and slipped him a twenty. It was a small tip, I guessed, by Augusta standards. But all I could afford.

Reaching the tee, I glanced at the three golf balls Clay was holding and instructed him, "I want you to give me one ball on the first tee, put one in your right pocket and one in your left pocket. After the first hole, give me the ball in your right pocket, move the one from the left to the right pocket and put the one I just played on the first hole in the left pocket. Do this for nine holes and then we'll start all over." I smiled then and asked, "You know who used to do that?"

"Ben Hogan."

I blinked in surprise.

"I read it in a book," he explained, then added, "My Dad gave me his books about golf. I've read them all."

We were interrupted by the starter, an Augusta member in a green jacket, who came over, introduced himself, and asked me who I was. There was a sheet of names on his clipboard. I told him who I was and that I was playing as a single.

"Oh, you're the Mid-Amateur winner!" he declaring, finding my name on his sheets. "I thought you might be one of those foreigners, you know, from Sweden."

"No, just Illinois. That's far enough away from Georgia," I joked. In a perverse way, I was glad he didn't know who I was. There was a certain virtue to being obscure and unnoticed at the Masters. The pressure was off. Nothing was expected of me.

I slid my cell phone into my back pocket. I didn't want anyone to see me using it, but out on the course, I could text-message home. I needed to keep in touch with Kerry.

Straightening up, I saw Clay had seen me pocket the cell phone. I winked at him and then, to distract his attention, I asked, "What's that? Homework?" nodding to the thick pad in his right hand.

"Yardage," he said.

"Yardage! Did you chart the course?"

He nodded. "I walked it yesterday."

"I've got my version," I said, as if to keep up with the kid and pulled my book out to show him what I had—a bright, Day-Glo-colored book of yardage at Augusta. It had been put together by a caddie who made his living charting courses on the PGA Tour. I explained how "The Book " had been given to me by the golf coach at the college where I teach. Flipping it open, I showed Clay the laser-measured distances on every hole, the diagrams of the greens, hazards, and small notations in the margins pointing out danger spots.

"Listen to this," I said, marveling at the scholarship that had gone into preparing this little book. "Here's what this caddie has to say about number 12. 'Don't pay any attention to the breeze over your left shoulder. That wind is coming down Rae's Creek, around those pines, and comes back over your shoulder. Always play it long on 12, or you'll be in the creek.'" I nodded at Clay. "A good caddie," I said, "is more knowledgeable than his player."

"Have you played Augusta?" Clay asked.

I shook my head. "There's a first time for everything," I said, acting more confident than I felt.

I'd been invited by Billy Payne to play Augusta National after I won the U. S. Mid-Amateur. But back then, in the fall, I hadn't had the time off from teaching or the money to drive to Georgia and spend a week playing golf.

Clay pointed to my yardage book and said, "The trouble with those things is that they only chart to the front of the green. This morning, and every morning, the groundskeeper calls Ray and tells him where the cups are cut. Ray gives us that information." Clay gestured to his book. "I've got it here."

I shook my head and smiled at Clay's eagerness, still I was impressed that he had the yardage. I knew there was a lot he didn't know about Augusta National, and one round of golf with me wasn't going to turn him into a caddie legend, but he was making a good start.

I stepped away from him and the other caddies so I could get a full view of the first hole. It was the first time I had really seen it up close and personal, as the sports announcers like to say on TV.

The first hole stretched away in one perfect carpet of emerald green, sweeping down from the tee then rising again 250 yards away. It was a slight dogleg right, with one right-side fairway bunker.

In 2006 the tee had been pushed back twenty yards in defense of high-tech drivers, four-piece balls, and the way Tiger Woods dismantled the course with his record score in 2002. The par-4 first hole was now 455 yards long.

In the distance was the enormous rolling green, all mounds and valleys. The cup was cut toward the back edge on the right side.

Opening day, I knew, the pin would be tucked behind the left-side bunker, the traditional placement.

"There's wind against you," Clay commented, coming to stand beside me on the tee. Charles Howell III and Brett Quigley, both PGA Tour players, were hitting off number one. Both of their drives came up short of the right-side bunker. That was the spot to be, Clay whispered. Standing there, I knew I didn't have to worry about the bunker. I didn't have the distance to reach the sand.

"Should I hit a draw," I asked offhandedly, "and keep away from that bunker?"

"You hit everything with a fade."

I glanced over at him, surprised again.

Clay stared back before breaking into a grin as he admitted, "I looked you up on Wikipedia."

Even the Internet knew my shortcomings.

"Okay, how do I play this hole with my Wikipedia fade?"

"Bobby Jones said to play to the right side and keep away from that left front bunker up by the green."

"I don't have the distance to reach that fairway bunker."

"You won't get any roll. The grounds crew cuts the fairways toward the tees, so the grass is growing against you." He sounded sure of himself, as if he had my drive under control. The only problem was that I was hitting the ball, not him.

"Yes, sir!" I tossed off, and stepped over to the tee. Howell and Quigley were heading down the fairway, taking most of the early-morning gallery with them. Back in Carbondale, at the public course where I played, the only people who ever watched me drive off number one were my playing buddies. I didn't mind being alone on the tee.

I teed up, stepped back, and slowly began to loosen up, feeling the stiffness in my arms and shoulders as I swung my new TaylorMade R9 driver, with its 10.5 loft and Fujikura FI shaft. The new driver was Kerry's idea. She told me that if I wanted to make the cut at Augusta National, I had to have some pro equipment. She had gotten me the R9 as an early Father's Day gift.

And so, with her gift in my hands, I drove off the tee at Augusta National, and my drive did what all my woods do: It faded left to right, landing safely in the middle of the velvety fairway, and rolled to a quick stop. At least I hadn't jerked it into the pines, I thought, and nodded to the few early-morning patrons applauding around the first tee, I then leaned over, plucked up my red tee from the smooth grass, and walked straight off the tee box as if I had been playing golf at Augusta National all my life.

Clay shot ahead of me. My big barrel bag bounced off his

back, and when he reached my ball, he swung the bag off his shoulder and paced the distance from the sprinkler head to where my drive had stopped, getting the yardage to the green for my next shot.

"What do we have?" I asked, slipping my driver into the bag and staring up at the green. From deep in the hollow, all I could see was the flag fluttering on the horizon. The wind was against me.

"You're looking at 168," Clay answered confidently. "It's all uphill. The pin is cut way in the back; you need to carry to the flag. You're not going to get much of a roll, not unless you hit your irons low." He paused to look down and saw my ball was perched on the lush rye fairway grass. I had a perfect lie. "It's a half club longer than it looks," he added.

Picking the right club was the secret to playing any golf course, and especially this one. The grass surrounding the greens was shaved to fairway length. There was no rough, or second cut, it's called at Augusta. The clean fairway made the course look easy, but the tightly mown aprons meant any shot that missed the green would roll off the putting surface and down into the hollows.

"Eight?" I asked.

Clay's face was half hidden beneath his cap. "I think it's a seven."

I pulled the 8-iron. A seven was too much club. The ball was a few inches below my feet. That wouldn't help my fade. The bunker to the left front side of the green had to be carried on the fly. I could carry it, and the spin would check the roll.

What I had going for me was that I hit the ball high. On Augusta's big undulating greens, that was to my advantage. A great player like Lee Trevino faded his shots the same way I did, but he hit everything low. He could never score at Augusta.

I aimed at the bunker. The ball had to carry 154, which wasn't a problem. I had enough room to maneuver on the green. Getting it close was the challenge. All I was doing anyway on the first hole at Augusta National was hitting and hoping, but then again, most of my game was just that.

"The wind's picking up," Clay noted, nodding toward the tall pines behind the hole. Down in the valley of the fairway, we couldn't feel anything.

I closed the club face and bent my knees to lower my hands, then, staying quiet and centered over the ball, I clipped the eight cleanly off the carpet of green. It was perfectly hit, one of those shots where you can feel the ball against the face of the club, feel the impact on the shaft channel through your hands and arms. It was pure, clean, and thrilling. And the ball in flight was a vision. With one simple swing, for one moment, any golfer on any fairway in the world can feel in control of his destiny. I held my finish, watched the ball sail over the rise.

"You're short," Clay commented, bringing me back to earth.

"You're sure?"

"Hit the seven."

Without waiting for me to agree, he pulled the iron and tossed me another Titleist.

"Helluva shot, though," he added. Being a smart ass, I would learn, would be his way of keeping me relaxed.

I toed the Titleist into place, and stepping behind the ball, started my routine again to hit the second approach. It was Kerry, who in all her life had never once hit a golf ball, who had taught me to have a set-up routine, borrowing the technique from the drama courses she taught at Southern Illinois University.

One day at Hickory Ridge, she followed me around the course and watched me jump from the cart, bang the ball, then drive after it. She told me I didn't have a playing method. Golf is like the theater, she said, and I had to get myself into the role before I hit the ball.

With her help, I created a pre-shot routine that transformed my swing into what looked like a piece of acting business, but it was really a way for me to settle down and play. I blocked out everything from my mind and my line of sight, drew down my field of vision to the ball, the flight, and my target. I drained off all the distractions beyond where the ball was being played.

But that was only one part of the method, she said. I had to also "get into character." Kerry taught me how to control my breathing. She taught me to feel the weight of the golf club in my fingers, to find the moment when the club became an extension of my arms. Only then did I draw up from my subconscious the memory of great swings I had made, and only then, while riding this wave of memories, of all that I had done in all the matches on all the other golf courses of my life, did I play the shot.

"Nice," Clay commented, watching the arc of the 7-iron. The ball carried to the top lip of the bunker. I saw it bounce on the green. It would run up the ridge, I guessed, and might even be close to the cup.

"Good enough?" I joked as Clay scooped a cupful of sand from a small sack he had tied onto my bag. He dumped the sand into my divot, then followed me up the hill. When I reached the crest, I saw the 7-iron shot had stopped within four feet of the flag. Clay might be a neophyte at Augusta National, but he had one thing going for him: The kid knew how to club me.

And then I spotted him. Sitting alone in the empty observation stands, still dressed in his green jacket and yellow tie, was the man who'd smoked a cigar up in the Crow's Nest, the man who claimed to be the former chairman of Augusta National.

I ignored him. Clay handed me the putter, talking the whole time about the speed and breaks of my four-footer. He didn't seem aware that we had an audience of one.

"Short putts are the hardest ones to make at Augusta," he advised.

My ball was below the hole. It was a straight putt on fast, bent grass. I had promised myself on the flight to Georgia that I wouldn't leave anything short. I didn't mind missing if I got the ball to the hole. Never up, never in was the golfing cliché every player lived by.

"Pull the flag," I instructed Clay.

"You should read the putt from both sides," Clay instructed. Like most teenagers, he had a lot to say.

"I say it's inside right." I crouched down and studied the break a second time from behind the ball.

"It looks more like a two-ball break to the right side," Clay answered, standing on the other side of the cup. "The putt is going to run toward eight green, and it's fast."

I smiled.

My four-footer slipped off the ridge and missed the cup on the high side by a good inch. Clay tossed me another ball without comment, and following his suggestion this time, I aimed two inches above the hole. The second putt clicked into the white plastic cup.

From behind the green, I heard the man who called himself Charles de Clifford Roberts slowly clapping. I glanced into the stands. My late-night visitor had his cigar wedged between his teeth as he clapped and he gave me a little bow from his seat. I plucked the ball from the cup and asked Clay, "Do you know him?"

"Know who, sir?" Clay asked, concentrating on replacing the flag without damaging the edge of the hole.

"That old guy in the stands."

"Where?" Clay glanced over at the temporary green stands and shook his head. "I don't see anyone."

I looked again and, of course, Clay was right. The stands were empty.

8

ON THE HIGH TEE of the long par-5 second hole, I took the driver from Clay and suggested that he forecaddie on the dogleg left hole. It was customary to forecaddie when members were playing, but not for the Masters, and Clay hesitated and frowned, then nodded okay and headed down the left edge of the fairway, telling me over his shoulder to watch out for the left side woods. "If you miss it, miss right," he advised.

The hole was downhill and there was a bunker on the right side, 300 yards from the back tee. There was no way I could reach the bunker. If I made the ridge, I could take advantage of the falloff of the fairway and gain a few yards. Bobby Jones and MacKenzie had originally designed the par 5s so they were reachable in two, but they had been lengthened to make them Tiger-proof. While Woods and a dozen other young guys on the PGA tour could now get on in two, there was no way I could.

The hole, however, looked inviting—a wide fairway and a large expanse of pink dogwoods and azalea bushes, all brilliant with bright color in the crisp daylight. It was one of those early mornings when you think how wonderful it is just to be playing golf.

I spotted Clay far down the fairway. He was standing at the corner of the dogleg, on the left edge of the fairway. He had slipped my bag off his shoulder and was waiting for me to play away.

"You have to be careful with caddies," a voice beside me commented. By now I was no longer startled by my stalker. "Back in '53, Sarazen was assessed a two-stroke penalty in the first round when his ball hit his caddie. He double bogeyed the hole," the old man continued.

Without comment, I walked to the markers. There was a crowd circling the first green, and looking through the trees I saw Tiger Woods and Mark O'Meara on the green. They had played out and were taking practice putts from different locations on the green, knowing from experience where the pin would be cut during the tournament. They were also practicing early in the day, as was their tradition.

"Why don't you go disqualify Tiger and O'Meara for excessive practice? Like you did with Frank Stranahan," I commented. If the old guy was going to claim to be Clifford Roberts, I'd go along with him. Then I stepped behind my ball and focused on driving off the number-two tee.

I'd use Clay as my target. I'd hit my normal fade and let the ball work itself back into the fairway. I couldn't reach the right-side bunker, but I wanted to be far enough right that I had a clear second shot up to the green.

"All of those tournament decisions have been taken out of my hands," Roberts replied. "And unfortunately, attitudes have changed." He sounded glum.

"Yes, things really have changed. Now they let hackers like me play in the Masters." I swung the R9, loosening up and tried to refocus my attention. Half my mind was on the absurdity of what I was doing, blithely talking to the old guy as if I believed he was a dead man back from the grave. The rest of my mind raced with thoughts of how I could possibly score on a golf course set up for the Masters.

"You qualified fair and square," Roberts replied. "If Bob Jones were alive, he would have sought you out for congratulations. No, I'm talking about the whole goddamn world. It's a crumbling place, going to hell in a hand basket. We have our country being run by Democrats and a president of mixed blood."

The old man had worked himself into a lather. I stopped swinging and stared over at him. And then I said, "Well, if I were you, I wouldn't complain about that to Tiger. He's already won your tournament four times. Not bad for a guy of mixed blood, as you phrase it."

"Tiger's parentage is black and Oriental, not black and white," Roberts snapped.

"So, if his parents were black and white, you wouldn't let him play?"

"I ran the club from '33 to '77 the best way I saw fit. You won't find a golf professional in America, or a patron of this event, that doesn't believe the Masters is the finest tournament in the world. Ask Gary Player. What did Gary say? 'If there's a golf course in heaven, I hope it's like Augusta National.'"

"Well, then, you may as well kick me out of the Masters. I voted for Obama!"

I stepped up to the ball, placing my left foot and then my right into position.

"I can't kick you out. I need you."

There was something in his voice, a note of desperation that startled me. I stepped away from my ball and glanced over at the old man.

"I'm condemned to this place," he admitted, gesturing at the glorious azaleas.

"Condemned? A moment ago you were comparing Augusta National to heaven."

Roberts shook his head.

"I'm condemned by my suicide to this golf course. When we started the Masters tournament back in the thirties, Bob Jones remarked that when an amateur won the tournament, all my sins would be forgiven. He was making a joke of my personal misdeeds, but it hasn't been a joke. That's what has happened to me. I wasn't the most saintly of men, Mr. Alexander. I wasn't like Bob. Everyone loved him. I was weak, like my mother."

I stared at the old man, this figment of my imagination, then remembered the story of how Roberts's mother had committed suicide when Clifford was a child.

"You are my ticket to eternal rest, Mr. Alexander." A wan smile slipped onto his cold face. "No amateur—not even Bob Jones— has ever won the Masters. If you do, you'll release me from my curse."

"Mr. Roberts, I am in no way capable of winning the Masters."

Roberts waved his cigar impatiently. "I told you, I'll see you have all the help you need to win. Now go ahead and tee off," he ordered.

Flustered now, I forgot my setup and swung hastily, duck-hooking my tee shot into the thick foliage left of the wide-open fairway and down the bank into the ditch. It was a hacker's drive.

The man behind me tsk-tsked, then commented that it was the worst tee shot he had seen hit off number two since '48, when Sammy Byrd drove into the pine woods and took a ten on the hole.

I grabbed my tee and charged off without replying.

"Calm down!" Roberts ordered, matching strides. "It's only Monday. You have a long week ahead of you."

"I have no time at all if I keep talking to a crazy old man."

"Everything is under control," he managed to say. He was breathing heavily as he lengthened his stride to keep up.

I slowed and then thought: Why in God's name am I worrying about a dead man's heavy breathing?

"I've never played Augusta, and my caddie is a rookie," I answered. "Nothing is under control."

"I'll get you one of the caddies from the old days. You can't win the Masters with this kid on your bag."

Clay had disappeared into the tall pines and thick azaleas that bordered the left side. "I can't win even with an old-timer Augusta caddie on my bag," I said.

"I wouldn't be so sure. More than one pro has been carried to victory on the shoulders of his caddie."

Reaching my drive, I saw Clay standing over the ball, which was nestled in a pocket of pine needles. I never would have found it. The power of young eyes.

I glanced ahead. Through the trees, I caught glimpses of the bunkered green and the flag. There was no way I could go for the green unless I hit a rope hook, and I hadn't been able to hook my woods since the eleventh grade.

"You could pull a Mickelson," the old man suggested. "He hit a wonderful cut shot a few years back from a lie like this."

I glanced at Clay, who didn't seem to see or hear anyone.

"I'm not Phil Mickelson," I said.

Clay looked up.

"Say what?" he asked, frowning.

I shook my head, waved off his concern, and slipped the driver into my bag. "It's unplayable," I said.

"You've got a shot," Clay protested.

"A shot in hell."

"Punch it out this way." Clay pulled the bag away to show me where. There was an opening through the closely spaced pines.

I saw what he was suggesting—a punch shot that had to carry eighty yards to the fairway. If I could thread my ball through the opening, I'd have a long-iron left to the green.

"Keep it low," Clay instructed.

Why not? It's only Monday, I told myself, and pulled the 4-iron and studied the tight lie, thinking that I'd have to play the ball closer to my body and get more of a vertical impact to gouge the ball out of the needles. I set up with the ball off my right foot and my hands forward.

The old man urged me on, saying "That's the way, Tim. You can't win the Masters playing safe."

"I can't win the Masters by duck hooking my drives into the pines either, now can I?"

"What?" Clay asked.

"Sorry, I'm thinking out loud. It's a bad habit of mine."

I was in a pine thicket in Georgia, talking to either a ghost or a crazy person. Or maybe I was the crazy person.

I tried to calm down and focus on my shot. I read once that Bobby Jones had said there wasn't a hole at Augusta National that couldn't be birdied, if you just thought about it, and there wasn't a hole that wouldn't be double-bogeyed if you stopped thinking. So I started to think, concentrating on what Kerry had taught me about visualization. I pictured the ball coming low off the bed of pine needles, carrying safely to the fairway, landing beyond the right-side bunker, and leaving me with an iron to the par-5 green.

"The ball is going to skid off these pine needles," Clay advised, pulling the bag away to give me room to play.

The ball came out higher than I expected and carried farther than I desired, but it safely cleared the low branches of the pines, slipped through the stand of trees, and landed softly on the open fairway before running down the gully and across the short grass to the second cut. I had, at most, a 4-iron to the green.

"Okay?" I asked, relieved.

"Better than okay," Clay declared. He swung the bag onto his shoulder and took off after my ball.

I walked out of the woods with the old man at my heels, jabbering about great shots that had been made at the second hole. In 1989, for example, Nick Faldo sprayed his drive right and into the trees and recovered by playing a one-handed inverted clubface stroke with an 8-iron. The ball ran 70 yards toward the green. Then he sank a 100-foot putt, one of the longest ever made at Augusta, to birdie the hole. He won the Masters that year.

I asked the old guy if he was going to give me Masters history lessons all week long.

"It wouldn't hurt you to learn from the past, Mr. Alexander. That's the problem with you young people. You think golf began the day you picked up a club. You have no respect for what Bob Jones and I did here in Georgia."

"I know all about it," I whispered. "You two made Augusta National the most discriminatory and secretive country club in America."

"Thank you."

I laughed. Maybe he really was Clifford Roberts. He was cheeky enough.

My ball was sitting up in the carpet of Augusta's first cut. I looked at the green and studied the yardage.

I had a clear shot. The green was fronted by two bunkers, leaving a narrow opening of less than fifty feet. The pin itself was cut on the left side. If I landed on, I didn't know if my ball would hold, and I didn't know what trouble there might be behind the putting surface. What I knew about Augusta was that anything over the green was trouble.

"What's the number?" I asked Clay.

"Ninety-three to the left side," In caddie shorthand, that meant 193. He was also speaking as if he knew my game. But he didn't. In truth, even I didn't know my game when it came to playing Augusta. I pulled the 5-iron.

Clay nodded.

So did the old man. "It's an easy five, a hard six," he piped up. "Don't worry about the bunkers. They're not a problem if you come up short. It's easier to get out of them than pitching up."

I hit the five.

It was a solid hit, one of the better irons I had hit all spring.

When we were within 60 yards of the green, we spotted the results. The ball was within a yard of the cup.

Walking onto the green, I took the putter from Clay and waited for him to pull the flag. It wasn't a difficult putt. Back home in Illinois, I wouldn't have worried over anything of this length, but these were Augusta greens, fast and full of subtle breaks.

I studied the putt from both sides, as Clay had suggested, and I asked him what he thought.

"The grain breaks toward the pines."

Following Clay's advice I tapped the ball firmly and let the slope work its way. The ball clicked into the cup and there was a scattering of applause from the small gallery behind the green. I nodded in recognition, but was too embarrassed to tip my cap. Then I followed Clay off the green as if I were right at home playing in the Masters.

9

"WHAT HAVE WE GOT?" I asked Clay as we reached the 3rd tee.

He had his yardage book out and was flipping through the pages.

"You're looking at 350. Keep it short of the bunkers. If the pin is on the right side, hit a driver and try to carry those left-side fairway bunkers. If the pin is on the narrow left side, then you better use a long iron or a utility metal wood and lay back. The pin is cut on the left side today, so lay up short of the bunkers and hit a short iron into the green. It will hold." He spoke as if he were giving his orals in golf.

"I'll aim at the bunkers and let the ball work back into the fairway," I said, studying the slope of the fairway. I could see that with a decent drive, I'd have a short iron into the green. Coming in high, I could keep the ball on the green.

Clay pointed at the tall pines halfway down the fairway and said, "They're moving."

I stepped away from the ball and took a few practice swings, thinking that all those times I'd watched the Masters on television, I'd had no idea how much wind was generated on the course in the early days of April.

Against the wind, I didn't have the length to carry the left-side cluster of bunkers. If I hit my driver, it might fade into the right-side trees. All I had as a target was a narrow strip of fairway. It was the percentage shot. There was nothing to gain with a 1-wood, so I hit away with the 3-wood.

My high-flying fairway metal didn't fade. It didn't move freely into the center of the fairway. It caught the last bunker in the cluster, 275 yards down the left side. A white puff rose as my ball hit the soft white sand. It was the longest 3-wood I had hit since I was a teenager.

Clay rushed to tell me it was no problem. I could play a wedge and be home in two, putting for a birdie. This was the shortest par-4 hole on the course, he reminded me. He kept talking as he followed me to where my drive had come to rest in the left-side bunker.

The sand, Clay informed me, had been replaced in 2002 so that the traps would look better on television, once the club decided to telecast all eighteen holes of the tournament.

Clay wasn't trying to impress me with his Augusta National familiarity. He was simply trying, as any good caddie would, to keep me from fretting over my misplayed drive. We both knew I had to score on holes like number 3 to make it into the weekend.

"You're in trouble," the old man said, materializing at my side.

"If it isn't the bearer of bad news," I mumbled.

"It's never too early to be pessimistic when you're playing this course," he retorted.

When we reached the bunker I could see the ball was sitting up.

I had a full wedge to the target. If this were a friendly game back home, I would have chopped out the ball with my pitching wedge, let it run up onto the center of the green and played for par. I didn't have that luxury at Augusta.

From where I stood, I could see the green was on a plateau that sloped from right to left. If I came up short, my ball would roll back off the green and down the fairway. I had to be long and six or seven feet to the right of the flag to have a makeable putt.

I pulled the heavy wedge, stepped into the hazard, and my foot sank into the soft sand. This was not like the bunkers back home, where in the spring we chipped balls off hard, packed, wet sand.

I took a few practice swings to find my rhythm, all the while keeping the club face from touching the surface. Then I burrowed my feet into the sand. In my day, I could get up and down with the best of them. My sand-saves record was as good as Gary Player's. But it had been many years since it was "my day" on a golf course.

"Anywhere on the green is fine," Clay added encouragingly.

Standing beside the caddie, the old man offered his own advice. "Knock it past the pin. It will check up and come back to the cup."

I opened my stance and the club face, and picked a spot half an inch behind the ball. The secret of this shot—of any sand shot—was to let my right wrist hinge freely on the downswing so that I'd slap the sand behind the ball and keep accelerating through the shot.

This time, however, I caught the ball first and not the sand. It shot out of the low bunker and carried to the green, hit a half dozen yards beyond the flag but into the ridge, where it checked up and curled to a stop within twenty feet of the pin. I had mishit the wedge and gotten lucky. Wonders never cease.

I stepped from the bunker, dropped my wedge against the bag and pulled my big Ping putter while Clay raked the sand behind me and Clifford Roberts launched into a story about Henry Picard at the '35 Masters.

His story was interrupted by my cell phone vibrating for the first time since I arrived in Georgia. I pulled it out and saw it was a text from my daughter, saying that Dr. Kestin had called and that Kerry's numbers—her tumor markers—had gone up. The doctor wanted more tests. I texted back immediately, telling Peggy that I had gotten her message and what I was going to do. Then I turned off my cell phone. I walked over to Clay, and told him I had to call it a day. I handed him my putter.

He took it reluctantly. As quickly and simply as I could, I told him I'd had a message from Illinois, and that a problem had come up. I didn't bother him with details.

"You're not playing any more today?"

"Sorry to say, Clay, it looks as though I'm not going to be able to play in the Masters."

10

THE CROW'S NEST WAS DESERTED. The college kids were on the course. I was thankful for that. I didn't want to have to explain my sudden departure. I'd leave them a note and wish them well. Bobby Jones had dreamed of having an amateur win the Masters, I'd remind them.

When I had everything packed, I sat down on my unmade bed to call my older son Tyler and tell him I was leaving Augusta and I would call him again en route.

"I'm not going to let you leave," Clifford Roberts declared from the doorway.

"There's not much that you can say, now, is there?" I didn't bother to look up. I turned on the phone. I had forgotten to charge it the night before and now its battery was low. Like everything else in my life, it was running on empty.

"You can win, Mr. Alexander. You have the game. You can be the first amateur to win the Masters and save me from this purgatory."

"I think, not to be too blunt, you're beyond saving." I still didn't look at Roberts. I knew he'd have that same sad, pained expression on his face.

"Well, suppose we save Kerry, then?" He said it slowly, deliberately, as if he had been hiding a hole card until it was absolutely imperative that he play it.

Now he had my attention.

He moved a step farther into the room and lowered his voice, even though we were the only two under the cupola.

"Play the Masters," Roberts said. "Win the tournament. Win for me and I'll see that your wife is cured."

He stared at me. There was no sly smile, no slight nod to indicate we could seal a deal right then and there. He just looked at me, his sad eyes filled with his troubled past, his failed marriages, the sicknesses that at the end drove him to suicide.

"How?"

"There are ways."

"There are ways?" I started to laugh at the absurdity of this conversation, my delusions that a dead man could keep my wife alive.

"When your time comes, Mr. Alexander, you'll understand that you can't help yourself. You can only help others, and pray others will help you in return."

"You'll help Kerry if I help you?" I asked again, as if to clarify the deal.

Roberts nodded.

"How did I end up playing Faust?" I wondered out loud.

"Pardon me?" Roberts frowned.

I waved him off. I knew Roberts hadn't finished high school back in Kansas; no point in embarrassing the old man by explaining my English teacher joke.

"Why me? Why not ask any one of a hundred other amateurs

who have played here since your death? Any one of them had as much chance of winning as I do."

Roberts was shaking his head before I finished, but he took his time replying. That was his way. He was a man who had succeeded in life by being careful and cautious. No one could fault him, or worse, catch him in error. His suicide was the one mistake he couldn't fix.

"Uh-huh. You're right, there have been other amateurs at Augusta National who were very talented," he explained. "Some very gifted, like Tiger Woods, but the difficulty is that they have all been young and inexperienced. They were free of your burdens: family obligations, emotional debts, a lifetime of angst, and, most damaging of all, your love for your wife. You have a great need, Mr. Alexander. You will do anything to save Kerry. And I can save her if you'll save me."

That was his deal. He was as blunt as any businessman might be. It was not for nothing that he had made his money on Wall Street.

"Prove it."

"Prove what?"

"Prove to me that you have such miraculous powers."

"You mean, turn water into wine?"

"Something like that. Show me you're more than a figment of my imagination, more than some psychic episode I'm experiencing because I'm scared of losing my wife, because I'm out of my league trying to play with the pros here at the Masters."

He nodded, obviously deciding how he might gain credibility. Then, matter-of-factly, he remarked, "You'll receive a telephone call within a few minutes. It will be from your wife. She will tell you that under no circumstances should you leave Georgia. She will tell you that you cannot use her cancer as an excuse to escape Augusta. Will that be enough proof?" Cliff Roberts smiled his cold smile.

"How are you going to help her?"

"Miracles still happen."

"As if you believe in miracles," I answered. I stood up and continued. "I have watched my wife suffer far too long to believe in miracles, Mr. Roberts. What I have learned about suffering over these last years is that everyone suffers alone. No one takes away the pain by snapping their fingers or saying a couple of extra novenas. What I want is a cure, and I want it now. I've been crazy to think I could escape from what is happening to Kerry by playing in this tournament. There are no handy miracles, Mr. Roberts."

And then my phone rang.

11

I LEFT THE CROW'S NEST after talking to Kerry and having her tell me that under no circumstances was I allowed to leave Augusta. She was only having blood taken the next day and there was no need for me to rush home. "You have a tournament to play, Timmy. I won't be your excuse for not playing."

I went looking for Clay. The weather had changed. It was overcast, with rain threatening. Plus, it was cold. The sunny skies were gone. I felt chilled to my bones. But I played better in cold weather, I reminded myself, and that cheered me some.

Clay was outside the pro shop and I told him what I had decided to do. The grounds were crowded. Spectators had been coming through the gates since eight o'clock that morning, and there were long lines at the gift shop, while even more visitors crowded into a makeshift museum showing the history of the Masters.

From the shop and gallery the crowd filtered out to the course, passing the huge scoreboard to the right of the first fairway.

Looking up, I saw my name listed with the players who had teed off early that morning. I wished I had a camera. By the end of the day, my name on the board, on the first day of practice, might be the only indication I'd ever played Augusta National. I walked by a stack of Spectator Guides and picked one up, knowing that in the back, in alphabetical order, was a listing of the players.

Alexander, Timothy Jack started the list, followed by PGA tour players Austin and Baddeley.

I stopped walking and read the short paragraph about myself.

Alexander, Timothy Jack

Birthdate 11/04/63

Winner of the U.S. Mid-Amateur Championship last year at Midlothian Country Club.

An English professor at Southern Illinois University, Alexander played golf at Wake Forest University as an undergraduate. He holds the course record (61) at Hickory Ridge Public Golf Course in Carbondale, Illinois.

First Masters appearance.

My academic curriculum vitae ran for six pages and listed college degrees, professional associations, published articles and books, awards and honors. In some small circles within the academic world my name was respected, my work cited by other professors in their scholarship. I could fill a lecture hall at a Modern Language Association conference whenever I spoke. English teachers sometimes asked me for autographed copies of my books.

At Augusta National I was worth fifty-one words. They did spell my name right, but they got my record score at Hickory Ridge wrong: I had shot 60, topping by a stroke the round by Lance Williams, the young assistant pro. My 60 had won the Southern Illinois State Amateur Championship the spring before I captured the U.S. Mid-Amateur.

I tucked the guide into my back pocket and walked up the slope to the back of the pro shop. Clay was sitting on the bench, on the walkway between the shop and where the players' bags were stacked. He was alone on the bench with my clubs tucked between his legs.

When he saw me, he pulled himself together and stood. "You okay?" I asked.

He nodded but didn't look at me.

I sat down on the bench and gestured that he should join me. It was a busy corner of the club, with players and caddies coming and going, even though the throngs of patrons gathered around the clubhouse were kept away by green ropes and official guards. I had to flash my player's badge twice to get near where Clay was sitting.

I lowered my voice and asked Clay what was troubling him.

"Ray says you wanted a new caddy." He wouldn't look at me. Both of his hands were grabbing the bag, as if he meant to show me he wasn't going to let his player get away from him. "I have the experience to loop here, sir," he stated.

"I'm not sure," I said slowly, searching for the right words to let him down easy. I told him the Fuzzy Zoeller story and how I needed an experienced Augusta caddie, someone like Willie Peterson or Todd Bramson. "I don't have a chance to make the cut unless I have a caddie who has been all over this course like white on rice," I told him.

Clay was nodding, as if he agreed with my explanation, and I waited for him to find the words to say so. I had dealt with enough college students over the years to know that I had to give someone his age a few minutes to find the right words to express his feelings, to tell me he understood. We could shake hands, and he would agree that another caddie would be better for my game. But that wasn't what Clay wanted to tell me.

"It's because of my dad that I wanted to caddie in the Masters. He always wanted, you know, to loop at Augusta National. He never got his chance." He glanced my way. I could see his eyes tearing up.

"Your Dad was a caddie?" I asked, trying to show some sympathy to ease him through his disappointment, and remembering what Ray had said about his father getting killed.

"He caddied here, but it never happened for him. Then when he got called back to the Guard...."

His voice trailed off and I kept nodding to show him that I understood. Then he said, "You know he was killed in Afghanistan?"

I nodded.

"One of those roadside bombs," he added, and glanced away.

"I know, Clay. Ray Harper told me.... Look...," I started to say, and Clay raised his hand and interrupted me.

"Hey, listen, it's okay. I understand." He smiled. "This is your big chance. You need all the help you can get. I understand." He slipped on his caddie hat, ready to leave. I knew I should let him. I knew my job was done, the bad news successfully broken. But I knew how it felt to achieve my dream of playing at Augusta, and it didn't feel good to step on someone else's dream of doing the same. Besides, who was I kidding? I wasn't going to win, regardless of who my caddie was. Regardless of that old man's crazy promises.

"Wait a second, Clay, hang tight. How do you know about the course? You had all those suggestions on how to putt."

"I had notes from my pop. He caddied during the season, but never in the Masters. The pros have their own caddies. It's not like it use to be in the old days."

"What did you learn from him?"

Clay pulled out a thick pad and smiled.

"This was Pop's Augusta National Bible."

"The sacred text."

"Yep, something like that."

"Okay, let's give it a try." I smiled at Clay and nodded to his book. "Your Pop's bible, and you as my bag rat." I stood up, saying, "Let's go hit some balls."

Clay was on his feet, grinning in agreement, and thanking me.

I waved off his thanks and asked, "Where to now?" I was such a neophyte I had no idea where the range was at the course.

Leading the way, Clay explained that the members' range that bordered Magnolia Lane was now obsolete. It was only 275 yards deep and half of the pros on tour averaged drives of 325 yards. There were drive balls over the 105-foot-high netting guarding Washington Road, so the range had to be moved.

That wasn't my problem, I thought. The only way I could drive a golf ball 300 yards was in my Volvo.

Walking to the new driving range, we filed through the crowds coming onto the grounds through the main gate. The spectators parted like the Red Sea at the sight of a caddie carrying a player's clubs. I followed in Clay's wake as the patrons glanced my way, turned to catch my name Velcroed on the back of Clay's white caddie jumpsuit, then quickly flipped through their copy of the Spectator Guide to read my brief bio.

I stepped onto the new range, trailing Clay. We were in the old parking lot of the club, next to the new caddie shack. A putting green and sand trap had also been built, and half a dozen players were driving balls into the wide-open range and toward Berckman Road. Sergio and Vijay were position closest to me. Vijay was working on his alignment with his swing coach and his body was wrapped in a rubber sleeve to keep from over swing. The pro was famous on the tour for fussing with his golf swing.

Clay set down the bag, tossed his white towel over the clubs, and took off to where the practice balls were available at the opposite end of the spectator stands.

I pulled my wedge and tried to act as if I really belonged on the range. I kept thinking of the Roy McAvoy character in the movie Tin Cup shanking his drives on the range into the other players before teeing it up at the U.S. Open. If nothing else, I knew I wouldn't shank the ball. I had hit a lot of bad shots in my day, but I had never been plagued with the shanks.

"You need another caddie," Clifford Roberts declared. He was back.

"Clay's my caddie," I told him. I spoke facing the range so the spectators filling the viewing stands behind the tee wouldn't see me talking to myself. I slowly swung the wedge, getting my rhythm, loosening up in the chilly weather. "We'll qualify or we won't," I told Roberts. "End of story."

Clay came running back with two small green bags of balls.

"I got you Titleists." He spilled out the balls onto the ground.

I took out my wallet and handed him a twenty. "Go get us a couple of Cokes, okay? And buy yourself something to eat."

I nudged a ball into position with my heavy pitching wedge and hit an easy iron. Before it landed, I moved another ball into place, setting it next to my first divot. Down the length of range, caddies and swing coaches and agents were clustered around their players, working on "Band-Aid cures," to get them through today's round, trying out new equipment, talking casually about the week ahead. I was the only player on the tee with no swing coach, sports psychologist, or strength coach, let alone an agent or seasoned, professional caddie. I hit another easy wedge.

"You're going to need a good caddie to win this Masters," Roberts commented.

"Clay can do the job," I answered.

"I mean you'll need more help than a caddie can provide." Roberts lit a cigar and began to pace back and forth behind me as he continued to talk.

"When Ike ran for President, he wasn't alone. There was a gang of us who got him elected in '52. You knew that, right? You left-wing academics must know at least that much." He smiled wryly, enjoying himself.

"English literature is my field, not political science, but I do know Eisenhower was President." I smiled back and, stepping over the bag, set the pitching wedge aside and pulled my 9-iron. "Are you talking about the Augusta 'Gangsters' for Ike?'"

This was another tale from Augusta's history—the story of how Roberts and a group of wealthy club members raised money to enable Eisenhower to run against Adlai Stevenson.

"That's right!" He was grinning.

My knowledge about the famous Eisenhower coterie made him feel better, made him feel he was still part of history.

"All of us. All good Republicans except for George Allen, and he was an all-right fella for being a Democrat."

Suddenly enthusiastic, Roberts rallied himself to tell the story.

"There was Pete Jones, president of Cities Service Company at the time; Bob Jones, of course; myself. I was Ike's financial advisor. Slats Slater, president of Frankfort Distillers; Bill Robinson, he was the vice-president of the New York Herald Tribune. There were others who threw in their support, as well as their money—Bud Maytag; E.T. Weir of Weirton Steel; Charlie Wilson with General Motors; Gene Black at the World Bank; Bob Wood of Sears Roebuck." The old familiar names rolled lovingly off his tongue.

"My point is that this gang of guys, we made sure Ike had the money he needed. We didn't have all those silly rules they have today about financing a campaign. We knew how to get things done. We got Ike elected not once but twice, and I'll say it myself: He kept this country from turning communist. That was what we feared about Stevenson."

My swing with the 9-iron was too loose. I hit a clunker that sprayed left, enough so that it would have gone out of bounds, if there had been an out-of-bounds. I stepped away from the tee and refocused on what I was trying to do: hit golf balls, not listen to Roberts tell tales from the past.

I was swinging too fast. I wasn't paying attention to what I was doing. Small wonder, with Roberts pacing beside me, talking on and on. I returned to my basic technique of whispering one-and-two-and-three as I swung. "One" on the backswing; "two" at the top; "three" on the downswing. It slowed down my action, brought my tempo under control. The ball shot off the face of the club, carried straight.

The iron was hit with enough authority to quiet Roberts.

I glanced around and saw Clay returning. Carrying two large green cups of Coke as well as a sandwich, he had to walk slowly to keep everything balanced.

I told Roberts to make his point before Clay reached us.

Roberts permitted himself a small, self-satisfied smile. "I'm going to do what I did for Ike," he said. "I'm going to assemble a gang of guys to help you win."

"That would be helpful, I'm sure, but I'm the one who has to swing the club."

"Well, that doesn't really apply when you're dealing with dead people."

I stared at Roberts; for the first time in his presence I was speechless.

12

ONCE CLIFFORD ROBERTS DISAPPEARED, I shook my head to get rid of his image. Either he was crazy or I was, or maybe both, but none of it was worth worrying about—or falling for. Golf is not a team sport. I had to hit the ball. I had to make the putts. I had to keep my focus in front of thousands of spectators.

When I won the Mid-Amateur at Midlothian, there had only been 25 people watching, most of them my friends from back home in Carbondale. Whatever help Roberts had in mind, it couldn't possibly lead me to victory against even the lowest-ranked professional, much less Tiger or Phil.

I went back to practicing, with Clay dutifully fetching me more balls and cleaning each club as I finished with it. By the time I started hitting my driver, I had been on the practice tee for over an hour. Sergio and Vijay and a couple of others had already left the range. Other pros had arrived.

It had also begun to rain—more of a mist than drops—but it

drove the few spectators off the metal stands and further thinned out the pros hitting balls into the faraway netting. The range became very quiet and I asked Clay if he felt like he was really at the Masters.

"I know I'm at Augusta National," he said.

"Why's that?"

"Because everyone here thinks golf is a religion, and pros are like the cardinals."

"And Tiger is the pope?" We both laughed.

"Well, maybe not anymore."

I had to agree.

I stepped up to the ball and swung slowly, paying attention to my tempo. On this drive, the ball faded far down the range, but I had missed where I was aiming and ended up too far to the right. At Augusta National, I couldn't just be hitting and hoping.

"I know what you're doing wrong," Clay offered.

"Who said I'm doing anything wrong?" I teed up another ball and, stepping back, aligned myself again. I stood behind my ball and slowly swung the driver. With each club, I started over, loosening my shoulders, extending my arc. It was what I never did as a kid. In college, I never needed to think twice about how or where or why. The arrogance of youth—if only I still had it.

I stood behind the ball and picked a spot on the distant mesh fence, 350 yards away.

Clay said, "You're picking your spot, but then you stare at the ball and not where you want to drive. Don't look down. Keep your eye on the target."

I didn't say anything. I stepped forward, this time making sure I kept my eye on the distant target, glancing briefly down to set the club face, then gripped and regripped the club. I stayed fixated on the spot I had picked out on the fence. Only then did I look down at the dimpled ball and swing.

My drive carried on line.

"Not bad," I said to Clay. "Do you play?" I teed up another ball.

"Only with my Pop."

"Was he a good golfer?"

I stepped behind the ball once more to get my line. I took my time. I had learned with age that what mattered was not how many practice balls I hit, but how well I executed every swing.

"He was great, but what he really liked to do was caddie for me. He taught me."

I paused and looked over at Clay. "Do you have a big family?" I asked, slipping my driver into the bag.

"Just me and Mom and Dad." He wiped the face of the metal wood with his big white towel and then pulled on the head cover. "Now there's just Mom and me."

I thought about Kerry, as I always do when I hear something that is heartbreaking about another person's troubles. Her sickness made me feel Clay's sadness as if it were my own.

"The thing about life is that it gets real complicated at times," I said, trying to make sense of what was happening to him as well as myself. "That's what's great about golf—the simplicity of it. It's played on a landscape that is peaceful and calm and there's an order to the day—eighteen holes to play, and everyone knows what to do.

I motioned to Clay that it was time to leave. "Let's go putt," I said, pulling my Ping from the bag.

We joined the throng of spectator traffic filing out from the gift shop and onto the course itself. Another crowd was clustered by the scoreboard, checking to see which players had already teed off and who was yet to play. We worked through the patrons and walked uphill, past the pro shop and the old oak tree that fronted the clubhouse. We went around the dining tables and umbrellas set out on the lawn, where lunch was served when it wasn't raining. I asked Clay what made him think that he was such a good caddie.

He didn't answer at once. He was thinking, perhaps, of how he might answer, or perhaps he was embarrassed at having been caught bragging. But then he said, rather calmly, and with the assurance of someone who had been around a lot of players, "Because I know what you need to do to win the Masters."

13

SPECTATORS, PLAYERS, CADDIES, the event staff and the few diners at the outside tables—everyone ran to whatever cover they could find when the mist turned to real rain. Clay and I went to the locker room and I decided to call it a day. With all that had happened, from the scary numbers Kerry had received to Clifford Roberts playing Mephistopheles, not to mention having hit balls for over an hour, I felt worn out. I needed a long shower and a short nap.

I told Clay I'd see him early in the morning and that I'd get a game and we'd play eighteen holes of practice. I paid him for the day and took my clubs with me, though Clay suggested that I could leave them in the bag room.

I shook my head and Clay grinned. "I guess without them you're just another hacker," he joked.

"Listen, with them I'm just another hacker, but they're all I have."

"Hey, you got the game." He said it enthusiastically, as if he really meant it.

He was a good caddie.

"Well, let's say I've got the sticks. Tomorrow we'll see if I've got the game."

With that, I waved goodbye and crossed from the pro shop to the clubhouse, dodging the shallow puddles and braving the sudden downpour, running for the warmth of the old colonial mansion. The vast expanse of Augusta National Golf Club was suddenly empty.

The college kids weren't in the Crow's Nest when I got upstairs. I stashed away my clubs and went ahead and took a long shower. Afterwards, wrapped only in a towel, I glanced through the bookcase, looking for something to read myself to sleep.

On the shelf was a copy of The Story of the Augusta National Golf Club written by Clifford Roberts. I pulled it out and, going into my room, put on pajamas and crawled into bed. It was chilly on the third floor, and it was raining harder. Above me, in the eleven-by-eleven-foot cupola, the rain beat hard against the windows. It wasn't a day for golf, and soon it would be too dark to play.

Having something to read calmed me in ways that always surprised me. Here I was, a player in the most important tournament in America, and I wasn't fretting about the rain or cold weather or not being able to practice. I was happy to be curled up in bed with a book, and this book especially—one that I expected would tell me more than I wanted to know.

I flipped it open and read the first line:

Like all golfers—or, as one might more correctly say, like all Americans—I was an admirer of Bobby Jones.

Of course it would begin with Bobby Jones. Everything at

the Masters began with Bobby. At best, Clifford Roberts was no more than a handmaiden to the greatest golfer of his time.

I read a while and then fell asleep. When I woke, the guys had returned. I could hear them whispering, trying to talk without waking me.

I swung my legs over the side of the bed and sat up, then paused and waited for my head to clear. I could feel the stiffness in my shoulders and lower back. It had been a long time since I had hit so many golf balls in one day. I didn't need dinner as much as I needed a massage.

I pulled on my trousers and opened the door, greeted the guys, and asked if they were heading out to eat. They glanced at each other, looking nervous. Zack Trout explained that they were planning to go to a country-and-western place they had heard about called Coyote's. They asked if I wanted to go with them, but I knew they didn't need an old guy like myself hanging around when they were trying to pick up girls. I told them to go ahead, that I was hoping to turn in early.

"The old man needs his beauty rest," I said.

"Let's play tomorrow," Zack suggested, glancing at the others, who all nodded in agreement.

"The Crow's Nest foursome," I said, thinking that at least I'd have someone to play with the next day, even if I was eating alone tonight in the clubhouse.

After they left, the Crow's Nest was quiet high above the rush of tournament activities on the lower floors. It was like being home in Carbondale, studying up in Morris Library, with the rain beating hard against the windows.

I went back to Augusta's history, to read Roberts's published, and longer, version of the Eisenhower story he'd told me earlier.

Less edifying was the story of boxing matches organized as entertainment for the wealthy white members at the Bon Air Vanderbilt Hotel in downtown Augusta. Roberts would hire a half dozen poor black kids from the poor section of town, put them blindfolded in a ring, then let them battle it out until only one was left standing.

The kid who was always left standing was Sidney Walker, nicknamed Bo. A shoe-shiner at the club, Bo was trained to fight by Bowman Milligan, the club steward. Milligan, Roberts explained, had been the first person he hired at Augusta because Milligan was "large and strong and a fine-looking black man."

It was Bowman Milligan who gave the young boxer, Bo, a new nickname, Beau Jack. With financial backing from twenty club members, including Bobby Jones and the sportswriter Grantland Rice, Bowman trained Beau Jack to become lightweight champion of the world.

Roberts's history also covered 1931, the first days of the Depression, when black men were hired for fifty cents a day to build the golf course. They would work "from can to can't," wrote Roberts—from the time one could see until the last light of day.

Roberts had published his book in 1976. One year later, he put a bullet in his head.

I glanced at my watch. It was almost eight o'clock. They might be closing the Trophy Room soon, if they still followed Roberts Rule, and I knew for a fact that they did. I had been at Augusta long enough to discover that the only thing to change at the club since Clifford blew his brains out was the length of the holes.

I got up, got dressed, and went downstairs to have dinner alone. But I wasn't alone.

"So, did you learn everything about Augusta from my book?" Clifford Roberts asked. He was sitting across from me in the nearly deserted Trophy Room. There were a few other diners, and waiters hovering by the door.

"I read what you wrote," I whispered. I was sitting in a corner with my back to the main room "But what I'd really like to know is what you left out of your book."

Roberts smiled, pleased that he'd taken his secrets to the grave. He seemed healthier and younger than before; he looked more like the portrait that hung on the Trophy Room wall. In his right hand he was holding a thick cigar, unlit.

"Why have you made such a fetish out of secrecy?" I asked.

Roberts leaned forward, as if to bring me into his confidence.

"Why should we be concerned about transparency? What we do at Augusta National is our own damn business. We don't need a lot of snoopy people prying into our affairs."

"You're happy enough to make a profit off these snoopy people with your tournament."

"When Bob and I started the tournament, we didn't make enough money to cover the cost of the prizes. I had to pass the hat among the members to come up with the $5,000. We lost money for nine straight years, and only stopped losing money because World War II came along and the tournament was discontinued."

He was agitated now, but I was enjoying myself. It was oddly liberating to get his goat.

"Have you thought about my offer?" Roberts asked next, changing the subject.

"You mean selling my soul to ensure that my wife lives?"

"You don't have to worry about your soul."

"Ah!" I realized now what the man was negotiating. I sat back and stared at him. There was no wry smile. I thought of how the players nicknamed Herman Keiser, the pro who beat Hogan in the '46 Masters, the Missouri Mortician, because of where he was from and because of his hound-dog looks. They should have saved the name for Roberts.

"Doing this good deal for me, saving my wife, will clean your slate, erase all your injustices to blacks at this golf club, is that right?

"You'll not find a colored employee at Augusta who would tell you I wasn't a fair employer."

"As long as they stayed in their place."

"The South is not the North, Mr. Alexander. It never was; it never will be. I remember when Governor Faubus trapped the President into sending federal troops into Little Rock. I knew from the very beginning that Ike was determined never to do that. But Faubus created a situation where Ike had no way out. He had to send troops, and that sealed his fate with all the southern voters. They hated him for doing that. To everyone down here, integration meant only one thing. Mixed marriages."

"You're not a fan of interracial marriage, Mr. Roberts?"

"No, I'm not. You go down to Brazil and see what has happened there. Ask any businessman who runs a corporation and he'll tell you, if they had their choice, they'd hire white people to work for them or they'd hire black people. But they don't want to hire mixed-race people. Those people are nothing but trouble. They don't know who they are. Black or white!"

"You better not tell Tiger Woods."

"I'm not a racist, Mr. Alexander."

"No?" I pushed my plate away. "What are you, then?"

Lightnin' appeared to clear my dinner plate, and Roberts said, "Ask Lightnin' what the coloreds thought of me. Go ahead, if you think I'm such a racist."

I looked up at Lightnin' and then pointing to the portrait of Clifford Roberts, asked the man was the founding chairman of Augusta National was like as a human being.

Lightnin' hesitated. The question had caught him off guard,

but he was still going to be careful about what he said to a white stranger.

"Mr. Roberts, he was a stern man, but fair. We always knew where we stood with Mr. Roberts. He didn't put up with any back talk, no sir, but he treated us fair and square."

"He wasn't a racist then?"

"Well, I won't know about that, sir. I didn't know the man's mind." Lightnin' stepped away from the table. "Coffee, sir? We also got some mighty fine peach cobbler, if you have room for dessert."

"Coffee will be fine, Lightnin'. Decaf, if you please. I need to get to bed."

The tall man smiled and asked good-naturedly, "How are those college boys treating you, sir?"

"So far, the old man is doing okay," I said. "Thanks for asking."

He nodded and, as he headed for the kitchen with the dishes, added, "Well, you go show those young ones how to play, Mr. Alexander. There's plenty of life in those bones of yours, God willing." He was smiling, enjoying the exchange.

"From your mouth to God's ear," I called after him.

"Amen!" Lightnin' responded, laughing before disappearing into the kitchen.

"What did I tell you, Mr. Alexander?" The familiar cold smile washed across the dead man's face.

"If you're not a racist, then why did Charlie Sifford say back in the '50s, that you'd said as long as you were alive, there would be nothing at the Masters but black caddies and white players?"

"Sifford never qualified for the Masters and, since his time, more than one black man has played in the tournament. I think we can lay that racial ghost, so to speak, to rest." He lit his thick cigar and took a puff.

"But you're dead now. None of that happened when you were alive."

"Lee Elder played here when I was alive."

"Do you know who Frank Hannigan is?"

"Of course I know who Frank Hannigan is!"

"After Hannigan retired from the USGA, he wrote that you were innately suspicious of blacks, Hispanics, and even Italians. He said you thought Italians' shortening their names was evidence of some sort of sinister behavior."

"It's possible. Why would they change their names if they had nothing to hide?"

"I don't know. Why didn't you ask Eugenio Saraceni?"

"What in the world are you talking about?" Again there was a pained look on the old man's face.

"I'm talking about Gene Sarazen. He changed his name from Saraceni to Sarazen because it sounded more like a golfer. Does that mean his famous 'shot heard around the world' in the Masters doesn't count?"

Roberts crossed his legs and dragged deeply on his cigar. He looked annoyed by my questioning. Then he said, "If my offer to help you win the Masters is so distasteful, if you don't want to align yourself with an alleged racist, then I will have to speak to one of the other amateurs."

"No you won't."

He watched me without speaking. He had the eyes of a predator: They never blinked. Before he could speak, I continued, "You didn't randomly pick me, Mr. Roberts. You knew I needed you."

Now he smiled. He leaned forward, and slowly, deliberately, tapped a wedge of cigar ash into the tray. I thought then that the Trophy Room at Augusta must be the last place in America where diners could smoke while they ate.

"You're much more intelligent than I realized, Mr. Alexander."

"I'm a professor of literature, Mr. Roberts. I was schooled in the seven types of ambiguity."

"I wasn't afforded the luxury of studying ambiguities, Mr. Alexander. I made my career by straight talk and square deals."

"Everything was black and white in your world, right? No mixed metaphors or mixed races."

"We all have our shortcomings. Otherwise, we wouldn't be human."

"On that profundity, I think I'll call it a night." I pushed back from the table.

"We haven't settled the terms of our agreement," Roberts said. "And, besides, Lightnin' hasn't returned with your coffee." Roberts glanced around, showing annoyance at the black's man slowness, as if the standards of the club had slipped since his death.

"What terms?"

"You'll take the help I provide on the golf club, follow my instructions."

"And if I do?"

"I'll see that your wife is cured."

I stared at him incredulously. How could he think I would take him seriously?

"Oh, there's one more thing," Roberts added, looking up. "Your caddie."

"I told you. Clay is caddying for me this week."

"It will make my job that much more difficult."

"It might make your job more difficult, but not mine. I promised the boy. I won't go back on my word. And that is not even one of the seven kinds of ambiguity. Good night, Mr. Roberts."

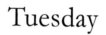

Tuesday

14

THE NEXT DAY, playing with the college kids for a sawbuck a side, I had a double-bogey 5 on the fourth hole when my utility wood landed in the front green-side bunker and I failed to get up and down. Trying to play too cute a shot with my sand wedge, I skulled the ball over the green and lost the hole. I was now two down to the kids in our skins game, and while I wasn't looking forward to losing to the college boys, I mostly didn't want to lose a round to kids half my age.

Standing on the tee of number five I was the last to drive, which was okay, as it gave me a few minutes to calm down before I had to hit off on another of Bobby Jones's patented dogleg left holes. All the holes at Augusta National were named after flower or trees and this hole was called Magnolia. It was a par 4 that was only 455 yards long, but it played all of that, Clay told me. "You can't cut the corner here. It's 319 to carry that left-side bunker, and you won't make par if you land in it."

"You need not worry about carrying those left-side bunkers," Clifford Roberts said, making his first appearance of the day. He had a cigar in his mouth though it wasn't yet nine o'clock.

I wasn't sure he was right. The hole had been overhauled before the 2003 Masters, years after his death. The tee was moved back 30 yards, and the bunkers were moved, deepened, and enlarged. I remember reading that Tom Watson had given up trying to win at Augusta because he couldn't hit the ball far enough off the tee to leave himself a short iron that would hold the green. Still, he was good enough to put together a great round in 2010. If Watson couldn't manage number 5, I had no chance.

"Line up off those three magnolias on the far left side of the fairway, and you'll be fine," Roberts said, then told me another tale about the old days at his course; like every member of every private country club in America, he had an unending supply of stories about their golf course. This time it was about the hole I had just double-bogeyed. The last thing a player needs is be reminded about a badly played hole, but that didn't concern Roberts. He would talk golf and Augusta National, regardless.

"One year on number four when Hogan was playing with Ken, Venturi hit a 3-iron and it landed twelve feet from the pin. This was back in '54. Venturi was still in the army and an amateur. Hogan sees what Ken did, so he pulls out his 3-iron and hits a great shot, but his ball ends up in the front bunker.

"Now Hogan can't figure out why his drive was short and asks Venturi if he can look at his club. With one glance, Hogan sees Ken's club is stamped as a three but has the loft of a one-iron. Hogan should have known not to trust another player's clubs—even an amateur's—because every player works on his equipment."

With that, Roberts nodded toward the three college players standing by the markers and told me not to try to keep up with them. I realized what he was doing: using his Hogan story as words of wisdom for me.

"I wasn't trying to keep up with the kids," I explained. "I was just trying to get on the green."

"Four plays long; this hole plays longer."

Zack Trout hit away and I walked up to join the others, and to escape Roberts' chattering. Clay had already pulled my driver.

With my game, I had only one shot on this dogleg, a gentle fade. I had to aim down the left rough, hug the tree line, and then let the ball work itself into the fairway. What I concentrated on was trying to keep my ball away from the deep left-side bunkers. I'd have no shot then to the target. All the greens at Augusta National were big and undulating, but 5 was famous for its false front and camel humps. There wasn't a flat putt to be had. I needed to get the ball close and below the flag.

I hit a good drive—not as far as my playing partners, but okay for me, and I kept it out of trouble. As we headed up the fairway, I saw I had gotten it out far enough to give me a relatively level lie, making it slightly easier to go at the pin.

I caught up with Clay and gave him my driver. He said I'd be hitting first, then added, "Drive for show; putt for dough." He grinned, repeating the golfing cliché.

"If only I could putt." I had meant to be ironic, but my comment sounded more self-pitying than sarcastic.

"We'll learn the greens," Clay answered. "It's early. We haven't played the backside, right?"

It wasn't early enough, I told myself. Now I regretted that I hadn't come a few days sooner to play Augusta National.

"Don't worry about the greens," Clifford Roberts offered. Clay had moved ahead and was walking with the other caddies in the foursome.

"Why, are you planning to have Bobby Jones read my putts?"

"Something like that."

"I'm not sure the USGA will think that's kosher."

"Keep the ball in play and you'll be in contention come Sunday afternoon." Roberts sounded full of confidence.

I reached my drive, where Clay had left my bag to pace off the distance, and waited to hear Clay's yardage when he came back to me.

"It's 185," he said. "Pin is back. You need to fly it at least 180 to carry the false front."

I pulled the 5-iron and paused, and waited for him to agree. The ball was set up on the smooth fairway, and I thought again how the fairways and greens at Augusta were nothing like the raggedy turf I was accustomed to playing on back in southern Illinoois. I could eat dinner off this grass.

The pin was cut to the right side on the upper tier. For the opening round on Thursday morning, I knew the flag would be jammed into the left side and much more difficult to get anything close.

Clay nodded okay to my club selection, and I stepped over to play the ball, which was only an inch above my stance. I'd aim right to compensate for the lie and choke down on the club to keep the plane of my swing.

Of all the clubs in my bag, I hit the 5-iron best. It was my magic wand. I had given up trying to play long irons. I didn't have the strength left in my arms for the 2- and 3-irons, but then, most of the pros had also given up playing long irons in favor of hybrids. If I couldn't play like a pro, I told myself, at least I could carry the same equipment in my bag.

From behind me, Roberts told me what I already knew, "That's a false front, and the ball will come back to you if you aren't high enough on the hump. Go for the center of the green and take what's left. Play for a par."

I laced a draw to the right side of the green. The ball landed short but kicked forward and ran to the hole, curling to a stop well below the flag. I was on in two and putting for a birdie on what most pros called the most difficult par 4 at Augusta National.

Across the fairway, Ron Gulaskey applauded my shot, and I lifted my club to acknowledge his praise. Zack gave me a high five from where he stood beside his drive, and Smith shouted out that I was playing like a pro.

"Great shot!" Clay exclaimed, taking the club from me. He wiped the face clean and slipped it back into the bag. I stood with him in the middle of the fairway, while the other three played up feeling that intense satisfaction all players feel after hitting a great shot and knowing that they are safely on the green. The college kids had drives that were all clustered together, all thirty yards ahead of my pop shot. They hit safely onto the expansive green, but none were inside my high-flying draw.

When we reached the green, I motioned for Clay to come over and asked him what he thought. It was an uphill eighteen-footer. I could see that it would break to the left, just before the cup. It was makeable, though I wasn't sure I was the one who could make it. Clay read the putt from both sides and, when he came back to where I was crouched behind the ball, leaned down and whispered, "It looks like it will break to the left, but it won't. Pop told me there's a lot of ghost breaks on these greens, and not a straight putt on the course outside of twelve inches. Remember, ninety percent of putts break toward Rae's Creek. You want to aim for the inside right corner of the cup and remember it's fast."

I followed Clay's instructions and knocked in the long putt for my second birdie on the course. Even if it proved to be my last, I'd at least have the satisfaction of telling my Carbondale buddies for the next twenty years that I had birdied the toughest hole at Augusta National.

15

I HAD THE HONORS on the sixth tee.

"The old man is waking up," Chuck Smith kidded me as I moved to the par-3 tee. "What do they say about sleeping bears? You don't want to wake them from their winter naps."

I smiled, saying nothing and thinking that it would be nice to beat the kids, even if only in practice. But one birdie didn't make a round.

On the scorecard, the hole was called Juniper and listed at 180. Clay had already stepped off the distance from the yardage plate.

"It's 176," he said, giving me the exact distance to the big green that was fifty feet below the tee. "It looks like it plays short, but it won't. Play to 76."

"Seven?" I asked, continuing to stare down at the huge green. The pin was cut on the lower left side, away from the hump.

"The green slopes down from the back to the front, and right to left," Clay said softly, confidentially. "You've got to be up or you'll put it in that front bunker. At least we don't have to worry about the right-side hump. They'll save that placement for Sunday. Hit the seven."

I could feel the wind coming from right to left and over my right shoulder. It would be a helping breeze if I hit a draw. But I didn't want to be short in the front left bunker. I pulled the 7-iron and Clay moved away to give me room to tee up. From the corner of my eye, I saw that the others had not selected a club. They were waiting to see how I'd fare with my club, and use my results to educate themselves. It was the way to play tournament golf.

I dropped my Titleist on the smooth turf and toed it onto a level spot. I wouldn't use a tee; that would only give me more loft, more distance.

When I stepped behind the ball to get my line, Roberts was standing next to me. As if we were in the middle of a casual conversation, he asked, "Do you remember William J. Patton? We called him Billy Joe."

I shook my head in disbelief. There wasn't a serious golfer in America who didn't know about Billy Joe Patton, the amateur from Morganton, North Carolina, who with his homemade swing almost won the Masters, finishing third behind Hogan and Snead.

"Back in '54, on Sunday afternoon," Roberts continued, oblivious to my incredulity, "Billy Joe hit the stick on this hole and the ball slid straight down and wedged itself between the cup and the flagstick. When he removed the bamboo, it dropped in for an ace."

I stepped up to the ball, hitched my left pant leg and carefully set the clubface, getting my line. Roberts would never stop talking, but I was delaying play for a reason that was apparent to no one on the tee but me.

"What's important about that ace was how Billy Joe couldn't get set on this tee. He moved his ball three times before he felt comfortable. That's my point, Mr. Alexander. Get comfortable over the ball before teeing off here. It's a deceptive little hole."

I nervously moved my ball an inch, then reset myself. Half of me wanted to step away to restart my routine, but already I knew I was taking too long to hit a simple 7-iron off the par-3 tee, even if it was the 6th hole of Augusta National.

"Easy," Clay whispered from just beyond the right marker. He had caught my uneasiness on the tee.

His quiet manner had a calming effort. I took another practice swing and then played away, hitting a hard seven to the wide-open green.

My ball was on line all the way. As if it had eyes, I thought, watching its pretty flight in the bright early-morning sky.

"It's long," Clay said, even before I realized I had hit it too strong. For all my intention of playing a safe shot, the adrenalin racing through me had given me too much club. My ball carried the flag, hit behind the pin, slammed into the ridge and bounced left, leaving me a long, downhill putt.

"Okay," Clay said encouragingly. "You're on the green."

I smiled. The eternal optimism of a good caddie. You've got to love it, I thought, taking a deep breath and thinking ahead that I was capable of knocking my putt off the green, once it gained speed coming downhill.

Zack was teeing up, and Charlie Smith told him to knock it inside the old man's ball. These guys were having fun. They could pick on me, now that my birdie on the last hole had proved I was worthy of a match. It was how they played golf on their college teams. Lots of trash talk between swings. I had been there once myself.

Zack hit a beauty. It came high off his club and short of the pin, leaving him a makeable uphill putt.

What did he hit, I asked him when he stepped over to me.

He showed me the 8-iron before slipping it into his bag.

The kid was surprisingly strong. He wasn't six feet tall, and couldn't have weighed more than one-fifty, but, like Ben Hogan, Zack was able to generate swing speed with his quick hands and great agility.

Charlie Smith resembled an English rugby player: a thick wedge of a body, short clipped hair and a shiny red complexion. It looked as if his face was on fire. And he played with fierce, angry intensity, as if he had something against his ball.

On 6 he pulled his drive. It hit the bank left of the green and bounced down the hill almost into the trees. He followed that drive with an onslaught of creative cursing that reduced the other kids and their caddies, even his own, to peals of laughter.

Clifford Roberts stepped out of whatever celestial zone he occupied to tell me about Bob Jones's father, the Colonel, whose ability to swear was so famous at Augusta that members waited until he was off his game to play a round with him, just to enjoy the Colonel's ability to weave a barrage of swear words into a piece of southern poetry.

Roberts kept talking about the Colonel as Ron Gulaskey, the British Amateur champ, teed off.

Gulaskey looked like a farm boy, and he was one. Growing up in rural Pennsylvania he had learned the game by caddying at the local country club. He was a poor kid who had gotten ahead in golf, and in life, through dogged determination. He didn't have the game to keep up with the best players, but somehow at the end of the match he was always still there.

And here he was again on the green at six, hitting a high floater that dropped down inside of us all, leaving him a three-foot-birdie putt. He charged off the tee, leading us through the avenue of azaleas and up to the green.

Walking to my ball, I saw Ron was closer than I realized. At home in Carbondale, I would have knocked his ball away for his birdie, but this was Augusta, and the younger roommates had side bets with each other.

I walked up the slope to where my ball had stopped, marked it, and tossed it to Clay as I surveyed my downhill putt. I hadn't a clue how to play it. There was a cluster of patrons, as spectators are called at the Masters, watching the action; they had set up their green folding chairs and claimed space beyond the green. The hole did not offer the excitement of a viewing spot, but it drew people with its scenery. And on this pretty little par-3 they could get close to the pros as they exited the green and headed to the seventh tee.

Charlie was charging to his ball, still angry for misplaying the iron. He had a tough chip. His ball needed to go up the slope and then hold the green. A hole like this could ruin his whole day.

From the left and below the hole, twenty yards off-target, Charlie's ball came up low and hot and skidded across the green. There was no way of staying close unless it hit the metal pin. It didn't. The ball ran twenty feet behind the hole. He had a putt coming back that was downhill, like mine.

Clay walked over and handed me the clean ball. I raised my eyebrows. How should I play it, I was asking. We were both standing behind my coin marker eyeing the downhill putt. Charlie came up onto the green and marked his ball and tossed it to his caddie. Zack was standing off the green. He crossed and re-crossed his legs. Everyone was waiting for me.

"Start it straight toward the tee," Clay said under his breath, as if he was sharing a state secret, or even more confidential, an Augusta National secret. "It will curl to the right."

"If I get the line, I'm home free," I said, trying to be positive.

"If you don't, you're off the bottom of the green," he chimed.

"Aren't you a big help." I glanced his way and he was grinning. I knelt down and carefully replaced my ball. I had thirty feet.

If this had been on television, they would've flashed the length on the screen down to the inch.

"Knock it in," Zack said encouragingly from across the green. Once the Masters started there wouldn't be much cheerleading, even among the amateurs.

I could see the roll. I could see the sheen of the grass. I was going with the grain. I couldn't have put my ball in a worse location.

Over my shoulder, Clay instructed. "It's four cups left of the left edge."

"It doesn't look it." I kept staring down the sloping green. Already I could picture my putt cascading by the cup, gaining speed as it ran off the green and back down the hill.

"See that white fleck on the green four feet ahead?" Over my left shoulder he pointed out the mark. He told me to tap the ball toward it. "Let the slope do the rest."

I had no better answer, that was for sure. Most, if not all, of putting is confidence—standing up to the ball and stroking the putter with optimism, if not bravado. Being timid never got a player anywhere. So I did what Clay suggested, as if it were my own idea, as if I could read the greens with the best of Augusta National's caddies.

The ball curled over the white petal and kept rolling, maddeningly slow at first, then gaining speed. I read the word Titleist off the dimpled Fusablend. My heart was in my throat, watching the ball gain momentum as it rolled downhill.

Clay had the flagstick out and had stepped away, but he never took his eyes off the spinning ball. We all watched as it tracked perfectly toward the hole. That ball wanted to hunt, as they say in the South. As it got closer I realized I might make the putt. It was in the zone. It was dead, solid, perfect. It was all of golf's clichés.

The Titleist hit the cup, bounced straight up a good four inches, dropped down and hit the bottom of the white plastic with a whack. I had made an impossible putt. I had birdied the par 3, my second birdie in a row. I was playing as if I actually belonged in the Masters.

The college kids broke into applause, as did the patrons. Charlie Smith let out a hoot and doffed his cap, and I plucked the ball from the cup. I gave my putter to Clay, grinning at him, shaking my head, marveling at how well he had read the line for me. The kid was good. I thanked whatever better instinct I had for no replaying him on my bag.

"You're killing us," Charlie Smith complained, replacing his ball.

"I'm killing myself," I answered, taking a deep breath. I knew my luck couldn't hold.

And that was true enough. My luck was tested on the next tee, the par-4 number 7 named Pampas because of the sharp grass growing left of the fairway. Most of the pros had considered it the easiest hole at Augusta until it was lengthened by forty yard, in '06, again because of Tiger. The green was small, originally designed to accept a short iron, but when the hole was lengthened and trees planted on both sides of the fairway, the green was redesigned so a pin placement could be tucked into the back right corner.

Standing in the tee box, I stared out at the chute of trees and the distant green framed by bunkers. Clay stepped up beside me and said I had to be on the left side of the tight fairway to have a level lie for my approach iron. All I could see, and think about, was the narrow corridor of trees that stretched, it seemed, as far as the eye could see.

"Hit the three," Clay suggested.

"I'm too short off the tee; we're looking at 450." I kept shaking my head as I pulled the hood off the one metal.

"Hit the three," Clay said again.

"I need to be hitting a short club to hold the green."

"Keep it to the left-center and you'll have a level lie. You hit the ball high, it will hold."

I smiled back at him, thinking that if I were his age I might be as confident about my game as he was, but despite my misgivings, I did what he said and pulled the 3-wood.

"Keep it out of the Pampas," Clay advised with a grin. "That grass will cut me to pieces if I have to go look for your ball."

I hit the 15-degree fairway metal. It clipped some of the branches on the left side of the tight fairway and lost some distance, but it was safely on the fairway. Now what I had left was a long second shot into the postage-stamp-size green bunkered like a military fortress.

"You've got a shot," Ron said encouragingly, as he moved to the tee. I saw he had an iron in his hand. He might be young and strong, but he wasn't reckless. I noticed Charlie Smith had already pulled his King Cobra. Of the four of us, he had the length to leave himself a wedge, even a sand wedge, into the green, if he could keep it in the fairway. Of us all, he was the least likely to keep his ball safe, but he wasn't afraid to gamble. His recklessness had the same appeal as Indy car racing. Auto wrecks were mesmerizing.

Ron's 2-iron split the fairway but left him a long iron to the green. He didn't carry a utility club in his bag, but he could play a cut 4-wood and have it come in high. He had a difficult second shot any way he played it, hitting up the rise to the bunkered green. I had a tough shot too. My only hope was that I had gotten the ball out far enough that it might have caught the downhill slope, gained another twenty yards, and given myself a level lie at the bottom of the valley. Ron would be hitting first, however, and I might learn a thing or two from the college kid.

I stepped further back in the tee box to get a better angle to watch Charlie Smith's drive. It was impressive that he would hit his driver. For some of us, this was only a practice day, a time to experiment. But Charlie wasn't experimenting. He was someone who didn't play for fun. The kid wanted to win, even if it was only a few bucks off of us.

Using a long tee, he teed up his Nike and stepped back and took three practice swings; that was his routine. As he approached his ball, he set his right foot, then his left, then quickly hitched his right shoulder, as if cocking his whole body. Always the same routine. He wasn't even nineteen, yet he'd mastered the patterns of a pro.

Charlie launched his drive. That was the only verb to describe it. He hit the Nike hard and high down the right side of the tight chute, and the tee shot never faulted. It came out of the trees, wasn't buffered by the slight wind blowing into us, and landed safely in the shallow valley of the long par 4.

We gave Smith a round of applause; he deserved it. Hitting the driver off 7 was risky, and he had gambled and won. Winning was his game. And it was his Achilles heel. Now I just had to figure out a way to metaphorically spear his foot.

"This used to be the easiest birdie hole on the course," Cliff Roberts commented, appearing at my side and matching strides with me as I walked toward my ball. "Back in '37 when Byron won, he drove the green and shot 66. Of course, the hole was only 340 then, and the green hadn't been raised, but nevertheless…."

I kept quiet, surrounded as I was by my playing partners and our caddies. I didn't mention to Roberts that I'd read that Nicklaus thought the hole had been ruined when it was lengthened. Jack had loved the small green and the precision short iron that it required.

"You could hit a wedge into this green back in the old days, but now it's one of the tightest driving holes on the course." Roberts continued, sounding pleased with himself, as if he personally had put something over on the professional golfers.

Of course, I knew that the hole had been lengthened in 2002, and again in 2006, in two fruitless attempts to bolster Augusta National against the pros playing with Dymo woods and lightweight graphite shafts. Like every other traditional golf course in the world, Augusta National was trying, and failing, to keep up with technology.

I kept walking in stride with the others and Roberts kept talking, telling me how the 7 green had been redesigned so there was a pin placement in the back half, and the putting surface had been contoured so players couldn't throw the ball deep onto the green and have it spin and hold.

Seeing him chuckle at his cleverness, I wanted to tell him that it didn't matter how many new designs the members came up with, or what trickery the Augusta National Grounds Committee thought of, there was already some young kid on the links who would get matched up with some club designer and outplay the course.

I reached my drive and stopped and stared at the flag, taking in the pretty canvas of pines framing the hole, and the five pockets of golden sand in the deep bunkers wedged around the green.

It was sights like this that always lulled a player into complacency. Great players, I knew, never fell in love with any golf hole. If you want to win, you must always see the course as the enemy. What had Hogan said about winning at Oakland Hills? "I brought this monster to his knees?"

"You have 221," Clay informed me, returning to my bag.

I snapped out of it, bringing myself back to reality. I'd been mulling over golf like an English professor. It was no way to play well, much less win.

"I'll hit the 4-wood," I said, reaching for it.

"I wouldn't," Clay advised.

"Listen to your caddie," Roberts added, materializing again at my left shoulder.

"The Ghost of Christmas Past," I blurted out.

"Pardon me?" Clay glanced around. We were alone. Zack and his caddie were twenty yards away, contemplating their approach shot.

I waved Clay off; let him think I was talking to myself.

"Use the utility wood," Roberts instructed. "The wind isn't helping. You want to aim for the left corner of the green. The grain breaks toward that pine on the back right side. The green is shallow, fifteen paces from front to back."

I ignored him and asked Clay, "Can I carry the front bunkers?"

"Yes!" Roberts declared.

"I think so," said Clay, nodding, and checked the distance again in his yardage book. We couldn't see the putting surface from where we were standing in the hollow of the fairway.

"I'll hit the four," I answered, disagreeing with both my visible and invisible advisors. "I'm uphill and into the wind. The ball will come down softer because of that."

To my right, Zack played away, hitting a long iron. It looked good in the air but before it reached the target Clay said that the ball was short. There was a puff of sand when it caught the front left bunker. Not enough club.

"You're right," Clay said, ceding to me.

I pulled the four and played it before I could start to doubt my own decision. The ball came high off the fairway and floated into the target, easily carried the left front bunker and hit the green. I saw it bounce once, then disappear.

"Did it hold?" I asked. At that moment, it didn't matter to me who answered, my teenage caddie or the ghost of Cliff Roberts.

"It will play," Clay said. "The green breaks toward the pin."

From deep in the valley, I could see the fluttering flag but little else.

I handed Clay the wood and he wiped the face, then slipped

the club into the bag. We both looked over to watch Ron Gu-laskey hit up. I wanted to ask Roberts what he thought, was I on the green or not, but I had no way of addressing him without drawing stares from Clay. I was going out of my mind, I thought, plotting how I could get my ghost to weigh in on my ball.

Gulaskey drove down on his long iron. He was trying to hit a cut shot into the elevated green, which didn't make much sense. Perhaps he thought he had a better chance of holding on the small green. Even without seeing the ball land, I knew it had carried the green and perhaps even the backside bunkers. If nothing else, he would be playing his third shot out of trouble.

He glanced my way when he finished his swing, smiled guilt-ily, as if I were his teacher, and then shrugged as if to make the point that this cut 3-iron was the best he could do. It was true, of course, that there were some golf shots, regardless of how long we played the game, that we just couldn't master.

That left Charlie Smith. He had arrived at his ball and, without pausing, pulled his wedge to play from less than 110 to the high green. He had been waiting all of us out and he was anxious to get on the green. The hardest part of golf is not the swing, but the waiting and walking, the long delays, the irregular rhythm of the game.

It wasn't a game for extroverts, Kerry said, following me around the course in my first amateur tournaments. She had been driven crazy, she said, waiting for something to happen. She couldn't grasp the beauty of a well played chip shot, the simple elegance of a lob wedge.

All that she really appreciated were my drives. Brute power she understood. She could understand the subtleties of good acting on the stage, but not that of a downhill putt taking the break on Bermuda grass.

Charlie Smith pounced on his 52-degree wedge. He was a

strong kid, and strength, not subtlety, was his game. His wedge
was high enough, long enough, and dead straight on the flag
stick. Perhaps he had played it too cute, I thought, as we followed after it, climbing the rise to the green, but his ball must
have been close, given the scattering of applause coming from
the early-morning patrons parked behind the green. They told us,
before we could see ourselves, that Charlie Smith had hit it stiff.

I wasn't, however, thinking about Charlie Smith's ball, the short
five-footer he had left for a birdie. I could see when I stepped
onto the green that I was looking at another tester, over twenty
feet, and all downhill on a slick surface. Just looking at my putt
made me dizzy.

I marked the ball and stepped off the left side of the small
green, giving the play over to young Zack and Ron, both of
whom had missed the putting surface and had to play up. Zack
came out of the front bunker with a poor sand wedge, leaving
himself another long putt that he blew. Gulaskey's chip from
behind the green was long and he 2-putted coming back. It
wasn't until they both walked off seven green with bogies that I
carefully replaced my ball on the smooth grass.

"It will break, what, four inches, left to right?" I asked.

We were both hunkered down behind the ball, studying
the line.

"Six inches from the left edge," Clay said.

I stood up and walked around to the other side and looked
at the line from that angle, then came back and studied the
line from halfway, giving myself a third view. If I had done as
much studying in college as I did lining up an Augusta National
putt, I told myself, I could have graduated summa cum laude.

"It's going to break ten inches," I told Clay, coming back
to where he stood behind my ball. He had a white towel in
his hand, and I half expected he might raise and wave it, sur-

rendering any chance of my making this downhill slider. I was half hoping Cliff Roberts would make another ghostly cameo, but he was, I was grasping, never around when I needed him. Clay shrugged and nodded, but he didn't look convinced. He finally admitted that it all depended on how hard I hit the putt.

True enough. The correct line was only one gauge. More depended on the speed of the putt as it gained momentum going downhill with the grain.

From the get-go, my lengthy putt didn't have a chance. I was so worried about the line that I didn't stroke it. The ball just piddled off the putter, rolled erratically as it gained speed, then drifted off line and away from the hole as if it had no purpose at all for being on the green. It stopped outside of Charlie Smith's ball marker. I was still away but now I was putting to save par.

Miraculously I make that putt and, walking off the green, turned around in time to see Charlie make his birdie. Without wasting time surveying the line or break of his four-footer, he jammed his putt home. Then he walked straight off the green, letting his caddie retrieve his ball.

I must admit the kid was beginning to annoy me. His Torrey Pines cockiness wasn't his best quality. The three of us followed him to number 8, which was called Yellow Jasmine on the scorecard because of the flowering vines that grew the length of the left side. The hole was 570 yards. It was the second longest hole at Augusta National, and playing all the way uphill and into a dogleg left made it more difficult than number 2.

Still, the hole had given up the second most famous double eagle in Masters history, back when it was 530 yards and Bruce Devlin holed a 4-wood for a two in the first round of the '67 tournament. Devlin, playing from deep down in the fairway, never saw it go into the cup. He had lost sight when it hit in front of the elevated green. The ball took one bounce, the gallery told him later, rolled up to the cup, hesitated at the lip, then tumbled in. Golf should always be so easy.

Charlie had pulled his King Corba again and teed up a long tee. The ball stood perched high, like a miniature water tank outside of any small farm town in Southern Illinois. Smith could reach the green in two, driving like he did, another young golfing Turk. But he'd have to carry the right-side bunker, 315 yards from the tee, in order to have a clear shot to the target. There was, however, something of a helping breeze, and I knew that with his cockiness from the last hole, he'd go for it. And he did.

16

CHARLIE'S DRIVE CARRIED 300 yards, long enough to catch the sand trap. From the tee we saw the puff of sand when it hit near the edge of the bunker.

He was swearing to himself even before he leaned forward and snatched his tee off the grass.

"It will play," I told him, being friendly.

Charlie grunted.

I teed up on the far left side of the markers and stepped back, letting him stew and watching as he shoved the Corba into his bag.

I didn't think I'd make the Masters cut, given the history of amateurs at the tournament, but I knew Charles Jacob Smith of San Diego State had no chance. Augusta National was difficult enough, and he wasn't helping his case with his adolescent outbursts.

My drive did what I wanted, hugging the left side, then my fade brought the ball back into the fairway. I was short and left of the only bunker on the hole.

Both Trout and Gulaskey missed the fairway, and both missed on the left side as they drove to keep away from the bunker, though neither one, I thought to myself, had Charlie Smith's length off the tee.

I stepped off the tee box with them; Charlie again had charged ahead, as he had on every hole on the front side.

"He's like a farm horse," I nodded towards Smith's bulky back. "He can't get to the barn fast enough."

"I beat Charlie last year and won the Haskins. I think he's still mad at me," Zack said.

"But you both made Golfweek's first team," Ron replied.

"You got screwed," said Zack.

"Next year, maybe."

They were talking college golf, and I kept quiet, afraid of embarrassing myself.

"The Haskins is like the Heisman," Zack went on, sensing I didn't know about the award, which, in this case, wasn't true. I knew all about the Haskins. "Chuck thinks he should have won but that there's a southern bias, because I'm from Alabama and the award was started at the Country Club of Columbus here in Georgia and named after this old-time pro."

"Fred Haskins," I said, "from Hoylake, England. He was the pro at the country club, and before that he had been an assistant at East Lake in Atlanta, where Bobby Jones first learned to play golf."

"Oh," the two of them whispered. My burst of information silenced them. Like all kids, they thought they had invented history.

"You didn't win the Haskins, did you?" Zack asked, realizing then that there were college winners before him, and I might be one.

I smiled wryly and shook my head. "I finished second to Scott Simpson. You know where Scott went to school?" I glanced over.

We had paused in the middle of the fairway. They shook their heads.

"The University of Southern California. So, let's forget about southern chauvinism when it comes to the Fred Haskins," I said, and moved to the right side of the fairway to give Ron enough room to play away.

Both Gulaskey and Trout took the safe route to the green, hitting fairway woods. Looking across at Charlie Smith I saw he, too, had a fairway metal in his hands, and he was going for the green from the bunker. I shook my head and walked over to my drive. Clay was waiting for my arrival, as was Roberts, who told me immediately how Bob Jones got Haskins the pro job at the Country Club of Columbus. In Clifford Roberts's world, everything revolved around Bobby Jones.

I let his comment pass and focused on my next shot. My ball was sitting up on the green carpeted fairway. I stared at the green. Only the tops of the trees were visible.

"Hit the driver off the deck," Clay told me.

I smiled, thinking I had not heard that term in years.

"You can do it." He was full of confidence about my ability.

I glanced over at Charlie. He had stepped out of the bunker and was watching and waiting for me to play. He was still holding his 3-metal wood.

I pulled the hood off my R9. I was thinking that if I managed to catch it, I'd put pressure on Smith. Let's see how good he was standing up to pressure.

"Keep the knees flexed," Clay advised, pulling the bag away.

I carefully set the club down behind the ball and widened my stance. Roberts was standing off by himself, smoking his cigar and silently watching. I half expected him to say this shot was not worth the gamble. All I was trying to do, he must have guessed, was show up the cocky kid. I took another easy practice swing. Out of the corner of my eye, and across the fairway, I saw Charlie Smith cross and uncross his legs, growing impatient with my deliberateness. I lowered my head and smiled.

I set up going to the edge of the pines on the left side. I couldn't see the green because of the elevation, and because the green was tucked behind the left-side trees. Everything was going against me: distance and direction. There was no way, with my fade, that I could manufacture a drive that would work left around the tree line. Playing blind, however, gave me a certain amount of freedom. I couldn't see what trouble I might be getting into.

I swung slow and easy and kept my balance with my sweeping swing. The ball came off the carpet without a hitch. It climbed the rise, rode the morning breeze, and bore toward the deep contoured mounds that encased the green, much like ocean waves edge an island.

"Is it there?" I asked, knowing Roberts would reply. He had the history of this hole. What I knew about Yellow Jasmine I had only read in books.

"Fine shot!" Roberts declared. From the tone of his voice, I knew he was impressed.

"Close," Clay added, grinning. "You're safe." He nodded appreciatively as he took the driver from me. Trout and Gulaskey, farther up the fairway, turned and tipped their caps; Charlie Smith stepped back into the bunker.

Going for the green from the sand with a 3-wood wasn't the smart play. Charlie's ball came out fat from the soft sand and carried less than a hundred yards. His third shot would be a long iron into a narrow target.

The green was narrow and deep, but there were no bunkers. It was a hole I could birdie. I was beginning to understand what holes I could challenge at Augusta National, and where I should be wary. This was a golf course that took away as much as it gave.

Charlie hit a 5-iron that was too much club. The green was deep, more than thirty yards from front to back, but there was a ridge beyond the front left pin placement. Charlie hit into it and the ball checked up.

Zack and Ron were both closer to the target, and on the right side of the fairway. They had clear shots to the cup, the easiest pin placement of the week.

I walked up to the pin and took in the slope of the green, picked a spot where I wanted my ball to land, then walked back to where Clay was waiting beside my ball. I told him what I had in mind: a high, soft lob wedge with as little spin as possible.

"Knock it stiff," Clay answered, encouraging me.

I set myself up for an explosion shot, an open stance with my feet, knees, hips, and shoulders pointing well left of the target and setting the ball midway between my feet. I didn't open the face of the wedge; I needed the distance.

I glanced once more at my target and swung slowly, lazily, up-and-down, and kept my wrists stiff throughout my languid tempo. The ball came off the club face soft and high and landed short of the pin and checked up. I was below the hole and within two feet of the cup. An easy birdie putt.

The other three finished up with pars, dropping another shot to me. Walking to the ninth tee I needled Charlie Smith, telling him that the old man had the honors again.

It was the wrong thing to say to Charlie and I was immediately sorry that I had kidded him. He was staring ahead, steaming at himself and his play. His anger had silenced the foursome.

Reaching nine, I went straight to the tee box and took in the hole. It was another of Bobby's doglegs that favored his draw. The hole fell away from the tee and turned left 250 yard out.

"There's Roberts's Ridge," Cliff Roberts announced, appearing beside me. He pointed with his cigar. Two hundred yards out, there was a level mound bulging up the sloping fairway. "I had that built," he announced proudly. "When we built the course, this was number eighteen, and I wanted a level lie to play my wood into the green. No hanging, downhill, or sidehill lies when I played against Bob."

It was a true story, but with the hole having been lengthened, the mound was passé. A flaw, if anything, on the flowing fairway.

I was looking beyond the mound, picking a spot to place my drive. I had to keep the ball to the right side to have a decent approach into the green, which was an easy enough target. There were two bunkers on the left side, the green sloped from back to front, and there was always wind at this high end of the course.

I turned away from Cliff Roberts and pulled my driver.

"Keep it in the fairway," Clay advised.

I didn't. I did something I rarely did. I jumped all over the R9 and ducked hooked it, sending my ball into and through the pine trees to the left of the fairway. It headed toward the first fairway until the last pine kicked it down.

It was a hacker's tee shot, and the college kids knew that well enough and kept silent. To his credit, Chuck Smith didn't needle me. He teed up and hit a beauty that split the fairway and carried over 300, leaving him a mid-iron to the green.

Tramping to my ball I had no doubt I'd find it sitting up on the pine straw like an abandoned ostrich egg. And I'd have no shot. I'd be chipping back into the fairway and still have a long iron to the green. Or I could take an unplayable and go back to the tee and drive off again. The only way I could save par would be to do something creative, but what that might be, I had no idea.

Reaching the ball, I asked Clay what he thought, but Cliff Roberts responded, saying, "Do what Gary Player did."

I glanced Roberts's way. I had no idea what Gary Player had done, and Roberts took my puzzled look as an invitation to explain in detail how Player, in the third round of the '61 Masters, was also in the left-side pine trees 160 from the green. Instead of punching his ball back out onto the fairway and settling for a bogie, he had the marshals clear the gallery from the left side of the green, then hit a big slice up the first fairway. His ball came in over the bunkers and over the green, but he chipped back for one putt and went on to beat Arnold Palmer and win his first Masters.

I stepped behind the ball and looked left, not right, studying the tree line to see if I had an opening through the Georgia pines.

"He hit a four wood," Roberts said.

If I hit a four wood, I'd be in the middle of Washington Avenue.

I turned to Clay and asked what he thought about playing up the first fairway.

"Like Gary Player?"

"You know about that?"

"My Dad told me." Clay gestured towards my exit route, adding, "but there were fewer trees back then."

I looked the other way, toward where my playing partners' balls were in the wide fairway. They were clustered together, caddies and players, waiting for me to disentangle myself from the trees.

"It's not a 4-wood," Clay said, mulling my club selection. He left the bag standing and moved around to stand behind the ball and see the angle of attack. I saw his eyes darting up and down the tree line, checking to see how low I had to keep the ball. The beauty of pine trees was their stately height and thin, bare trunks. They were like Paris walkway models.

"You don't want to try and reach the green," Clay said.

"No?"

"Too many variables. The bunkers. The slick green." He kept shaking his head. "You want to come up short of those two bunkers, in the second cut, then lob a wedge onto the green." He sounded certain. "Hit the five and keep it low," he instructed.

Without waiting for my answer, Clay pulled the club and handed it to me, asking, "You know the way to play this shot?"

I knew the basics. Every player knew how to create a slice: Play the ball forward, punch it out, cut across it. My hope was that Clay might have some new way of playing off the slick pine needles that carpeted the forest floor.

"The ball is going to skim on you," Clay advised, "like soft butter off a knife. You can't control it. Play the ball forward and aim ten yards left of the target." He pointed toward the Crow's Nest. "Keep the back of your left hand square and don't turn the club over. Drive down and through impact. Don't worry about anything. Let it fly."

I stepped up to the ball, aimed at my bedroom in the Crow's Nest, and swung away. The ball started left, cleared the pine trees, then worked right. I had 200 to the left side bunkers. I could never hit a 5-iron that far. And I was right. I came up twenty yards short of the sand and safely in the famous second cut of Augusta National. I had a difficult pitch to the difficult finishing hole on the front side, but it was a helluva shot and walking back up one fairway, I asked Clay how he knew I should play the cut slice out of the trees.

"I saw it on TV."

"Television?"

He nodded. "On the Golf Channel. A film done by Bob Jones back in the '30s on how to use hickory shaft clubs."

I glanced around, thinking Cliff Roberts might have more to say, but he didn't materialize. The golf instruction films Jones did in Hollywood, I guessed, had come before Roberts met up with Bobby Jones.

We were still walking up the rise when Charlie played his ball from down the fairway. He came up between the mounds, hit short and ran onto the green, but it didn't have the distance and it tumbled back, gaining speed as it rolled off the green.

"Jesus," I whispered, seeing the results of Charlie's approach. The pin was cut on the front ledge. Nothing would hold.

"Play it like O'Meara did," Roberts advised, appearing at my side, "when he won in '98 against Freddy Couples. Hit twenty feet above the stick; it will come back to the pin."

His instructions were too simple to work, but strangely, I knew I could do it. I could see the shot I needed "to execute" as Kerry would always tell me when I practiced at Hickory Ridge.

I pulled my 52-degree wedge. Roberts kept talking, restating how O'Meara had played the shot. I stepped away from the ball. I didn't have the same angle as O'Meara. I was coming in from the left side and out of the second cut, not from the middle of the short carpeted fairway. I had to clear the left side bunkers and have the ball check. I was worried that the ball would jump and not take the roll.

I glanced over at Clay.

"Any ideas?" I asked. The kid was on a roll. I didn't want to break my string of good luck by not listening to him.

"Go with the wedge. Play it six feet left of the flag. The ball will hit on that fringe and tumble forward, then catch the slope." He studied his caddie book for a moment, then added, "The pin is twenty-one feet from this side. If you're lucky, you'll be close. If not, you'll be off the green."

"Thanks," I grinned over at him.

Surprisingly, his flippant attitude relieved my tension. There is something to say about being too serious about the game. I hit the wedge with a full swing, fully relaxed. I hit it the way Mickelson does, looking as if he is sleepwalking through his round.

I had to hit the ball far enough to clear the bunker, high enough to land on the fringe of the narrow green, and left enough to catch the slope and come back down to where the hole was cut in the front of the green.

It was one of those impossible chips that you just play and take whatever you can get. Sometimes you're lucky and the ball behaves, and for a few minutes, or least until your next shot, you believe you can really play this game, and golf isn't that difficult. Then, of course, just when you have convinced yourself, the scenario changes and you are back with the rest of mankind, hacking away, struggling to make par.

The ball landed past the lip of the bunker, bounced and kicked up, then took the gentle slope to filter down to the cup. It curled to a stop four feet below the pin, giving me a makeable putt.

My cozy wedge into the ninth green unnerved Charlie. He pressed his approach, trying to knock it in, then missed his downhill putt and settled for a bogey. I stepped up and knocked in my par putt and to win the front-side Nassau.

17

AND I WON THE BACK SIDE as well. I took the kids to the cleaners, I joked to Kerry when I called her after my round. I had found the secret of scoring at the Masters, I told her.

"What's that?" she asked.

"My caddie. He's a genius at reading these greens. I was three under today."

I told her about Clay, how his father had been killed in Afghanistan, and that it had been his dream to caddie in the Masters. And now Clay was caddying for me.

"Oh, dear," Kerry said, probably thinking his dream was my responsibility.

"Don't worry," I said, "If I don't make the cut, he can still say he caddied in the Masters."

"Is he with you?" Kerry asked.

"No, I'm in my room. I had lunch and now I'm up in the Crow's Nest." In the cellular age, no one knows where anyone is. "I'm done playing for the day, but I might go out and putt later this afternoon."

"What did you have for lunch?" she asked, like all wives worried that their husbands were eating right.

"I'm having the best food in the south. I had a Masters pimiento cheese sandwich, in one of their famous green wrappers."

"Why green? Is that the Augusta color?"

"I guess so. It's because of Clifford Roberts. He didn't want to see trash on the grounds, so everything, including the napkins, is green to blend in with the grass."

"Who's Clifford Roberts, the groundskeeper?"

"Hardly. He ran Augusta National and the Masters for 46 years."

"Where is he now?"

"Dead. He killed himself in '77, but when they make a decision around here they still ask themselves, 'What would Mr. Roberts do?'"

I had more to say about Roberts, but that would have to wait until I was back in Carbondale. Then I'd say something like, "The strangest thing happen to me at Augusta."

But now I could hear in her voice that she was weary from talking, and I told her I loved her and that I'd call again later. Then I said I wanted to say hello to Peggy.

When I got my youngest child on the phone, I asked how her mother was doing. Peggy had come home from college to be with her mother while I was away. I knew Kerry would have instructed Peggy not to say anything to upset me, but my baby was incapable of not being forthcoming with her father.

"Dr. Kestin thinks Mom may have to go back to Barnes." She had lowered her voice, but I guessed she had also left the bedroom and gone into the second-floor hallway to talk. "He did some more blood tests and he's waiting for the results."

"More blood? They're draining her dry," I shouted, suddenly furious. "What in God's name are they looking for?"

"I don't know!" Peggy exclaimed, and started to cry.

Ignoring her tears, I made her tell me everything that had happened since I'd last called. I had her go over again why Kestin needed more tests.

"He said some levels had gone up or something."

"What does that mean?"

"I don't know, but Mom said maybe the cancer has come back."

"Christ!" All my strength left my body. I was sitting on the edge of the single bed in the Crow's Nest, running my hand nervously through my hair.

"It might not be anything," Peggy rushed to add. "Dr. Kestin said it could just be a faulty test; things get messed up at the lab."

I took several deep breaths, as I always did on the golf course when I had a difficult shot, and told Peggy I would call later. My daughter-in-law Janet would stop by the house after picking up my granddaughter Laura from school. It was easier to talk to Janet. She had an emotional detachment about Kerry that wasn't possible with my kids. Their mother was going through hell and it was tearing us all apart, and here I was 600 miles away from home playing a game of golf. I was some kind of husband.

I snapped it shut, closed my eyes, and forced myself to calm down. I pictured myself back in Carbondale, playing at Hickory Ridge, and I had to make a downhill three-footer to win all the marbles.

When I opened my eyes again, Clifford Roberts was standing in the doorway of the tiny room. His face was stony, and he looked as if he couldn't wait to tell me more bad news.

"You're scheduled to play early on Thursday, one of the first threesomes off," he informed me.

"I don't like playing early," I told him.

"There are advantages to being first off the tee. You won't have to stand around the clubhouse all day and fret."

"That's what I like about you, Clifford. You have all the answers. Well, I have a different answer for you: Change the time." He started to protest, and I added, "Let's see how much authority you have at Augusta. Let's see if you can still run this country club from the grave."

"Golf club, not country club," he interrupted.

"Whatever," I shrugged, then added, "You say I can win this tournament? Well, let's start small, Clifford. Let's see if you can change my tee time." With that, and a cold smile of my own, I grabbed my putter and a handful of balls from the bag and headed for the staircase. There was a lot that I couldn't control in my life, from my wife's health to my first-round tee time, but I could learn how to putt the greens at Augusta National.

Wednesday

18

ON WEDNESDAY, I hit balls in the morning, then played in the par-three tournament with the other amateurs from the Crow's Nest. It was more fun than serious golf, and afterward I worked o n the speech that Billy Payne, the chairman of Augusta National, had asked me to deliver that night at the amateur dinner. Organized by Bobby Jones in 1948, at the suggestion of Charles Yates, who had won the British Amateur Championship in '38, the amateur dinner was held on the night before the opening round of the tournament.

That night the dinner took place in the new grand ballroom of the clubhouse, with the tables full of Green Jackets—as I had started to call the members—as well as Augusta officials and the dignitaries of other golf associations from around the world. Representatives of the USGA sat beside those of the Royal and Ancient Golf Club of St. Andrews, the European Golf Association, and a half dozen other organizations. It was a dinner given for the young amateurs, but we were in the minority. The room was filled with wealthy old men.

Lightnin' was working the dinner, dressed in a freshly pressed butterscotch-colored jacket. All the wait staff were dressed the same way, but now there were also white men and women working the tables.

After dinner Billy Payne began the evening's program. He was a handsome man, dignified in the way of small-town bankers and mayors, built solid and big like a defensive end, which he had once been at the University of Georgia.

His speech was slow and southern and he spoke as if his mouth were full of grits. It took me a few minutes to begin to catch and understand his careful delivery.

Payne welcomed everyone to Augusta National, then addressed the spirit of Amateur Night by telling a Clifford Roberts story. In 1957, Roberts had received a letter from a South African man who said that his son, age 22, was a great admirer of Bobby Jones and would love an invitation to play in the Masters. The father told Roberts his son couldn't afford to travel to America, but if he received an invitation, his father would pass the hat and come up with the money.

The young man's golf record was uninspiring, but taken by the story, Clifford Roberts did invite him. The young man, Payne said, was Gary Player. He played in the 1957 Masters and finished twenty-fifth. Four years later, in 1961, he won the first of his three green jackets.

It was a nice, heartwarming story, followed by a long, impressive list of Masters champions who had first come to Augusta as amateurs and stayed in the Crow's Nest: Jack Nicklaus, Ben Crenshaw, Curtis Strange, Mark O'Meara, and Tiger Woods.

Next, Billy Payne introduced the four of us amateurs. Speaking without notes, he described each of our backgrounds. The man had done his homework. Then he smiled at me and, as he and I had agreed, invited me to say a few words on behalf of the amateurs.

"Tim, you're obviously not the average player at the Masters, what with your PhD. Could you describe, with all the reading you have done on golf, why you think the game holds such a fascination, and why the Masters, especially, draws the attention of the world to Augusta every spring?"

There was a shuffling in the room as the crowd turned toward me. I slid my chair back and took my time getting up, giving myself a moment to collect my thoughts, giving everyone time to center their attention on me as I stood at my seat. It was an old trick that any professor uses when meeting a class of new students.

I began by thanking the members of Augusta National for inviting all of us amateurs to play in the Masters. I paid homage to Bobby Jones and Cliff Roberts and what they had given to golfers, amateurs and professionals, for all these years with their tournament that, I reminded everyone, announced the start of the golf season in America.

"There is something magical about Augusta and the Masters," I said. "People who don't play golf know that Augusta National is the standard by which all golf tournaments are judged. And players, regardless of their ability, go off the first tee believing that, yes, this is their year to break a hundred, to break eighty, to even break par.

"And the luckiest of all come to Augusta National in the springtime to see if they, too, have the game to play with the legends of golf."

I gestured toward the other amateurs, my roommates in the Crow's Nest and, including them with a sweep of my hand, continued, "We are thrilled to be here as young amateurs. Well, some of us are not so young," I let a ripple of laughter cross the room and then went on, "but all of us are fortunate to walk in the footsteps of Bob Jones, Ben Hogan, Arnold Palmer, Jack Nicklaus, and today, Tiger Woods.

"We idolize them because there is something magical about their ability to hit a little ball and make it behave, to make it go against the wind, or with the wind, and then, on the green, to follow the ebb and flow of a smooth surface and click into the cup.

"There's also a beauty to the golf swing, a self-contained artistry—a dance, let's call it. A smooth grace of arms and legs and body, all moving in a solo tango on a manicured lawn.

"And there is the sheer power of a drive. The whack of Titanium against Urethane. The thrill of following the flight of an arching ball, a well-played shot.

"That's golf. It's a game; a sport; a passion. It is the need to drive a little ball just a little farther, or beat another player, one on one. And best of all, it is a game played on pastoral land under sun-drenched skies.

"Golf draws us back into its history—to great matches won and lost, the stories of legendary players that have been passed from one generation to the next. Today, we are here where Bobby Jones once played, and Sam Snead won, and Gene Sarazen made his marvelous double eagle.

"But the truth is that, even for us amateurs who may never be champions, golf is a personal quest, an eternal quest to win, not against an opponent, but against one's own failings. It is the attempt to hit the perfect drive, strike the greatest iron, make the longest putt. And on the rare occasion when we have the satisfaction of having hit the ball better than we could have ever imagined, we realize it as a silent pleasure that can't be shared, but that draws us again and again to the game.

"We have all been there once or twice, at that perfect meeting of the mind and the body, of the clubface and the ball, and whenever we go out to play a round, we are on a quest to reach this ecstasy once again."

I nodded to Payne and sat down. There was a moment of silence before the room broke into applause. Billy Payne rose, waited for the room to quiet, and thanked me, commenting that if I played as well as I gave after-dinner remarks, then the college kids might have a run for their money this week.

"Now, to all of you playing tomorrow, I wish you the best of luck. Play well, and take the attitude I took a few years back when I suggested to President Clinton that we play a round of golf. When he agreed, I said to the President, just to get us on the same page for the match, 'I'm gonna whup your ass.'

"So, that's what I have to say to all of you—go out there tomorrow and whup their asses!"

There was a round of applause and cheers and a quick chorus of thank yous.

The guests were standing, stretching, shaking hands across the narrow tables. I saw Billy Payne circling the crowded room, smiling, accepting the best wishes of all the officials gathered in the room. He shook hands with the heads of the Brazilian Golf Confederation, the Canadian PGA, and the Golf Union of Wales. Then he was lost in a cluster of Green Jackets.

The doors opened and I felt the night April breeze.

Walking into the cool evening, I wandered over to the giant old oak tree on the front lawns of the old manor clubhouse and stopped there to gaze across the darkened golf course. And I waited for Clifford Roberts to find me, as I knew he would.

19

I HEARD HIS VOICE before he emerged from the shadows.

"Thank you."

"For what?"

"For what you said. You know, we built Augusta National in the middle of the Great Depression. It was a struggle. No one takes that into account when they write about us today."

"Some do. I do."

Then, as if succumbing to the nostalgia of the night, Roberts confessed, "Augusta was the only home I ever had. My father was the shiftless sort. He would buy and sell whatever he could. His ways finally drove my mother to her suicide."

"And what drove you, Mr. Roberts?"

It was a question I had been debating asking, and in the darkness, and having had two glasses of wine, I finally found the courage. "The papers said you had cancer and that was why you killed yourself. But accounts I've seen say that wasn't true—

no cancer, no dementia. You were feeble, yes, but many people are, and they don't blow their brains out."

Roberts was silent for a moment, and we both stared into the vast blackness of the course. The famous holes of Augusta were beyond our sight, but as my eyes adjusted to the night, I managed to make out the shape of the first tee.

"Family tradition?" Roberts asked rhetorically, making a joke of my question. Then he replied seriously, as if he, too, had been contemplating his actions since his death: "They were all gone, all my friends. Everyone I knew, Bob Jones, the President, all my friends. It was time to end it."

"You left your wife."

"Yes, and I loved Betty. She was my third wife, as you must know, and I loved her. I wouldn't be a burden to her or anyone."

"Let me presume to say that your wife should have been the one to decide if you were a burden. According to what I've read, your wife was quite capable of handling you."

Roberts chuckled. It was the first time I'd heard anything resembling gaiety emerge from the old man. Even in death, he held a tight rein on his emotions. The sudden drop of his guard emboldened me, and I said, "It wasn't that you worried about being a burden, Mr. Roberts. My guess is you were driven by other reasons."

The old man was silent for a moment and I realized I might have asked too personal a question when he cleared his throat and answered.

"All my life I had taken care of people, Mr. Alexander. I took care of my brothers and sisters when I was barely out of short pants. I took care of my mother until her death. I took care of Bob Jones when he developed syringomyelia, the disease that destroyed his spinal cord. I took care of Ike here at Augusta when he had his heart attacks. I took care of this golf course all my life.

"I didn't ask for the glory that was due Bob Jones, or the President, or even this old plantation. Being able to help made me feel good. I remember when I first met President Eisenhower. I wanted to help the man. I wanted to gain favor, perhaps, in his eyes, but truly I just wanted to help him."

He stopped and turned to me. "The great irony of my life is that I am just like Bowman Milligan or John Milton—those two who worked their whole lives here at the club, black men, faithful and obedient to wealthy white members."

"We all work for someone, Mr. Roberts."

"But you went another way, didn't you, Tim?" Roberts said, surprising me with his use of my first name, and with the suggestion that he knew more about me than I realized. I waited him out. "You didn't walk away from golf because of your father. That's the excuse you have manufactured for yourself over the years, and what you told the boys the other evening. Your father was proud of what you had done. When he died your mother asked you to keep playing, to play for your father. But you walked away from the game, not because of his death, but because of what I suggested the other night at dinner.

"You walked away from the game because you were afraid you couldn't measure up. You couldn't be the success that your old man had been. You have done the same with your academic career. You didn't have to stay at Southern Illinois. You are in Carbondale because you are safely tucked away in the obscurity of that downstate campus.

"You know you can't fail in Carbondale. I know that because you are just like me. I stayed all my life in the shadow of great men. I was close enough to Bob Jones and Dwight Eisenhower to be of service. I lived off the reflected glory, and never had to deal with the responsibilities of fame."

"Then why am I here in Augusta, Mr. Roberts?"

"You are trying to prove to your wife that you are worthy of her. That you are not a failure." Roberts answered.

"There are many in my profession who would not call me a failure, Mr. Roberts." I could hear the anger rising in my voice.

"But you don't call yourself a success, Tim. You have always kept your own compass when it comes to such matters. Now you are using golf to prove something to Kerry. Her cancer drove you back to golf, which as you say yourself is the only thing that you have ever done with any skill. God gives us one gift and one handicap, and we live our days trying to win against our own failings. Your gift was the game of golf. Your handicap was that you were afraid of success. You didn't want to become the person you saw in your father. So, you walked away from the game.

"But now you are back. Golf is the metaphor you need to save yourself in your wife's eyes. And you're afraid you can't."

Thursday

20

KERRY CALLED on Thursday morning to wish me good luck. I had gone downstairs to eat breakfast but couldn't handle anything more than black coffee. My nerves were a wreck, so I retreated to the Crow's Nest to calm myself. I was teeing off at 1:40 p.m.—

Cifford Roberts had somehow managed one of his small miracles and changed my start so I had time to hit some balls and loosen up. My roommates all had early tee times; they were awake and ready to play, their voices loud and anxious. All of us were nervous; this was the real thing. We had run out of days to play for fun. The Masters had begun.

We wished each other good luck, shook hands all around, joked about how poorly we expected to play. It wasn't a question of breaking par, Zack said, it was whether we could manage to break 100. Everyone laughed a little too much.

"Any words of wisdom, Doc?" Zack Trout asked. He was sitting at the card table, pulling on his socks and looking much too young to be teeing it up at the Masters. But he had won the U.S. Amateur, and that alone proved he could play with the best. Golf always favors the young.

I shook my head, and started to say something smart-ass in reply, and then realized that the boys, even Charlie Smith, were looking at me with anticipation, as if I might indeed have some words of wisdom.

"I think," I said, pulling my thoughts together as I replied, "that we have at least thirty-six holes of golf; we can't let one bad shot or hole get to us. The hard part of this game, as you know, is keeping focus on what has to be done. Look at the great pros. They're never out of the tournament. After a bad shot, a bad hole, they know they can come back and score.

"So, if I have anything to say, it is to try to break down the round into eighteen separate acts. Think of it as a stage play," I explained, and now I was repeating the advice Kerry had given me. "Every shot is one scene; every hole one act. Go out there and play it that way. Don't rush to the curtain call. Give yourself time to show the audience what you can do. And God knows, we'll have the audience."

I smiled and they laughed, for all of us secretly feared the Augusta galleries as much as we feared the greens.

"Okay?" I asked.

"Okay!" they chimed in and, cocky from my pep talk, they high-fived each other and I stood and shook their hands again. It was time to play.

When my cell phone rang I went into my room and took Kerry's call. Knowing how I react to pressure, she asked me immediately if my stomach was tied up in knots. I was legendary for throwing up before giving papers at MLA conventions.

Before I could ask how she was feeling, she plunged into advice, everything from drinking water, to walking slowly between shots, to visualizing where I wanted to hit the ball. She told me to compartmentalize the game so I wouldn't be overwhelmed by the people and players and the hullabaloo that went with the Masters.

"You're on a stage, darling, and you are in control of the scene. You're the star. Everyone wants you to succeed."

I paid attention as she talked, for what she had taught me nine months before had helped me win the Mid-Amateur and earn this invitation to Augusta. Golf isn't a metaphor for life, she had told me. It is the other way around. Life teaches you how to play the game. We live our lives with some semblance of order and wisdom, and I could apply that knowledge to a round of golf.

More important than her theories was the fact that Kerry knew me. She knew how impulsive I could be; how I could let my inability to make a decision replace my better judgment. On the day I proposed to her—the evening on which we both earned our Masters degrees from St. Louis University—she made me write out my proposal on a sheet of typing paper, sign it, then fold it and seal it in an envelope. She stuck the envelope to the refrigerator door with a magnet in the apartment we shared and told me we had two months to think it over. If either one of us changed our minds, we could remove the envelope and go on living as we were.

For two months, I glanced at the fridge every time I came into the kitchen, making sure Kerry was still with me. When the end of summer finally came, she admitted that she had held her breath, too, whenever she walked into the kitchen.

Her silly game had its purpose. She had taught me, that long-ago year when we were just kids, that it was worth waiting for dreams that needed time to germinate. It was a lesson from life that I needed now at Augusta. I had four rounds of golf ahead of me. I needed to take every round as it came.

Kerry wouldn't allow me to ask about her going to St. Louis for more tests. She said only that this was my day, my week. I wasn't permitted to worry about her. I told her that I would call as soon as I finished my round.

"Your tee time is 1:40," she informed me.

"How do you know?"

"You're all over the Southern Illusion," she said, referring by nickname to the Southern Illinoisan. "They reprinted that cute photo of you from Midlothian with the trophy."

"They won't be using it tomorrow."

"Come on, darling." In her voice I heard the tone she had used to encourage our kids when they were younger and going off to play in little league games. She said goodbye and wished me well again, and kissed me goodbye over the phone.

In the sudden silence I felt immediately and totally alone. I closed my room's door, though I was alone in the Crow's Nest. The others had gone off to play.

The sun was finally and fully out. It was warm and the air was electric. The old clubhouse felt alive. I could hear the patrons outside, an occasional burst of applause, and the hum of distant voices on the lawns beyond the building.

I took another deep breath to fortify myself and stood up. I had a lot of work to do before teeing off. Unzipping half a dozen compartments of my bag, I dumped out everything I didn't need—my rain gear, two sweaters, extra balls.

I took two new sleeves of Titleists and sat down on the bed and marked them for the round, circling the 'T' with red ink, as if I were grading my own examination papers. It was the mark I had used since returning to golf. With almost every golfer playing Titleists, marking the golf ball was the only way to be certain you were playing the right one. I marked six: three for each nine. If I needed more than six balls, it wouldn't matter— I'd be toast.

I knew what I was doing: delaying the inevitable. The idea

of playing in the opening round of the Masters sent a thrill up my spine at the same time that it left me terrified.

God, I was a mess. And, on that reassuring thought, I put on my good luck cap, the one from Midlothian, grabbed my bag and, carrying my spikes, headed down the narrow stairs to play my first round in the Masters.

21

CLIFFORD ROBERTS HAD another miracle for me, but he didn't produce it until later on Thursday. First I hit some balls, then I took a nap, ate a quick lunch, and finally, an hour before my tee time, I changed clothes and met Clay again at the pro shop. It was time for practice putts. We walked over to the green together, slipping through the crowd, and stopped on the apron, where I pulled out my Ping putter, dropped three balls and positioned them. I gave myself simple four-footers to make on the slippery bent-grass green.

If I couldn't make four-footers on the practice green, I wasn't going to get close to par on this course. I stood up straight and stretched my body, thinking, not for the first time, that perhaps I should have kept the belly putter in my bag. My legs and back weren't what they used to be, and for putting, steady legs were absolutely crucial. The long putter was saving the careers of half a dozen pros on the Champions Tour.

It even turned Bernhard Langer into a putter.

I reset myself and stroked the first of the four-footers, knowing that it broke severely right just before the hole. My stroke held firm and the ball clicked into the cup, as did the next two. I popped the balls onto the grass and paused, taking in the large green and the surroundings. Around me was a crowd of players, caddies, agents, coaches and sports psychologists. I had read where even amateurs had their own staffs. Drew Weaver was an undergraduate at Virginia Tech in 2007 when he became the first American in twenty-eight years to win the British Amateur. He had a swing coach and a sports psychologist helping him with his game.

All I had was a caddie trying to fulfill his old man's dream and a dead man trying to reach his final rest. I was a pilot for a TV Reality show.

I moved my three balls further from the cup on the putting green and looked over the line. This putt was ten feet, and while I couldn't see the break, I knew there wasn't a green at Augusta that didn't have one. Plus, these greens were lightning-fast. As Gary McCord once famously declared, Augusta National greens weren't mowed, they were bikini-waxed.

I missed the ten-footer. The ball didn't have a chance. It slipped by on the low side and ran six feet beyond. Clay left the bag and shagged the ball. On my second putt I was too high and the ball ran by the hole without, as they say, giving it a look.

Standing by myself on the big green, I felt as if all the patrons were watching me make a fool of myself. The gallery circled the green: men, women, kids, officials in pith helmets, all of them pressed against the green rope.

I moved the last of the Titleists into position and stared down the line. Ben Hogan once said that golf was two games. One game was hitting the ball. The second was putting. It was putting that finally finished him as a player. He lost his courage on the greens.

It wasn't courage that I lacked—I couldn't see the line. I missed one on the low side. I missed the next one high. On my third ball, I kept on line and drilled it dead center. If only golf allowed three attempts, I thought wryly, or allowed me to use the enlarged cup the USGA cut into the green they built for Eisenhower outside of the Oval Office.

Clay tossed me three balls and I asked him, "Get the other sleeve. I need more ammunition." The spectators closest to me laughed and nudged each other. At least I was entertaining the patrons.

While I waited for Clay I crossed my legs and leaned against my putter. There was a small commotion at the other side of the big green, closer to the first tee, and I saw several police officers break through the crowd, and following them, Tiger and Stevie Williams walk onto the putting green. When Tiger appeared a burst of applause greeted his arrival.

Tiger nodded and tipped his hat, recognizing the attention, but kept to his tasks. Like almost every golfer in the history of mankind, he first dug into his bag and tossed a few balls onto the green, then began doctoring his right hand, putting a strip of white tape on his middle finger. I looked around at the gallery that had just laughed at my little joke. They were watching Tiger's finger-taping as if it were open heart surgery. Scandal or not, Tiger was the player everyone came to see. All the patrons became to move away from where I was putting toward Tiger on the other side of the green to get a better look at him. I was left alone in my corner of the huge practice area.

"He puts on his trousers one leg at a time, Tim," said Mr. Roberts from behind me.

"When he's not taking them off," I quipped, then added, "it's not the putting on of his pants that concerns me. It's what he does once he has his pants on and picks up a golf club."

"Don't let the Tigers of the world dictate your game. Take responsibility. You can't tiptoe around Augusta National and win the Masters."

Clay had found the sleeve of Titleists and was coming back to me.

"Thanks for the vote of confidence." I held up my hand and Clay tossed me the balls, one at a time. I found another position on the big putting green. I was above and eight feet from the cup. I could see the putt would break two inches from left to right and, on the slick downhill surface, it also had to start on the right line or it was a goner.

Beside me, Roberts uttered his familiar "Uh-huh," as a way of announcing himself, then said grandly, "I've found someone to help you with your putting, Tim."

"I think I'm doing okay, thank you," I answered, not looking up.

Roberts kept quiet, waiting and watching me putt. Perhaps because I was so aware of him standing there, breathing down my shoulder, I jerked the eight-footer.

"As I said," the dead man continued, "I've found help for you."

It was the way he said it, the tone in his voice, that made me hesitate and look up. Standing beside my ghostly guru was a man I recognized from old black-and-white photos in golf history books.

Heavyset and dough-faced, he was dressed in gray plus fours, a long-sleeve white shirt, a narrow tie, white shoes, and stockings. He was wearing a gray cap, and hooked under his arm was a hickory-shaft blade putter. I knew his name even before Cliff Roberts introduced me: Bobby Locke, the first great player to come out of South Africa. Although his name is not well known today, in his time—the '30s and '40s—he was so good that the American pros banded together to keep him off the PGA tour.

Roberts nodded at Locke and said, "It's Bobby who coined the phrase, 'Drive for show, putt for dough.' He managed a smile, showing off the prize he had brought me back from the other side.

I was truly going out of my mind. First Cliff Roberts and now Bobby Locke. I leaned against my putter to steady myself.

Clay stepped over and asked if I was okay. He could see the startled look on my face.

I nodded that I was okay, but wasn't sure I was. I asked Clay get me a bottle of water.

"You're a little tense," Clay said, being nice. He said he would be right back with water. I nodded but didn't say anything. To regain control of myself, I focused on my putting and, without even thinking, stepped up and tried to make the downhill slider as Bobby Locke watched me with his small, dark, expressionless eyes. Not for nothing had the pros nicknamed him Muffin Face.

I missed the next half-dozen putts.

"May I offer a suggestion?" Locke finally spoke up.

"Please," I whispered, humbled by my inadequacy.

"Do this," he said, demonstrating with his hickory putter. "Set the ball at the toe and stroke out at it, putting, therefore, with topspin. You achieve this by bringing the club head back inside. You're hooking it, but you'll be square at   impact.

"Also, remember that all putts are straight putts. You aim to where the putt will break on the green. You can't make every putt out here, but you want to have a tap-in coming back."

"It's the breaks that I can't read," I confessed.

Locke nodded his heavy head and stared at me. His eyes were gray and set deep in his head. I recalled then how he had been hurt in an automobile accident in South Africa late in his life and had never played again.

"All of us have a different feel for the amount of break we'll take," he said. "It depends on the pace of the putter. How hard you strike the ball. It's different for all of us. I learned when

I played here at Augusta National that the ball will never fall in from the side; it must be dead center to drop. The sides of the cup are not doorways. If you stroke the ball from the inside, as I suggested, and hook it, you'll spin it to the hole."

I took my stance over the first of the six balls and stroked the first one, making sure my eyes were directly over the ball. This time my stroke was off. The ball slipped by on the low side, inches below the cup. I stepped to the next ball, set myself carefully, and took my time. I wanted to make it, but even as I thought that, I could feel the muscles of my arms tighten up. I should have stepped away, but I went ahead and jammed the putt. The ball went four feet beyond the cup.

"I have another suggestion, Mr. Alexander." Locke moved a foot closer, saying that he thought I had a fine putting stroke but could benefit from a few simple adjustments.

"Don't look at the ball," he said. "Stare at a spot just behind it. What you're trying to do is keep your head from moving. If you're locked into the ball, your eyes will naturally turn to track the ball after you've hit it."

I addressed the next ball, found a spot just behind it, and calmly stroked the Ping. I missed again.

Locke stepped forward again and said we should try something else. It was as if he'd brought a bag of tricks with him from the other side.

"Do you play basketball, Mr. Alexander?"

"I did when I was younger."

"Well, a basketball player knows that when you attempt to make a free throw, you concentrate on the rim, not the ball in your hand. So on the next putt, focus your attention on the cup, not the ball. Let's see if that works.

"One other thing. Try this." He handed me his hickory-shafted putter.

His club was lighter than my big Ping, and the leather grip was thin and worn. I held it carefully.

"That putter of yours has too much loft. Coming off the face, your ball is airborne and it skids before it starts a true roll. You need a putter that minimizes the time the ball is in the air. It lessens the chance of going off line."

Locke stepped away, and I repositioned myself. I could see Tiger on the other side of the wide green. He was working on three-footers, surrounded by Stevie Williams and two others. Beyond, standing on the fringe, was a state trooper. Well, I thought, in this particular area I'd done Tiger one better—he only had a cop following him. I had ghosts.

"Remember," Locke continued, "putting accounts for forty percent of your score. You have all those fancy new clubs in your bag for the other sixty percent of your game, but this one club is what you need to win. So treat it with respect. Now do this," he said, telling me to address the ball by placing the putter in front of the ball, then behind it to make sure the blade was square to the line.

I took his advice and watched the eight-foot downhill slider curl into the cup.

"Nice!" Clay proclaimed, arriving with my water.

I leaned the hickory-shaft putter against my thigh as I unscrewed the cap of the water bottle. When I looked around, I realized Roberts and Bobby Locke had disappeared. I was alone with Clay, and I told him I was trying something new, that I was concentrating on the cup as if it were the rim of a basket.

It's all about maintaining my focus, I went on, as if I had I been carrying that piece of golfing logic around with me all weekend long, ever since arriving in Georgia. Real players know you didn't arrive at the Masters and change your setup and swing, try new clubs, or experiment with a putting stroke.

"Where did you get that hickory?" Clay asked, frowning down at the club in my hand.

I lifted the putter up slowly, as if it were a treasured antique, which in many ways it was. The club was trembling in my hands.

"I got it from a friend," I said. "A new old friend."

It was enough of an answer, I knew, to thoroughly confuse him.

22

THE PRESS CENTER WASN'T CROWDED when I finished my round. The shadows were lengthening on the course, and the crowds had thinned out around the clubhouse. Only a few reporters were on hand, but the center was set up for many more, with rows of tables, computers, and phones. On one wall, a huge television screen showed the action on the course; on another was a digital scoring board. Beyond the press room was a special dining area for the sports writers and television crews. It was a club within a club, all for the working press.

It was six o'clock on Thursday of Masters week and for the first time at Augusta National I felt like a player. I had finished with a 73, one over par. That score made me the low amateur in the clubhouse and earned me my fifteen minutes of fame at the Masters when Chris Handley, who ran the media for Augusta National, invited me to the press center.

It wasn't as if I had shot the lights out. One over par was a respectable score at the Masters, but I knew Augusta National was trying to promote amateur play, and this first-day score had, if only briefly, put me on the second page of the leader board.

"Good afternoon, ladies and gentlemen," Handley began, "and welcome. We're delighted to have Timothy Alexander with us this afternoon. I'd like to remind everybody that all of these interviews are on tape and will be broadcast through our facilities, so we are live on tape."

He smiled over at me, then turned to the reporters and said, "This is Tim's first Masters Tournament and, as you all know, he won the USGA'S Mid-Amateur last summer. Today he shot 73, which is a wonderful round of golf, especially given the rain late last night. I believe, Tim, this is your first week at Augusta National?"

I nodded and sipped the Diet Coke that had been given to me. Sitting down, facing the writers, I was flying high. At the end of my first competitive eighteen holes at Augusta, my name was on the leader board and I was being interviewed by the press.

"Tim, why don't you tell us how you're feeling right now."

I hesitated, trying to think of the right approach to take. Leaning forward, I spoke directly to the writers, ignoring the small microphone on the table. "I would like to say, Mr. Handley, that I am extremely pleased to have the opportunity to play your wonderful and, given my score today, very welcoming course."

There were smiles, and Handley thanked me, then suggesting, "Tim, why don't you go through your round, and then we'll see who might have some questions."

"Okay." I smiled out at the writers. "Let me start with the birdies," I said, remembering how golf press conferences worked from the Mid-Amateur. "That's a short list," I added quickly. "The bogeys will take a little longer."

A few smiles. They were an easy bunch, I realized; they wanted to be entertained.

"I birdied number two. I had a good drive, but I hit my 5-wood fat and came up short of the right side bunker. I pitched up about forty yards and left myself a fifteen footer that I managed to make. I should say at the outset that I normally wouldn't have made that putt or a few others, but I have a great Augusta National caddie when it comes to reading the greens. I smiled at Clay who was standing up against the back wall.

"I managed another birdie on eight, which makes me feel pretty good since that, as you know, is the toughest hole. I knew I couldn't carry that right-side bunker, so I got it out about 280 and then, on my second shot, I kept it in the fairway and had a long wedge into the green. I made a big breaking ten-footer.

"The eighteenth was a big surprise. I got a gift there. I hit my natural fade and my drive came up about 285—I'm not a big striker—and my ball was too far over to the right to give me a clear shot to the green. I hit what was, for me, a nice 5-iron around the corner of the pines to get up onto the back plateau where the pin was cut. I landed in the slope and the ball checked up, and I made my best putt of the day.

"Those, ladies and gentlemen, were the only video highlights. Few and far between."

I looked over at Chris Handley and asked if I should go through my bogeys. He nodded so I continued with the details of my round. I was like almost every other golfer in the world. I would remember my shots into eternity.

"Well, I started my debacle on the fourth hole, which, by the way, I also bogeyed on my practice rounds. That hole has my number. I can't seem to find the green. I hit a 4-wood today and the wind caught it and drove the ball into the left-hand bunker. Getting out, I left myself a five-to-six-foot putt that I blew."

A reporter in the first row of chairs raised his hand. I nodded to him as I picked up the glass of Coke and took another sip.

"Tim, I saw you play out at Midlothian when you won there and you were using a belly putter. I saw you finish on 18 and you had a blade putter with a hickory shaft. When did you change?"

"I left the belly putter at home in the garage with my lawn rakes and shovels," I quipped, and the writers laughed. "I knew a belly putter wouldn't work on these big, sweeping greens. For me, it's a question of feel. The belly putter reduces my feel, especially on putts that are breaking five or six feet. You might have seen that putt I made on 18. I had to play it about a cup and a half outside right. With the belly, it's kind of hard to move that putter back and forth only two or three inches. Your whole upper body has to move.

"The belly putter is fine on smaller greens, the kind I play most often in Southern Illinois. I'm not going to run the table with that putter here at Augusta National. What I need on these greens is a stick that gives me lots of feel. It's as simple and as complex as that." I shrugged.

"Didn't Angel Cabrera use a belly putter when he won the Masters?" piped up another writer.

I nodded, then answered, "It wasn't strictly a belly putter, as I recall. He didn't brace the butt end against his gut like most of us belly users do. It was long, maybe forty inches or so. So, you're right in saying it was belly-style in term of length. Most of us older guys use the belly putter, I guess, so we can stand straighter when we address the ball. It helps us have a more consistent stroke, overcomes the shakes."

"Do you think belly-style putters are bastardizing the game, making it easier?"

I nodded slowly, trying to think through this landmine of questions. The reporter was fishing for a new angle, using me as an amateur to say that the pros weren't honoring the tradition of the game.

"Well, you know what e.e. cummings said." I smiled down at his puzzled face and before he could respond, I said, "Cummings didn't write poems about golf, but he does have a wonderful line: 'Progress is a comfortable disease.' Perhaps that's what's happening with golf. All this new technology is producing a comfortable game."

"So why are you using an old-fashioned blade putter for your first Masters?" another reporter asked. "It's a throwback club. It looked like Bobby Jones's old Calamity Jane. Did you lift it out of the Trophy Room?"

"I wish," I answered, raising my voice over the laughs from the reporters and the handful of green-jacket members who were standing at the rear of the press room. Now I had to be careful how I answered. My buddies home in Illinois knew I didn't carry a hickory putter in my bag.

How long did I have the putter, someone else asked. And where did I get it? The link to Bobby Jones with the same kind of putter was a news angle for the writers; they could write about that in tomorrow's sports pages. The amateur who arrives at the Masters with a throwback club.

"I got it from a friend," I answered vaguely. "He gave me the club for these greens."

"A member?"

I shook my head, trying to think of a story dull enough to make them drop the questioning. If the reporters thought I was hiding information, they'd be all over me for details. I told them how a friend from my days on the Wake Forest golf team had come to see me play. He had given me the blade putter, saying it was what I needed to handle Augusta National. I said just enough to satisfy their curiosity and keep them from questioning me more. Then a young female reporter asked about how I had double-bogeyed number seven, and I was saved.

"First, I should say I was told by my caddie that this hole was a lot easier in years past. Well, it couldn't have been tougher. Those pine trees framing the tee make it an intimidating drive. All I wanted to do was get my ball somewhere in the fairway and I almost managed that. I was on the right side, barely in the first cut. I think I hit it about 284, and that left me 176 into the pin, which was cut on the right side.

"I didn't know what to hit. It's a tabletop green, as you know, and I was sure I'd either plunk it in one of those three front bunkers or fly it over the green. I didn't know how to hold it on the green. I played an eight that hit the ridge and catapulted over—you don't want to be over on that hole or, for that matter, any other hole on this course.

"The rest, as they say, is history. But I want you to know I hit a good drive and a solid mid-iron and still double-bogeyed that hole. I missed the green coming back. What's the famous line of Seve Ballesteros about why he four-putted? 'I mees, I mees, I mees again. I made.'"

When the laughter died off, another reporter asked, "And you also bogeyed twelve, right?"

"Twelve was playing about 155 today, and I choked down on a nine and tugged it into the wind and missed it. I was trying to miss it left, worried about leaving one out to the right and finding Rae's Creek. I hit a good pitch to about eight feet and also hit a great little putt, but I missed it again, just by a hair."

"About your caddie," the same writer asked. "I saw him when you were finishing up. Is he someone you brought with you from Illinois?"

"No, at home I caddie for myself. I belong to the 'wheel it and deal with it' set. This caddie, Clay Weaver, was assigned to me. This is his first Masters, too, and I'm lucky to have him on my bag."

"How do you spell his name?" someone else asked. The story

of two first-timers—a player and his caddie—was triggering interest. I spelled Clay's name and waited for the next question.

Someone asked what it felt like to be playing in the Masters.

I paused to think of how to phrase my reply. My guess was that whatever I said would be quoted and picked up by the Southern Illinoisan. I didn't want to sound like an idiot to my golf buddies back home.

"When I got my invitation, it was just around Christmas, and it was a wonderful present to receive. However, playing in the Masters didn't really seem real. I didn't truly believe it until I arrived and saw Magnolia Lane, and then, I started to get a little nervous. It is one thing to dream about playing in the Masters, quite another to actually play."

I paused to give them a moment to scribble down what I had just said, as well as to give myself time to think of a closing line, some sort of zinger that would encapsulate the experience for me, give everyone an understanding of what it was like for an ordinary golfer to have a chance to play in this very special place, in this very special tournament.

I thought of what Clay had said when we were walking up 18 and we could see the white clubhouse up on the horizon and the pines bracketing the fairway. He said, "You know, it almost doesn't matter what happens next. We're going to always have this day."

I decided to use his line and replied, "So, I guess I'd say no matter what happens to me next in this Masters, or in my golf life, I'm always going to have this one day at Augusta National when the golfing gods looked kindly on an old hacker from the Midwest. They let me play the round of my life, and a guy can go for a long time on that kind of memory."

23

"WE SAW YOU ON TELEVISION!" Kerry announced when I called home. "We watched you on eighteen, when you made that great putt. Oh, darling, you were wonderful!"

I was outside the clubhouse again, standing alone under the big oak. It was after nine o'clock and it was dark on the course.

Kerry sounded as if she were in tears, and I guessed that she was. Lately, feeling any emotion seemed to dissolve her into tears.

"That was Clay with you?" she asked next.

"Yes, it was."

"He's a good-looking boy, isn't he?"

"I think the gallery was following us because of him. How are you doing?" I asked immediately before she could change the subject, or ask about my game.

"Oh, I'm fine. The same. Doctor Kestin wants me to go into Barnes for tests, that's all. It's a long way and a lot of time and money."

"Are you getting any sleep?" I asked next. Sleep was our touchstone. If she slept, she was well.

"Peggy tried to call you when you finished," she answered instead, moving the conversation away from herself. "You didn't answer."

"There was a press conference. They asked me to go to the press center to talk to the writers."

"Timmy, oh, how great!"

"Well, let's hope I don't blow to 85 tomorrow."

"Don't think that way."

"I know, and you're right. I found out something on the putting green that I think will help me. A new way of putting."

"That putt on 18 was wonderful. You have a new putter!"

I wondered how could I possibly explain Bobby Locke and his hickory putter to her, but unlike the reporters, she wasn't interested in the details of my clubs.

"What do you have to score to get to play on the weekend?"

"I have to be one of the lowest forty-four, or be within ten strokes of the leader."

"You can do that!"

"Hey, maybe we should be just a little realistic."

"Just shoot another 73. How's this for realistic: If you can do it once, you can do it again."

I was tempted to say that just because Mr. Roberts had conjured up one phantom legend of the game, he wouldn't necessarily conjure another tomorrow.

"Everyone here is talking about you," she said next. They were talking about you on WCIL. You're famous in Carbondale."

"Who would have thunk it! Well, if I'm going to make the cut I better get my beauty sleep."

"Okay, I guess." She sighed into the phone. "I miss you, darling."

"I'll be home soon."

"Not too soon."

We both laughed. But I couldn't hang up without adding, "You're going to be all right," I needed to say that out loud just to reassure myself. Still, I couldn't make it sound possible that she would be cured, nor did I have words in my vocabulary to help my golf game against Tiger and all the other pros. I was just a college teacher living in a fantasy world at Augusta National.

When we hung up, I stood without moving under the big oak. I could hear voices from the clubhouse, people going to dinner, having drinks in the bar. Their laughter carried into the cool night. I was totally detached from what was happening. It was like being in the eye of a hurricane. If I could live within the green ropes and away from the world beyond the dogwoods, azalea, and magnolia trees, I might be safe forever.

"But you can't hide from your responsibilities." It was Roberts. This time, his words were undercut with a touch of compassion.

He stepped out of the shadows to join me under the tree. He was wearing as always his green membership jacket and a fresh white shirt. Looking past the massive branches of the old oak, I asked him if he'd ever read All The King's Men by Robert Penn Warren.

"I saw the movie," he answered. "Broderick Crawford, I believe, was in it."

"In the first film version, yes. The novel was based on the life of Huey Long, who, as you know, was once the governor of Louisiana. If Long had played golf, I'm sure he would have fit in here nicely," I jabbed. "In the novel, the last line said by the narrator after all the calamities have occurred is that what he had to do, what we all have to do in life, is to go out into 'the awful responsibilities of time.'"

I glanced over at Roberts. He had one hand dug into the pocket of his fine linen trousers. His other hand held his short, thick cigar. He looked content and self-satisfied and in good health. Since I had met him at Amen Corner, he appeared to be turning back the years; he looked younger with each passing day.

The old man permitted himself a wan smile, and then, with his little finger, tapped a wedge of ash from his cigar. When he replied, it was in a voice full of the knowledge learned from a lifetime of hard work, misfortunes, and small victories: "Whatever the novel says, that hasn't stopped you from hiding."

"You think that's what I've been doing all these years in Carbondale, hiding from my responsibilities?"

"Weren't you?" He asked it kindly, like a friend.

I shook my head.

"No?" Roberts looked surprised.

"I was hiding from my father, that's true enough."

He nodded and answered, sighing, "Aren't we all?"

"I believe you're right, Mr. Roberts. That's what children do when they can't live up to their parents' expectations. But at some point the piper must be paid."

I nodded goodbye and started toward the side door that led to the back stairs and the Crow's Nest.

"Mr. Alexander," Roberts called after me. "If you don't mind, would you please call me Cliff. All my friends do."

As I took the stairs two at a time, heading for the top floor of the old manor house, I thought, Well, how about that. I had made a friend at Augusta National, even if he was a dead man.

Friday

24

THE DOWN SIDE of having Cliff Roberts arrange a late tee time for me on the opening round was that I had to tee off early on Friday. Waking at dawn, I slipped out of the Crow's Nest and went downstairs to grab breakfast in the Trophy Room.

In the far corner, I spotted Charlie Smith eating alone. I hadn't heard him get up that morning or, for that matter, come home the night before. I did notice that the three kids each went off on his own after their opening rounds. Now it was competition time, and the friendly banter was put on hold.

I nodded good morning to Lightnin' as I slipped through the tables. I would join young Smith for breakfast. It was the only sociable thing to do. The room was filling up, mostly with Green Jackets, and while it was crowded, everyone in the early hours was keeping their voices down, speaking softly.

"Do you mind?" I asked Charlie, arriving at his corner table. I smiled at the teenager.

Smith jerked up from his plate of food, scowling at the intrusion.

"Sorry to interrupt," I said quickly, shoving the heavy oak chair against the table. I turned to walk away, but he got up to stop me.

"No, hey, it's okay. Sorry." He sat back, gesturing for me to join him. "I'm a little jumpy."

For a moment, I thought of leaving anyway, but knew I had to be the grown-up.

"Nice round yesterday. Seventy-six is lookin' good," I commented, sitting.

"Not as good as 73."

I picked up the menu and shrugged, "I made a few no-brainers."

"Yeah, sure." He sounded angry.

I glanced over at him. It was not quite eight a.m., and I didn't have the patience to handle this surly kid. Still, I held my tongue. I didn't need roommate problems, not at my age.

Lightnin' saved me by appearing to take my breakfast order. He was full of good cheer and ready to talk about the weather, the golf course, and how the chef made great eggs, sunny side up.

When Lightnin' left, Charlie mumbled another apology for his manners.

"Stressful times," I suggested, then asked, making conversation, "Where did the gang go last night, Coyote's?"

Charlie shook his head. He didn't say anything. Whatever had set him off wasn't my concern. What little I knew about him from a couple dinners and a round of golf was that he was a wise-ass kid who didn't think before he spoke. It was an attitude I often saw in student athletes at Southern.

"I was thinking about what you said the other night at dinner." He didn't look up from his coffee cup as he spoke. "You know, what you were saying about your old man, how you needed to win just to spite him."

I realized then that perhaps it hadn't been smart to unburden myself on these kids five minutes after meeting them. But I also knew it was a relief to tell strangers I'd never see again, and knowing myself, I understood that playing in the Masters was some sort of finger in the face of my dead dad for what he had put me through as a kid.

Still, it didn't make me feel better. Being angry at a parent is like lugging a golf bag around in the rain.

"My dad's not like your old man," Charlie said, beginning to explain himself. I could see some anger now on his round, soft face. It was boiling to the surface.

"My old man is all over me about playing and winning. It's been that way since he gave me a golf club when I was five or six. It's not the game that matters, it's winning. That's what counts." He pushed back from the tight corner table, as if to shove himself away from his burden. "You know the story of Sean O'Hair and his old man?"

I nodded. The young PGA touring pro had been pressed so hard to play golf that he finally walked away from his family.

"That's my old man." Smith shook his head. "I can't win enough for him."

Now I felt guilty about having taken quiet satisfaction in winning my match against Charlie earlier in the week.

"Is your dad here?"

"Oh, yeah. Mom, too. They've got a suite over at the Marriott. Dad wanted me to stay with them, but thank God for the Crow's Nest. I can get away from him for a few hours. On the course I've got the ropes keeping him off my butt. He got hold of me after the round yesterday and reamed me out about that double bogey I had on thirteen when I went for the green and caught the creek." Charlie glanced up, looking guilty. "I had seen the score you posted, so I gambled with my second shot. It was better than having my old man all over me for letting you be low amateur on opening day. That killed him." He smiled then, and added, "He couldn't believe a player pushing fifty beat me."

"What did you hit off the tee on 13?"

"A 3-wood. I can't draw my driver, and if I push my tee shot with the driver, I'm in nowhere land."

"No one can draw those titanium drivers. Metal woods won't draw. And on top of that, hitting a one, you won't have a level lie on your second shot, not the way that fairway slopes. You did the smart play, lay up."

Charlie Smith kept nodding as I talked strategy. He acted as if he agreed, but I could see he wasn't buying.

"So what's not right?" I asked.

"My Dad thinks I'm another Rory McIlroy. He says with my strength I should be driving the ball 320 plus, should have shaped it around the dogleg, gone for the green. He thinks that everything Tiger did before he was twenty years old is what I should be doing."

"Did Tiger qualify for the weekend when he was nineteen?"

"I don't know. I'm not Tiger anyway. No way, no how!"

Lightnin' returned with my eggs and toast and the two of us fell silent as he cleared away the dishes. When he left, Charlie confessed, "I wish I could do what you did—you know, walk away from the game. Go ahead with my life. That's what I want to do."

I didn't respond at first. I knew, as I suspect only a teacher might, that Charlie was waiting for me to give him permission to do just that, to turn his back on golf and his old man. He wanted an adult, and a college professor at that, and one who had shared his fate, to tell him that it was okay to walk away from his family.

I kept buttering my toast. I was less a shrink than I was an English teacher, and what I learned from literature had less to say about leading a long and happy life than about unhappiness, hardships, and dysfunctional families. What I needed to tell Chuck

Smith was not some fancy literary example, but what we all learn about life from playing golf.

"Did you ever see Chi Chi Rodriguez play?" I asked. I looked over at Smith so he would see I was being serious, that this question out of left field did have a purpose.

He shook his head.

"I saw Chi Chi play a few times back in the Western Open up around Chicago. A club in his hands was like a magic wand. He could make a golf ball dance. But he never played golf the easy way. He always made the game difficult. For example, if he was in the middle of the fairway with 150 to the green, he'd try to hit a high fade or a low hook. He would never hit a safe, simple, mid-iron straight at the stick."

"Why?"

Like all golfers, Charlie was always in search of whatever secrets other players might have about the game.

I cut into the soft eggs, spilling yellow yolk on the plate. "I don't know," I said, shaking my head. "Maybe it was to amuse himself, maybe to make the game more of a challenge, but it didn't always work. He failed more than he succeeded. The fades didn't always fade. The draws didn't always draw. You can't pull off great shots all the time, unless you're Ben Hogan.

"What you want to do in life, Charlie, is what you want to do on the golf course. You want to make the game simple. Play the safe shot, go for the par, play conservative."

"That's not what you did."

I nodded. "True enough. But I was like you are now, impetuous. I didn't know that sooner or later something would go wrong in life and I'd need to be ready. It's like hitting a great drive and having it bounce into a hazard. Once you start a family, one of your kids might be diagnosed with a rare disease before they're out of diapers, or you find yourself out of a job with a mortgage to pay."

I stopped to pull myself together and then said softly, trying to sum up my ramblings, "You want to have some money in the bank, so to speak. You want a reservoir of good feelings and past kindness to others that will carry you through the hard times. That's why a par on any given hole is good; it gets you to the next tee where maybe you'll have a chance to make birdie."

"So, how's that going to help me get my old man off my back and give me room to live my own life?"

"Your father isn't going to become another person, Charlie. You have to accept that and you have to deal with it. Don't complicate your life with a lot of emotional baggage. Don't be another Chi Chi.

"I wasn't smart enough to let my old man be who he was going to be," I said, explaining myself. "No, I had to fight the very existence of the son of a bitch! And what did it get me? A lifetime of carrying around a lot of baggage I didn't need. I boxed myself into an emotional corner. I've been where you are. Don't let that shape the rest of your life. Those are my Masters Week words of wisdom. Cheaper than a shrink." I smiled, hoping to soften my lecture about fathers and sons.

Charlie didn't say anything. He studied my face for a long moment, then glanced off. He looked across the crowded room full of Green Jackets and players and TV personnel. Everyone was dressed for show, wearing ties and white shirts—everyone except the two of us huddled in the corner. We looked like who we were, two guys ready to go play some golf.

I knew what I had said to Charlie wasn't what he was expecting to hear, or wanting to hear. He wanted me to pat him on the back, to tell him he was right to hate his old man for interfering with his life and his game of golf.

"That's it?" he asked.

"Yep. That's it!"

I returned to my eggs and let Charlie mull over what I had said. When I finished and reached for my coffee he asked me in a soft voice, all his earlier moodiness dispersed for the moment, "How do I do that?"

"How do you play a simple mid-iron from the middle of the fairway without complicating the golf shot?"

"Yeah, something like that." He smiled at my metaphor and his own quandary.

"You play life like you play golf, Charlie. You go at it one day at a time, one shot at a time. You don't press; you don't complicate the situation. You accept the fact that sometimes a well-hit wood will land in a fairway divot—remember a few years back how that happened to Trevor Immelman on the final hole here at the Masters? A divot should have been repaired but it wasn't, and Trevor played it where it lay on the fairway and managed to make par and win the Masters."

"What if you can't just deal with it?"

I stared across the table at Charlie and made my last point as if I was summing up a graduate seminar back at SIU.

"That's what I did, son. I walked away from golf, the one thing I really loved. I gave up a lifetime of satisfaction and pleasure and success because I couldn't differentiate between playing the game I loved and being my father's son.

"You see, Charlie, I wasn't playing just golf, I was trumping my old man every time I won a tournament, and then when he was gone…" I stopped talking and took a deep breath. I could feel a rush of tears to my eyes.

I realized that I hadn't talked so much about my father in all the years since his death, nor had I known that my recollection of my childhood was still so vivid and close beneath the surface of my memories. It was a sign of aging, I guessed, my past life closing in on me.

I pushed away from the table and, before I could say good-bye, Charlie said quickly, "Thanks." He nodded and stood up too. "And good luck today."

"You too!"

"You think that old member was right? That an amateur is going to win it this year?"

I glanced around, half expecting to find Cliff Roberts hovering near our table, listening to my discourse about golf and fatherhood. Given his story, I suspected he, too, had a lot to say about erring dads.

"Yes, I believe he might be," I smiled, trying to leave our breakfast on a positive note. "That's another thing about life," I said. "Sometimes miracles happen. But first," I added, "you have to go practice to make them happen."

25

"I GOT AN IDEA," Clay said as we walked to the practice tee after breakfast.

I nodded, but didn't reply. My mind was still swirling with what Charlie Smith had told me, and like a typical parents, I was worried now that my advice might not be what the boy needed to hear.

"About your R9," Clay continued, ignoring my silence. "I jumped on the Web last night and started reading this article by Fred Tuxen."

"Who in the hell is Fred Tuxen?" I glanced his way.

We were filtering through the early crowds arriving for the second day of the Masters. There were coming in clusters, moms and dad, and their children, who the Green Jackets, in their wisdom, had decided to allow in to the tournament free.

"Tuxen is the guy who invented the TrackMan."

"What in the hell is a TrackMan?"

"It's a golf-club-launch monitor device. He wrote this article that says that when you hit a ball the initial direction that the ball takes is eighty-five percent face angle and only fifteen percent swing path."

We had reached the range. A handful of players with early-morning tee times were hitting balls out toward the end of the empty range.

"And?" I asked.

Clay gestured to my driver. "Your R9 is an adjustable-face metal wood. This guy proved with his launch monitor that a player can hit a straight drive even with a twelve-degree inside-to-outside swing path, if the face is set two degrees closed."

I shook my head, grinning.

"Look," Clay went on, determined to have his say. "why have a TaylorMade R9 and a ratchet hosel if you don't adjust the face to control that fade of yours?" He gestured toward the driver, and continued, "You can change the angle and the loft; you can change the flight by forty yards."

"I like my fade. It gives me control of the ball."

"But not at Augusta. You need to draw your drives to win here. You've said so yourself. All you have to do is change the FCT between the neutral and left settings."

I shook my head. "Clay, I can't start messing with my driver in the middle of the Masters."

Clay shrugged and spoke carefully, as if he had prepared himself for my answer and had a response ready. "I was thinking last night that you could try it, make a slight adjustment from neutral, and if it was too much, change it back." He shrugged again and asked, "Why have all this fancy technology if you don't use it?"

"You can't cure a swing with simple technology, Clay. Masking a flaw in the driver won't stop my swing from infecting how I hit the other clubs in my bag."

"A quick fix is what we need to play this course. Augusta

National is set up for Bobby Jones's draw, not your fade. You only have three days, maybe only one."

Clay glanced down the range, nodding to the other players banging out balls. "Those pros are tinkering all the time with their clubs. They've got Butch Harmon or Hank Haney, or Leadbetter, three of the best instructors of the game, working with them. What do you have?" He grinned. "Me!"

I was tempted to add that while the pros might have the best instructors in the world, I had Clifford Roberts and Bobby Locke. Instead, I answered, "I need more than a wrench to my clubs to help me."

"Think about it," Clay answered and, setting down my bag, jogged off to get a bag of practice balls. He was like my wife. She would pose a problem as a question, then leave it to me to mull it over, to let the question chew away at my subconscious.

I pulled my gap wedge from the bag and began to loosen up, swinging slowly, well aware of how tight the muscles were in my shoulders and back. Also I knew somewhere in my cerebral hemisphere that Cliff Roberts was waiting to speak. I was sure that he was always around and listening to what I said. This time he waited until Clay Weaver was well out of hearing range before appearing.

"The boy has a point. You've been fighting that fade all week."

I took several more easy swings with my heavy wedge, feeling a new soreness in my right hip. I was one of the walking wounded. Maybe what I needed to do was get a hip replacement like Tom Watson. Look what that did to help him at the British Open.

"I thought you were a traditionalist, Mr. Roberts," I replied, speaking under my breath even though there were no spectators in the stands behind the range tee at the moment. The few fans who had turned out this early in the day were at the other end of the metal stands, crowded together and watching Zach Johnson bang drives into the wide-open range.

"I am a traditionalist," Roberts replied, "but golf, like everything in life or death, needs to move with the times."

"Hey, I bought a new driver for this tournament!" I joked.

"Then use it! We have someone who can help you, right here at the course."

"Who's that? The pro?"

"Mitchell Golf. They have a workshop over by the caddie house. Ed Mitchell has been coming to the Masters to repair clubs since '94. You could see him about making an adjustment to your driver."

I knew a whole fleet of club manufacturers followed the tour, ready with replacement clubs or repairs. They were part of the traveling circus of vans: a fitness center, a caddie wagon, and the army of agents, swing coaches, and shrinks who moved with the tour from coast to coast all year long, a giant caravan of vehicles crossing America, following the sun.   .

At every PGA tournament stop the vans and trailers were parked on the other side of the driving range, beyond the caddie shacks, away from the clubhouse and the tournament sponsors' big white hospitality tents, ready to help the pros keep in physical and mental shape, to get their clubs adjusted and repaired.

Clay came running back with the bag of Titleists and dumped them on the ground. Without responding to Roberts, I moved a ball into position and hit a high soft wedge fifty yards down the range. When it hit, a trail of overnight moisture sprayed up and followed the roll of the ball. I hit another wedge and another until gradually I could feel my muscles loosen. Even my hip felt better. I reached for another club, thinking that I didn't want to leave all my good swings on the range.

"Maybe you need to change your grip." Clay commented, watching me work my way through the bag and begin to hit my R9.

"My grip is fine, Clay," I said, not looking up, and then I told him the truth. "I would never mess with my grip."

"Golf is a lifetime of habits, Clay. When you get to my age, you don't reinvent yourself. I am who I am." I hit another high fade that floated toward Berckmans Road, but came up well short of the end of the range.

Clay didn't protest. Like any good caddie he knew when to keep his mouth shut.

I slipped the R9 into the bag and smiled to show him that there were no hard feelings, and before I could say anything else, he spoke up, "Do me a favor? Let's go over and just talk to this guy who fixes clubs."

"Ed Mitchell?"

"You know him!" That surprised Clay.

I nodded, saying nothing. I didn't know anything else about Ed Mitchell beyond what Cliff Roberts had just told me. "His repair shop is parked by the caddie house, right?" I added.

"Right!" Clay grinned, as if he had won a small victory.

I took a deep breath. "Well, okay, let's go. It wouldn't hurt to talk to the guy."

"Now?"

"Better now than later. I tee off in an hour. And I have only three rounds left to fix my fade so I can play this course. Remember, Trevino never could play this course with his swing."

Ed Mitchell looked less like a PGA pro than the small-town banker which he had been before he started manufacturing and selling the club repair machines he invented to fix golf clubs. Nor did he look like the shop boys I knew in my younger years when I had been hanging around pro shops and bag rooms.

He looked surprised when Clay and I stepped inside his mobile workshop.

"May I help you?" he asked. He was wearing a long-sleeve blue shirt, a tie, and an apron. There was nothing to suggest he knew anything about club-making or how to re-adjust stainless-steel metal woods.

The workshop was crowded with equipment, and the two of us, plus Mitchell and his assistant, were wedged against wooden benches and heavy metal machines. I slipped around Clay and put out my hand to shake Mitchell's, explaining as I did who I was and that I had come for his help. Mitchell watched me with bright blue eyes, shifting his glance to Clay and my clubs and then back to me, taking in everything that I had to say about my natural fade and my R9 metal wood.

He had to be impressed by my clubs, though it was obvious my name meant nothing to him. Still, he kept silent until I finished a convoluted explanation about my natural fade, and what Clay tossed into the conversation about TrackMan. Finally, I asked, "What do you think? Can you adjust a metal wood to tame my fade to play this course?"

Mitchell smiled, then said carefully, "You remember what Ben Hogan said? 'In selecting clubs, always look for one that suits your swing.' I agree with Hogan. However, we can adjust your metal wood to fit your swing. A lot of people say you can't bend a metal wood, but within limitations, you can. The problem you have here is that the R9 is adjustable and not bendable as the other TaylorMade models are. May I?" he asked, reaching for my driver.

He pulled the club from the bag, explaining as he did that forged titanium is also bendable as long as the hosel is long enough to allow the bending bar to fit over its length, saying, "Direction is all about the face angle and the lie."

He gestured toward the array of metal equipment. "The truth is, with most clubs, you can adjust the loft and lie angle as much as you want. We do it here. We've been repairing clubs at the

Masters since '94. So, if you want to eliminate your fade, we can do it. Do you fade every club in the bag?"

"Pretty much, but it's the driver I'm concerned about. I've got to work the ball off the tee from right to left on half a dozen holes on this course, but I can't start messing with my swing in the middle of the Masters." I nodded at Clay, and added, smiling, "My caddie says we can do it with technology, but maybe he reads too much."

"It can be done," Mitchell answered. "When I came into the golf business back in '62, the Cushman riding golf cart was the only real innovation. The next big change was the Eaton slip-on that changed the club's molded-rubber and leather wrap grips. Now a player can't keep up with the innovations. That's why you have tour repair vans following the pros. A week doesn't go by without some manufacturer thinking of a new twist or tweak for a club. There's no such thing as standard in the industry. Everyone needs custom-built clubs, what with these hybrids. In fact, I've seen where players have replaced the golf carts with Segways! What next?" He grinned and shook his head. "But I'll say one thing for golf innovations: It keeps me in business!" Then he asked, "What's your tee time?"

"We've got an hour," Clay answered for me   .

"Then I better get to work. But let me warn you: Once a player starts tinkering with the clubs, it never stops. It's an incurable disease."

26

I MADE THE TURN AT 9 at one over. Stepping to the tee at 10, I felt I could work around the back side close to par and, with a good break or two, maybe be a couple under. Even one or two over would get me into the weekend. Clay had been right. The readjusted R9 was working. I was keeping the ball in the fairway. And I was enjoying myself and my playing partners.

Agesilao Senese, the young Northern Italian, who was playing in his first Masters after winning the Deutsche Bank Players' Championship, was one of them. Agesilao spoke little English beyond "hello" and "good luck" but his smile was warm, and his dark, Mediterranean looks had attracted a gallery of young women who trailed us from hole to hole. While Clay had attracted a few beauties in the practice rounds, I told him that now he would be lucky to pick up the Italian kid's castoffs.

Senese had played careful golf in the first round, but on the front side of the second round he had slipped on a few holes, and going into number 10 he was 4 over. He would be on the bubble to make it to the weekend. And judging from his face, he knew it.

Playing with us was Bill Vicars, a seasoned pro who had won the week before in New Orleans and was the last pro to qualify for the Masters. It was his first trip to Augusta, and he shot 6 over on Thursday, and was now plus 9. Vicars was toast, but he appeared not to mind. He had begun to kibitz with the gallery between shots, as if playing in the Masters was something he did every spring.

I had the honors on 10, and I stepped between the markers and teed up, then walked over to Clay and raised my eyebrows, waiting for him to suggest a club.

The 12, the Golden Bell, was the most famous hole at Augusta, but it was on 10 where Ralph Stonehouse entered the history books. He was the first player to tee off in the Masters back in 1934 when the nines were reversed at Augusta National. Ten was also another of Bobby Jones's right-to-left holes that did not favor my fade, but so far Ed Mitchell's work had served me well. My hopes were high as I teed up.

I looked down the long, sloping dogleg, framed by corridors of pine and azaleas and dogwood all in full bloom, all sparkling in the sunlight. The fairway fell away from the tee and then just over two hundred and fifty yards out, it turned left and disappeared.

I pulled the driver and stepped back between the markers to get my angle on the hole. What I had to do was hold my drive to the left side of the fairway, catch the slope, and pick up another twenty yards as the ball bounced down the incline. If I did that, I'd have a mid-iron into the green. Even Bobby Jones's guide for the patrons watching the tournament said anything hit right meant a second shot with a longer iron.

I swung the R9 slowly, standing behind the ball and parallel to its flight. I was seeking with my simple routine to find the center of my swing. It was another of Kerry's techniques, a lesson she had learned in the meditation classes that she had started taking after she found out about the cancer.

"It's that space we have inside us," she explained, "the space beyond the busyness of life."

She taught me how to relax when I had to face a four-foot putt on a slick green. She showed me how to breathe deeply to calm myself. When I found my center, standing on the 10th tee, it was almost magical the way my whole body changed. My centering technique was to have the driver become an extension of my arms, the ball an extension of the club.

I hit a beauty. The ball hugged the left side and, just before the dogleg, it drifted right, caught the slope, and ran. From far down the fairway, the applause came back to me, a gift from strangers. I glanced over at Clay. He was smiling, nodding his approval.

I slipped the wood into the bag, conscious that everyone was watching me. I was sure that in the TV tower behind 18 Jim Nantz and Nick Faldo had already labeled me the old guy playing against the kids, giving them a chance to recall how at age 59 Tom Watson had almost pulled off the miracle of the ages at Turnberry.

Or they might be framing their narrative another way, talking about the amateur in the era of the professional. I was a throwback, another Bobby Jones taking on the professionals; maybe they'd make the point that, while I was an English teacher, Bobby Jones had majored in English at Yale before spending his life working as an Atlanta lawyer.

Teeing off next, Vicars hit a drive that dwarfed mine. His ball climbed into the sky, hung up there forever, then landed a good thirty yards beyond me. He was 320 down the left side, leaving him 165 to the elevated green. Young Senese didn't catch his ball and hit a screamer; still, he carried to the dogleg and, thanks to topspin, ran on the low, sloping fairway. It wasn't pretty, but it worked.

We stepped off the tee together, but Senese charged ahead,

with Vicars following, trying to keep up. There was a surge of others in our wake—Augusta National members in green jackets, caddies, security wearing white pith helmets, the score keepers. Forget about it taking a village, I thought. It took a small city to put on a golf tournament.

I moved to the left of the sloping fairway and slowed down. It would do me no good to race after them. I had to keep my own pace. Whatever else might happen, I had to play my game and not get wrapped up in the excitement of others. Besides, I didn't have the strength to match strides with the young pros.

To cheer myself up, I thought about Julius Boros lumbering around San Antonio Country Club, moving at the age of 48 like an old bull elephant across the African savanna, and beating young Arnold Palmer at the '68 PGA Championship.

Clay joined me on the left side of the fairway.

"How are you doing, kid?" I asked. "How're you holding up?"

"Better than you."

I laughed and said under my breath, "I keep waiting to blow up."

"You're not going to blow up. You're going to pull this off." He was full of confidence, but then, he was so young he didn't know better. Hollywood endings on a golf course only happen in movies.

We reached my ball, and I leaned over to check the lie. If there was a bad lie on any fairway at Augusta National, I never saw it. Still, I had a problem. I was 212 to the green, the ball was below my feet, and the pin was cut in the back left side. If I was anywhere with my second shot, I wanted to be over, not short on the front edge and having to putt over hill and dale to reach the cup.

"Utility?" I asked Clay. It was the club we had played twice in practice rounds without a great deal of success   .

Clay set the bag down and went to check the yardage against the metal markers in the middle of the fairway.

"Easy, Tim, easy. Take your time," Clifford Roberts advised, appearing for the first time on the course.

"Where have you been, Cliff?" I said. "I thought you'd given up on me."

"You didn't need me until now."

"Why, thank you, Cliff." I smiled.

Clay returned to the bag and, catching the end of my comment, said, "You talking to yourself again, Tim?"

"Wouldn't you be if you had to make this shot?"

In the blinding bright light of mid-morning, my eyesight wasn't good enough to see how the trees were reacting to the April breezes.

"The tips are blowing both ways, on both sides. You'll have to keep it low. If you hit it high, the wind will knock it down. If you hit it low, the ball will run like a scared rabbit." Clay told me.

"You need better advice," Roberts commented, more to himself than me.

Ignoring him, I laid my hands on my clubs, having no idea how to play the shot. Back at Hickory Ridge, this shot was a no-brainer. But golf courses are like women—no two are alike. What I might do at Hickory Ridge would never work here. I stared down at my bag, clueless whether to go straight for the green or hit it high and get it up to the top ridge. The green favored my fade, but if I cooked it the shot would end up in the right-side bunker.

Then I was distracted by Cliff Roberts. He was waving toward the gallery behind the green ropes. I glanced in that direction and saw a man emerge from the thick Georgia pines, slip like a shadow through the thick gallery, and walk down the slope toward where I was standing in the middle of the wide fairway.

He was wearing a green blazer, a white Pima cotton shirt, neatly pressed gray gabardine trousers, brown tasseled loafers, and his famous trademark, a flat white hat that I knew he bought decades before at a shop called Cavanaugh on Park Avenue in New York City.

"Ben," Roberts greeted him. "Would you mind giving Tim some help on how to play this shot?"

I stared at Ben Hogan.

Hogan nodded imperceptibly in greeting, took a drag on his cigarette, and stepped behind my ball to see the angle of my shot. With half my mind I realized I was certifiable; with the other half I wondered what Hogan would tell me.

In a voice that was soft and southern, he asked calmly, "How far can you hit a 1-iron, fella?"

Of course Hogan would want me to hit a 1-iron.

"I don't carry a 1-iron, sir."

Hogan took another long drag of his cigarette. He was in no rush. There's a story told of how, at the '54 Masters, in a playoff between Hogan and Sam Snead on the same hole. Sam had knocked his approach over the green, then made a 65-foot downhill chip for a birdie. Meanwhile, Hogan, who was on the green in regulation with an uphill 25-foot putt, smoked a whole cigarette to calm himself before trying and missing his birdie putt.

"Hit your two," Hogan finally advised. "Play it back in your stance and drive it toward the left front edge of the green. It will kick right."

"You think I can reach the back ridge with a two?"

Hogan nodded. "You swing flat like me. Keep the ball low; it will run up that ridge." He moved away; as in his life, he said his piece and then stopped talking. I pulled the 2-iron and a frown washed over Clay's face, but he kept silent, sensing that I had made up my mind.

My 2-iron came off the velvet fairway low and hard and with just enough of my natural fade that it worked itself back to the corner of the green. The aprons at Augusta were cut close, so anything short of the green would run. I hit my 2-iron better than stiff.

A roar funneled down the fairway to where Clay and I were standing. I sensed the gallery knew they might be witnessing history. The old man was throwing down the gauntlet to the touring pros. One good shot made all the clichés of the game seem possible.

Senese pulled a club and set himself to play. Clay and I fell silent with the hundreds of others who lined the fairway and circled the green. All eyes were on the Italian kid. The right-side bunker was not a problem; neither was the wide amoeba-shaped bunker carved into the fairway well short of the putting surface, a bunker left over from the days of hickory clubs.

Senese's approach got caught up in the swirling winds at that southern end of the course and came up short, rolling back down off the sloping green. Seeing that, Vicars played a 4-iron fade into the green, but the ball didn't fade, it sliced, and Bill was in the right-side bunker and had to play a long sand wedge that came out hot and ran beyond the cup. He missed his putt coming back. And Senese, too, 2-putted.

Following Bobby Locke's putting lesson of setting the ball at the toe and hitting it with topspin, I drilled home my six-footer. Thanks to Locke, and Ben Hogan, I was heading into Amen Corner even par.

27

GLANCING UP at the huge scoreboard tucked into the tree left of the fairway I saw I was tied with Phil Mickelson and Hunter Mahan, all three of us just making the top ten. Rory McIlroy was leading at 5 under, but also on the leaderboard was Chuck Smith. I smiled. The kid had come out of the pack with three birdies on the back side. He could be one of the early leaders in the clubhouse.

Tiger, however, had yet to tee off, and most of the field was behind those of us who had teed off early. Fair enough, but Smith's old man could still get a photo of his son's name up on the big board by the clubhouse.

I stopped walking to study the scoreboard. It was mesmerizing. I could have stayed there and stared at it all afternoon. The big board was like the stock market ribbon on a cable station. A ceaseless flow of numbers, changing from black to red, going back and forth as each player's stock rose and fell. There were stories to be written behind all the birdies and bogeys on the big board. The numbers

went red when the play got under par. It was Cliff Roberts who had
come up with the idea of putting up red numbers for the players,
another of his Masters innovations adopted by the PGA Tour.

I glanced around to see if Roberts or Hogan were following me, but neither one was in sight. I half expected Ben to be
there on 11 tee when I arrived. It was Hogan who had taught
the pros how to play this hole. But he was nowhere in sight
when I came out of the woods and reached the tee box.

I was still thinking about Hogan as I stared down the long
tunnel of trees to the open fairway. He had once said that if
he was ever on the par-4 11 in 2, he had misplayed his second
shot. What Hogan feared, as did everyone who played at Augusta
National, was the small pond to the left side of the green, created
from a tributary of Rae's Creek.

In 1951, when Hogan arrived in Georgia, he discovered Bobby
Jones had carved a new pond into the front left corner of the
green. To take the pond out of play, Hogan came up with the
strategy of hitting his second shot to the right side, then getting up
and down from there and being satisfied with par.

Ben kept to his plan—except for when he famously didn't.
Playing in '67, in his last Masters, he shot even-par on the front
side, then birdied 10. At 11, he went for the green with a 6-iron
that curled to a stop a foot below the cup, and he made another
birdie. He went on to make four more and shoot 30 on the backside, tying the nine-hole record. He was 54 years old and that tournament was his last hurrah.

I stepped between the markers. It was still my honor. I took out
a new Pro V1 and swigged from the bottle of water I had stashed in
my bag. It was quiet on the tee. I could hear birds in the high pines
and the soft muffled conversations of the few Augusta National
members manning the tee box. Coming from farther down the
fairway, from the stands to the right of 11 green and near the tee

of the par-3 12, I heard faint roars from the gallery watching the action on 12. It all sounded distant, like echoes from another golf course and another event. For those of us deep in the dogwoods that framed the entrance to 11 fairway, we might as well have been in church, far back in the pews waiting for the service to begin.

At the rear of the tee box, young Senese leaned over and whispered something in Italian to his caddie. The caddie was an older man, and I wondered if it might be his father. More fathers and sons. Then Vicars distracted me by pulling his wood from the bag and pounding it lightly on the tee. He was ready to play, ready to be done with the round and out of Augusta and on to the next tournament where he could tee it up.

I glanced over at the white-haired green-jacket member directing play, and he smiled nicely and gestured that I should play away. I re-teed my ball and forced myself to quit thinking of the lovely setting, of Cliff Roberts, of how Hogan had played this hole decades ago, of what my playing partners might be doing, or whether young Smith would finish as low amateur after two rounds.

Golf is all about focusing, the shot that has to be made. Concentration is also one of my great failings in life. I closed my eyes and took a deep breath. I opened my eyes and looked down the length of the narrow opening to the faraway fairway.

The day before, playing in the heat of the afternoon, I had laced my drive on the left side and it had held up, caught the slope, and run. I'd had a clear shot to the target. With a helping wind, and just over 225, I hadn't followed Hogan's strategy but rather had played to the right front fringe with my 3-wood. And with the flag cut on the high side, I managed—to everyone's astonishment, including my own—to reach the green.

My problem was that I didn't know how to hit my drives more than one way. Most of the pros playing on the PGA tour could hit the ball nine ways to Sunday, everything from a low cut to a high draw. But I was locked into my "educated fade," and trying to match skills with pros just wasn't going to work.

Still, with my readjusted R9 I could keep the ball straight through the trees and into the open. All I wanted from number 11 was to get my par and move safely through the first hole of Amen Corner.

But just when you think you have it all figured out, the golfing gods remind you that you are only mortal. Driving off, I felt my left side opening too soon, and I pushed the shot, driving my ball deep into the pines to the right side of the fairway and beyond the first cut.

I picked up my long tee and walked off the box. Vicars followed in my wake. When I glanced around, I saw he had a fairway wood in his hands. That's what I should have done. Hit a 3 or 4 to make sure I didn't lose it right. It was a familiar golfer's refrain: Wisdom comes only after the ball is in flight. I handed Clay my club and he whispered, "It's okay."

"Yeah, sure."

"It's okay," he said again, as if he had inside information from down the fairway.

Bill Vicars split the fairway with his 3-wood. The old pro wasn't done yet, and that more than anything separated the pros from the rest of us. They know the game is always in the next shot, that golf is not a history lesson but another chance to shoot the lights out, to get it up and down, to birdie the last hole and win it all.

We fell silent as Senese teed off. I felt the whip of wind when he swung, a quick world of young strength that made me blink. He charged off the tee, following his drive that, unlike mine, rode the wind into the wide fairway beyond the tight corridor. He had driven beyond both of us.

I moved off the tee, headed not for the safety of the fairway but to the right side, where I could see several of the marshals had already rushed into the woods to find my misplayed ball.

Clay reached it first and signaled that I had a shot.

Catching up, I found my drive had come to rest in a nest of pine needles in the middle of the trees, but that I had room to swing. If I was lucky, I might be able to thread it through a dozen thin pines and safely back onto the fairway.

"Why are you grinning?" Clay asked, staring at me.

"Clay, you don't play on muni courses in all kinds of weather without learning how to hit off rocks and clay and baked sand and everything else when the course isn't much more than a cow pasture."

I grabbed my 5-iron. The five was my go-to club when I was in trouble. I had always joked with Kerry, telling her that when they buried me, I wanted my 5-iron in the casket. It had gotten me out of more trouble than my honorary membership card from the Southern Illinois Sheriff's Association.

"Watch this," I motioned him to move. The three marshals had already cleared out. I looked back into the fairway. On the other side, Bill and Agesilao were standing together, waiting for me.

I looked at my lie. There's a trick to playing off pine needles— or, for that matter, off tarmac or any other strange surface. As Walter Hagen termed it, you had to hit the ball as if it were simply the top of a daisy.

I had one shot, and that was to cut the ball out of the trees. I was still 225 from the green and I had to guard against driving into Bobby Jones's green-side pond. I wasn't good enough with my mid-irons to sculpt the ball around the trees and fade it into the flat fairway below the green. As I thought about it, I realized that maybe my muni experience wasn't enough to save me. I might have to take an unplayable after all.

"You can play it," Hogan spoke up, appearing as if out of cyberspace, and reading my mind. "Here's how."

Holding his cigarette in his lips, he demonstrated the shot. "Weaken your left hand and, on the backswing, exaggerate a clockwise rotation of your left arm to create a power fade. The ball will work around the trees. Hit your five. You know how to play off this lie." He gestured to the bed of needles.

"Oh, yeah," I answered bravely, as if talking to myself. I remembered seeing Ballesteros on television playing out of waist-deep azaleas when he won in '80, but Seve, as the announcers always said, had more imagination than most, and certainly more than me.

I waved my hand at the CBS crew to move, motioned that I was coming their way. Clay swung the bag onto his shoulder and slipped through the azalea bushes toward the fairway, forty yards from where I was standing alone in the pines, so he'd have a clear view.

I stepped behind the ball and tried to envision the shot. I imagined the flight from the azaleas, up and through the pines, then carrying onto the fairway and coming up short of the green-side pond. All I'd have left then would be an easy pitch-and-run to the flag. In my mind's eye it looked simple, but a half-dozen things could go wrong and I'd be left in the bushes or the ball wouldn't work left to right and I'd catch the water.

Clay reached the fairway, and with the assistance of the marshals, moved the camera crew from my line of flight. I set myself to play. From behind me, I heard Hogan again, this time telling me to move the ball up in my stance. Next, he realigned my position and reminded me to rotate my left arm. I focused on the narrow avenue of escape. It was the first time in a long week that I was in serious trouble. I had had a few misadventures in the bunkers, caught close lies in the second cut, and been in the trees on nine, but for the most part I had kept the ball in play playing conservatively. I had kept myself in contention.

I backed away from the ball again, having lost my courage to swing.

"It's okay," Ben reassured me.

No one could ever rush him, and he would not rush me.

"Play when you're ready."

I thought of the cameras and the gallery focused on me as I stood deep in the white dogwood woods. It was quiet on the course, a lovely afternoon in Georgia. I was the whole show.

"Play it off the left toe, not the heel," Hogan added.

I addressed the ball once again, plucked at the left sleeve of my shirt to free the fabric from my shoulder and set the 5-iron in position. Following Ben Hogan's instructions, I focused on my thin window of escape from the forest.

Taking a deep breath, I settled myself down and then clipped the ball neatly off the bed of needles and it shot out of the pines and clear of the woods. It moved left to right as if it had eyes, caught the fairway, and ran. I was safe with only a knockdown wedge left to the pin cut in the back corner of the deep green.

The gallery was still applauding when I emerged from the trees. I tipped my cap and handed my iron to Clay.

"Okay?" I joked.

He was grinning too as he wiped the face of the 5-iron clean and slipped it into the bag. We paused to watch Vicars play. His drive had landed in the middle of the wide fairway, where Bobby Jones had originally placed a small pot bunker. Bobby's idea was to place a hazard on the hole that couldn't be seen from the tee. Only by luck or local knowledge would a player miss it. It was another piece of golf architecture Jones had borrowed from the Old Course at St. Andrews.

Now the bunker was filled in, and Vicars was safely in the middle of the smooth fairway with a utility wood to the green. He hit a beautiful little draw that curved around the small pond.

The ball hit hard into the left bank of the putting surface and checked up, leaving him a 15-foot uphill putt for birdie.

Playing now just to make the cut, Senese hit a flyer, going for a birdie to get back into the game, but his ball hit hard and bounced over the green, running down the back edge and almost into Rae's Creek. He was dead. I felt sorry for the kid, watching his shoulders sag.

Golf wasn't about strength, I knew; think how often John Daly self-destructed on a golf course. Golf was always played in the six inches between one's ears.

Reaching my ball, I waited while Vicars went up onto the green and marked his, then I asked Clay for the wedge.

"It's not a wedge shot," Roberts whispered in my ear. "With yesterday's warm weather, this green has dried up. You can't hold a wedge. You're better off with a pitch-and-run."

I turned to Clay. "What do you think? Wedge it or pitch-and-run?"

Clay shoved his caddie cap up off his forehead, looking distressed by my question. I realized I was demanding too much from the kid. He had only been looping a week at National. It took most caddies a lifetime to learn the mysteries and tricks of a golf course. As a good caddie, he didn't want to be responsible for pulling the wrong club.

Then he said, "I'd hit the wedge."

"Pitch it," Hogan told me, stepping into the breach. He was standing at my right shoulder. I didn't look his way, but I could smell the cigarette smoke as he exhaled. Not even death, I thought, could keep this man from his Chesterfields.

"I'll play the eight," I told Clay.

"You sure? It will run."

Hogan started giving me more instructions, talking over Clay's question. Ben pointed to the ridge on the green where I should land the ball and, up on the putting surface, Roberts walked over and gestured to the same spot, my two ghosts from Augusta National who had played this golf course more times than years of my life.

It was a long pitch-and-run—more than twenty yards to the front edge, then another twenty to the slope, which was 20 degrees higher, according to Clay's yardage book.

The only way to play the shot was to hit it hard enough to clear the front edge, then catch the slope to check the speed, while making sure it had the right angle and was going slowly enough to take the break. It sounds simple enough, but it was nerve-wracking to play.

I set up with the ball off my right toe and took a few careful practice swings.

"The grain grows toward Rae's Creek," Hogan added. "The ball will run away from you."

I backed away and glanced over at the next green. Mickelson was finishing off his putt, and I waited for him. I didn't need the distraction of a burst of applause on my backstroke. When he made his putt and walked off the green, I returned to my pitch-and-run.

"Keep it low," Hogan said, giving me his last instructions. "Get the ball rolling as soon as possible. The higher it lands, the harder it lands."

I chipped too long. The ball landed up the ridge and did not check but scooted forward, running past the hole as if frightened by the flag. It stopped a good twelve feet behind the cup. Any rank amateur might have made the same shot on any golf course in America.

There was polite applause from the viewers in the high stands behind 12 tee who had watched me play up. I was sure more than one in person the gallery was thumbing through their spectator guide, searching for my name and wondering how I got into the Masters.

I took my hickory putter and walked onto the green and marked my ball, then moved aside as Senese played up. Vicars circled the hole, studying the break of his putt.

The young Italian's ball came in hot and carried to the flag. It hit hard and dropped straight down into the hole. The roar of the crowd echoed across the water as they witnessed his unbelievable birdie. Senese's chip from the edge of disaster had brought him back into the tournament.

I nodded congratulations and applauded myself as the kid walked up and retrieved his ball, then I stepped over to my marker and replaced my ball. Senese's chip shot had a strangely calming effect on me. I kept thinking: Anything was possible on a golf course. Miracles happen, especially at the Masters.

I knelt behind the ball and looked at the line, remembering again what Locke had told me: All putts are straight. The only problem was finding the line, judging the break. I walked around the hole and studied the putt from the opposite side and, as I did, I glanced over to the edge of the green where Hogan and Clifford Roberts were standing together. I raised my eyebrows to indicate I needed Ben's help.

Hogan slowly shook his head, saying, "I'm no help to you, Tim. You probably know what I said before I died: In my last years of playing, I'd look at the hole and all I'd see was a cup full of blood."

Hogan's putting woes were legendary. Still, I needed help. I kept walking, circling the green, as if I knew what I was doing, catching the roll from every angle. When I was close enough to the old pro I told him he still had the best eyes in the game, and that I'd pull the trigger, I just needed his read. "Let me be your surrogate," I asked.

Without answering, he left Cliff Roberts's side and stepped over to me. It was the first time I had asked him to read a putt for me at Augusta National. With age, he had lost his nerve, but in his day on the tour, Ben Hogan was the greatest.

He leaned over my shoulder as I crouched behind the ball and told me that my putt would break six inches to the left of the cup. He pointed to a brown spot on the green where I should aim. He told me not to jam the putt as it would take the break and run toward the sun.

I set the ball at the toe of Bobby Locke's blade putter, moved the blade ahead and then behind the ball to get the right angle, and made my stroke, then watched, along with some ten million others on television around the world—and Kerry back home in Illinois—as the ball rolled twelve fee across the green and dropped safely into the plastic cup.

28

CLAY WALKED WITH ME from 11 green over to the tee at 12. We were greeted by a roar from the crowd in the stands behind the tee box. From that vantage point, they had seen my putt on 11 and there was a feeling now, I was sure, that perhaps I was for real and maybe could make a run for the green jacket, as Billy Joe Patton had done years before.

The cheers echoed off the trees and the water and the hollows of the fairways. With the sound coming at us, I kept thinking I was at home, watching all of this on television—watching myself on television walking to the tee of the second hole of Amen Corner, watching myself tipping my cap to the spectators.

I had spent most of my life as an observer, making comments and judgments on literature and life in classrooms and lecture halls far from any real action or drama. Now I was in the middle of it all, nodding and smiling and accepting applause and cheers, which once again, and after all my years of being away from the game, were for me.

Clay turned to me on the path and said, "You're the Cinderella Man. That's what they're calling you in the Chronicle. Did you read the paper this morning?"

I shook my head and told Clay I could be one of the ugly stepsisters by evening as I stepped between the markers on the tee of the hole named Golden Bell, the short par 3. It was 155 yards and, depending on the wind, required only a wedge or a short iron. Still, Palmer had made a 6 here in '59, and Tom Weiskopf hit six balls into the creek in 1980, scoring a record 13.

Standing on the tee, I felt as if I were inside a bandbox. The observation stand behind us was filled with fans, and more spectators were stretched three and four deep along the green ropes. Behind them, within the cluster of trees, were concession stands and picnic tables, and still more patrons. Spectators came to this far corner of the course just to watch the pros play through Amen Corner. That was all they saw of the Masters, but it was enough.

The green on 12 was eight feet lower than the tee and nestled pretty and peaceful in the shade of pine trees. It was lowest point of the golf course. Water blocked the front of the green, three bunkers added sand, and a garden of azaleas bloomed above and beyond the putting surface. It was as pretty a piece of golf architecture you could find anywhere in the world.

I studied the flagstick on the right side of the shallow green, six paces from the fringe, and asked Clay what he thought.

"It's a nine," Clay whispered. "Choke down and let it work left to right. You need to keep the ball on the right side to have a makeable putt."

After Senese played away, I pulled my nine and dropped the ball. Hitting the nine with some sort of divot would help hold the ball on the green. I stepped away and took in the full hole once more: the patch of green, the garden of azaleas. I studied the contour of the green.

The trick for me was to find the right spot and hit it stiff. Augusta National had great drainage, so I had to come in high to manage any kind of backspin.

I hit the nine but it wasn't stiff. Trying to guide the shot, I pulled the Titleist ten feet left of the flag. The ball rolled over the edge of the green, ran down the slope, and went out of sight.

I handed my club to Clay, who reassured me that I was okay.

All I could think of was how Greg Norman flew the green and lost his ball in the azaleas back in '99.

When Vicars teed off, I walked off the tee, down the short sloping fairway, and across Hogan Bridge over Rae's Creek. It was only at this spot at Augusta that was away from the spectators and the game returned to the players and their caddies. In these moments of relative isolation I could almost imagine what it might be like to be a member, one of the privileged few playing a round of golf without being surrounded by the tournament's circus.

When I reached the green, I saw my ball was safe, short of the bunker and not in the azaleas. And I was away.

Vicars's ball was also off the green, but he could putt. Senese had found the flat surface with his tee shot but had left himself a fifty-footer. I walked onto the middle of the green and assessed the slope. Mine was not an easy up and down; for one thing, the green was very slick. I thought then I might be able to play my approach as if Augusta were a links course, hitting the ball low and letting it roll.

I paced the distance from the cup, back off the green, and

down the slope to where Clay was already waiting beside the ball. I was thirty yards from the cup.

"Your 64 degree wedge," Clay told me. He was dead serious. This was crunch time. We were running out of holes on the back side, and we were both focused on just finishing the round and making the cut. At the moment we were in great shape, but disaster could happen, and there was no telling how many birdies other players could throw up on the leaderboard later in the day.

I walked behind the ball and studied the contour. I was below the green a good five feet. I could see the pin but not the cup. I left my ball and walked back up the bank to study the break. In theory, I had a simple shot. I would play the wedge as if I were getting out of a bunker, hit it high and short and let it trickle down to the hole, close enough to save par. That was what Amen Corner was all about. Players never wanted to hurt themselves with a double bogey at that far corner of the course.

I went back and addressed the ball.

Okay, I told myself. It's a wedge shot. A simple flop. A shot I had made thousands of times back home in Illinois.

I played it forward off my left heel, reminding myself to hit through the shot, to trust myself and the deep wedge to scoop under it, to lift it high and soft like a free balloon. I made a big arc, trusting my swing, trusting myself, keeping my arms stiff, and the ball came up soft and high and spun as if filmed in slow motion. It sailed effortlessly onto the green, landed way short of the flag, and rolled down hill to the cup.

From across the water and 155 yards away, back behind the tee, and up in the gallery stands, the fans cheered my recovery shot. I was on the green in two at 12 and close enough to tap in for a par on what the great Lloyd Mangrum once said was the meanest little hole in the world.

29

LEAVING 12 WITH THREE PARS, Bill Vicars, Agesilao Senese, and I walked off the green and across to the next tee, set back in the trees. Senese still had the honors and both he and Vicars had me on this hole. Even before teeing up, I knew I was the odd man out on number 13.

In 2002, this par 5 was lengthened by 30 yards and, again, it was all because of Tiger Woods. He had come to Augusta with his strength and ability and turned the old course into something that was only slightly more challenging for him than my muni courses in Illinois were for me. He was on the green in 2 on every par 4 with a drive and a short club.

Now, a new tee had been carved into a corner of pine woods, land that had once been part of the Augusta Country Club. The hole was still the same dogleg left that favored players who hooked the ball, only now it was longer. A drive of 265 down the length of Rae's Creek would get me around the corner to a flat lie for my second shot, but I wasn't sure that my new adjustment to the R9 would hold up. I was more likely to hit into the right-side second cut or leave it somewhere out on the fairway where I'd have a side hill lie. No matter where I put my drive I wouldn't have the length to get on in two. I didn't have the distance or the draw to play the hole.

I wasn't worried about Rae's Creek or the pine woods on the left side. I wouldn't cook my drive. On Thursday, I had played conservatively, getting my ball safely onto the fairway, then hitting up short of where Rae's Creek crossed the hole for a second time.

Senese, I knew, could hammer his drive and keep it left. Vicars, who appeared to have every swing in the bag, would work one of his big draws and find a level spot on the fairway for his second shot. All I had was my old faithful fade, which wasn't much good on this hole.

Cliff Roberts spoke to me as we took the long walk over to the tee. "You know who owns this hole?"

It was a rhetorical question. I waited for Roberts to tell me what I knew he would tell me regardless of what I answered.

"Jimmy Demaret. No one played 13 like Jimmy."

I glanced Roberts's way and saw he was smiling. He always smiled when he spoke about a player he liked.

"Jimmy owned this hole," he repeated.

Whispering now, as if he were afraid the others might hear his voice from the dead, he reminded me how Demaret had been the first pro to win the Masters three times. He was also the first player to shoot 30 on the back side. "That record stood for twenty-seven years," he said reverently; he took his Masters history seriously.

I didn't jab him with a wry comment. Augusta National was all he had of his life, just these great memories from past tournaments. Still it was more than what most men possessed, living or dead.

Teeing up on the hole that was called Azalea, I felt a certain amount of relief. I knew what I had to do: drive the ball into the open fairway and leave myself some sort of second shot to a spot further down the fairway, a spot where I could pitch it close enough to save par. Maybe I could squeeze out a birdie. At the least, I wanted to walk off 13 with a par, to get through Amen Corner without destroying my chances of making the cut.

I teed up and stepped over to Clay to pull my driver.

"Nice and easy," he said softly.

Clay knew players want to let it all hang out on long par 5s. He was gently reminding me not to cook it, not with an out-of-bounds hugging the length of the left side.

I nodded and stepped back to the markers and took in the fairway once more. If I laced my drive down the left side, far enough so it cleared the dogleg, I'd have maybe 180 to the green. It was a tempting thought. And I might be able to do it with my new R9.

I stepped up and repositioned my teed-up ball.

"What do you think?" I mumbled to Roberts as I fussed with my grip. I couldn't see the old man, but he was there. He was always there.

"Go for it," he advised.

"Really?" That surprised me. True, Roberts had been egging me on, but with the challenges of this hole, I'd be lucky to get out alive.

"Let me tell you a story," he said.

Perfect, I thought. The dead really do have their own sense of timing.

I ignored him and took another slow practice swing.

Roberts wasn't deterred. He began to tell, in his maddeningly deliberate manner, an Eisenhower story.

"The President only played bridge and golf. They were his two passions. He played both games the same. Take bridge, for example. Let's say Ike had the bid, and the bid was four hearts. The average person would be quite happy to play it most any way in order to make the bid requirement, which would be four hearts. But the General wanted to make that extra trick even though, money-wise, it didn't mean anything.

"Let's say we were playing for a cent a point, and, by making that extra trick, he got 30 points, 30 cents. But the amount of money involved had nothing to do with it. That extra heart trick meant something else to him: the satisfaction of getting everything out of the hand that was possible to attain.

"That was President Eisenhower. It was the secret of his psyche and the secret of his success. And this is how you have to play this game. Go for that extra heart trick like Ike did."

I wasn't Ike. I wasn't playing bridge. But I had one ace in the hole. I wasn't flashy like the flamboyant Jimmy Demaret, or as compulsive as Ben Hogan. But I was dogged. I'd never be a leading man. But I wasn't a character actor either. I was the rock solid next to the hard place. I knew how to get the job done.

I didn't bail out to the right off of 13, nor did I cook it. I drove straight down the left edge of the fairway. My drive hugged the trees to the corner and then worked right into the fairway. I couldn't have walked down the fairway and placed my ball in a better position. I hit a beauty.

I reached my ball before Clay did. He came hustling after me, clubs rattling in the bag.

I was again the first to play my second shot. Both of the young pros were up on the hillside. I stood beside my ball and looked down at the green. I took a half dozen deep breaths to calm myself. I had no idea what club to pull from the bag, or how to play my next shot. Earlier in the week, my drives had all been to the right side, and I had played safely up short of the creek. Now, with this drive, I had an outside chance of being home in 2.

Roberts was at my side the moment I paused, ready to tell me

what to do next. Though now, sensing that he might have unnerved me, he said nicely, "I have someone who you should listen
to before you play your next shot."

Before I saw him, I knew who it would be. Who else but
the man who owned the 13 hole?

And even as a ghost, he stood out. On a warm spring afternoon in Georgia, with the flowers all in bloom, this player's
outfit made the flora look pale.

He wasn't wearing a green jacket, though he owned three.
Jimmy Demaret's father had been a house painter in Houston, and
Jimmy had inherited a flair for color. He bought his clothes in New
York City, where Adolphe Menjou and Clark Gable once shopped.
He dressed, from head to toe, like a peacock. On the golf course
no one could ignore him, which, of course, was exactly what he
wanted.

But Jimmy Demaret had a game to match his flashy clothes. He
was so good that when pros played with partners Hogan always
wanted him.

And there he was, striding casually across the fairway to join
me at the bend of the dogleg.

I nodded hello and said it was a pleasure to meet him, as calmly
as if we were all at some weird cocktail party for the dead. He
smiled and looked around, remarking that I seemed to have gotten
myself in some kind of match. Then he told me how in 1950 when
he won his last Masters he was playing with Roberto De Vicenzo
and had hit his drive on 13 too far right, into what we called
no-man's land.

"I had a downhill lie," Demaret said, speaking in his thick
Texas drawl and enjoying the memory. "It wasn't much of a lie,
but I didn't have many options. I cut a 2-wood across that little
creek down there in front of the green, and the ball ran up to
the green. I didn't know how close it was, but there was this

tremendous cheer from the gallery behind the green. When I got closer, I could see why. My ball was about two inches from the cup. With my eagle I got back to two over par. Then I birdied the 15th and the 17th and, instead of shooting 77, I salvaged a 72, and that was good enough to turn the tournament around.

"But the most amazing part of that week was that I played the par 5s 10 strokes under par. I never did that before or since. I played this hole 6 under par that week."

"That's why I suggested Jimmy help you on this hole," Roberts piped up.

Without waiting for my agreement, Demaret glanced at my lie, then stepped over to my clubs and glanced inside my bag.

Jimmy said, "You're not like those young fellas. You'll need everything you got to clear Rae's Creek. Play that fancy hybrid club all you fellas have today and work it left to right. You might reach the green."

"I can carry the creek," I answered, "but my ball won't hold the green. It will end up in one of those bunkers behind the hole."

Clay snapped his head around. I was talking out loud again.

"For some reason, this green is softer than the others," Demaret advised. "Play the ball forward and swing more upright. That will give you lift."

I pulled the hybrid and said to Clay, "I'm giving it a try."

"Good!" he declared, grinning and moving the bag.

"You're not going to be so cheery if I don't make it." I stepped behind the ball and took two slow swings.

"You'll make it," he added with a caddie's full confidence.

A great caddie is like a great wife—he has blind faith that you can do the impossible.

My lie was level. I had found the strip of fairway at the near corner of the dogleg that offered me a perfect position. I set myself and aimed for the front left-side bunker. My ball would work itself back to the green, but what troubled me were the rear bunkers. I didn't know if I could keep the ball on the green.

"Swing easy and let the club do the work." Demaret advised. He was smiling. There were few players on the old PGA tour as obliging as Jimmy. "We all know, those of us on the other side of the fairway, so to speak, what you're living with, Tim. We're going to make it happen for you. The golfing gods are on your side."

My fairway wood came out high and too close to the trees. Luckily, though—with the golfing gods' help, perhaps—it cleared the branches and leaves and rode the late morning breeze. Still, I didn't think it had the distance. The hybrid wasn't enough club. The ball couldn't carry the creek.

But it did. Clearing the water, it hit the front fringe and bounced onto the green where it checked up and rolled slowly forward toward the cup. The din from the gallery was deafening, and why not? I had duplicated Jimmy Demaret's famous 2-wood. I was home in 2, with a chance for an eagle to go 2 under. I knew now that I would make the cut. I'd be playing that weekend at the Masters.

30

I DIDN'T LEAVE Locke's hickory putter in my bag after my round on Friday, I was too nervous to let it out of my sight. Someone might steal the club, which is what happened to Ben Hogan after he won the 1950 Open at Merion. The 1-iron disappeared from his bag when he left it in the locker room.

I carried my clubs upstairs to the Crow's Nest. If I had the putter in my grasp, I thought, then I could almost believe I wasn't losing my mind, wasn't imagining Bobby Locke, Ben Hogan, and now Jimmy Demaret coming from the other side to help me win a green jacket.

In the Crow's Nest, I glanced into Charlie Smith's room and saw he was stretched out on his bed. He had his spikes and his soaks offer the foot of the bed. His fingers were laced behind his head. I stopped and said, "Nice round, Charlie." I had spotted his name high up on the main leaderboard.

He glaced my way. "Thanks. You?"

I flashed my fingers and pointed them down to show him how many under I was. Charlie let out a long, low whistle and stirred himself, swinging his feet over the side of the bed and onto the throw rug beside it. My 68 had impressed him and made him at least momentarily jealous.

"Our roomies?" he asked.

I shook my head. "Zack is a dozen over. Ray, I think, is lost out on the back nine. I couldn't find his name on the board. Maybe he WD'd."

"We're the only amigos left?"

"I guess so. Do you have plans for dinner?"

He nodded without looking up. I understood what he meant. His father had plans. My guess, too, was that his parents would want him to stay with them at their hotel to make sure he was safely tucked into bed early that night.

"Okay, I'll catch you later. If not, good luck tomorrow. You're playing well."

Smith stood then and reached out and shook my hand. He thanked me for our talk at breakfast. It had been a big help, he said. He seemed embarrassed thanking me. I waved it all off and told him to focus on his game.

Then I added, smiling, "'Cause I'm gonna whip your ass."

He laughed, remembering the line from our Wednesday night dinner. It was the first really lighthearted moment I had seen Chuck Smith enjoy at Augusta National, and I could see now that I had misjudged him—he was a good kid.

"Good luck, sir," he said, shaking my hand again.

"You, too, Chuck." I tapped him on the shoulder and nodded and left him in his small room to be alone for awhile. My guess was his father already had a list of what he had done wrong that day. There would be no partying for Chuck even though he had made the cut.

Out on the second-floor landing, I dialed home on my cell phone. There was no answer. I let it ring until the answering machine picked up, just so I could hear Kerry's voice. Then I called Tyler. Again, there was no answer. I called Peggy's cell. No answer there, either. At twenty, Peggy seem to be always on the phone when she was home.

My whole family was unreachable, which wasn't a coincidence. Something was wrong. If Kerry was worse, Tyler would have called. My kids were under instructions to keep in touch. And then I realized what was happening. They were coming to Georgia. It was just the kind of crazy decision Kerry would make. She had come to Midlothian the summer before to watch me play my championship round and had hid in the clubhouse before I teed off, but I could feel her presence. That was the thing about the two of us. We were wired with this clairvoyant link. It was like parents who wake in the middle of the night and know something terrible has happened to their kid.

I walked into the empty second-floor lounge. The top floors of the old manor house were eerily silent. Cheers from spectators on the course reached the building like rumbling thunder. The Augusta National Club House was the eye of the storm, a peaceful oasis.

I suddenly felt immensely tired. I wasn't cut out for the craziness of tournament golf, I thought, and I wondered then if my walking away from the game at nineteen had had more to do with that than anything else. I was more comfortable sitting in the back row of events than being on stage. I knew that much from watching Kerry acting in college productions. She blossomed in the glow of footlights. I always felt slightly embarrassed by any recognition.

I set off to find a soft leather armchair and, stepping around the empty game room, I walked into the bar and there he was, waiting for me.

"Restless?" Cliff Roberts asked. His cigar was laced into his fingers like a baby's Binky.

Seeing me, Lightnin' walked over with a smile and a congratulations. Like all the staff in the clubhouse, Lightnin' knew what was happening on the course. All the TV sets were tuned to the tournament, and for these employees at Augusta National, golf was the only sport that mattered.

"How about a Heineken?" I asked.

"Yes, sir, one Heineken it is!"

I turned to Roberts. We had the corner of the room to ourselves. He sat forward and, lowering his voice, began to tell a story that he wanted only me to know.

"When I was younger, much younger than you are today, I was in Europe. It was the First World War. I was a private in the Signal Corps and I met a woman there. Her name was Suzanne, Suzanne Verdet. We were great friends from the first day we met in Paris. She saved my life once. I was in France and planning to fly to London. Suzanne wouldn't let me go. She had a premonition, she told me, and she kept me with her for another day. The plane I would have taken crashed in the English Channel, and all lives were lost."

Roberts stopped speaking. He was staring off across the bar, which in the afternoon light, was deeply shadowed. He looked sad and preoccupied and, without looking my way, he continued to speak.

"When I was alive, I was never someone who was willing to admit my mistakes. It was how I was raised. A poor boy in a dysfunctional family, I always felt I had to be ready to defend myself against everyone and anything. But looking back at the patchwork quilt of my life, I see I would have been a happier man if I had succumbed to my desires and married Suzanne, which was her wish, but one she never expressed.

That was not her way. And I was a man too afraid to express my feelings."

He fell silent. I saw the sadness on his face. Even in death, he could not escape his life. Now I was feeling guilty for my harshness with the old man.

"Where's Suzanne today?" I asked.

"She is waiting for me to leave the prison I'm in and join her—on the other side, as you would say." He smiled wryly.

I took another sip of my beer, and Roberts glanced my way. He had not, in all of our exchanges, been so forthcoming, or as open with his feelings.

"I believe we have had similar experiences with regard to making decisions. We are all failures, Tim. So don't be that so on yourself."

"Well, it matters to me," That is what death is like, I thought. The lives of the living are common knowledge.

"Yes, when you turned down that position at Yale, you turned down Kerry's chance to take her talents to a big stage. She might have been a star in that Yale drama school. Why did you turn down the job, Tim? That would have been quite a coup for a small town teacher like yourself, making it to Yale University."

I sipped the beer from the bottle, leaving the glass empty on the table. I could see that simple gesture annoyed Cliff Roberts. I also realized that Roberts knew exactly why I didn't take the Yale faculty appointment.

"Her decision was her decision."

"Please! If you had gone to Yale, then she, too, would have had opportunities. She would have been playing in a bigger arena and not stuck out in a backwater college. Broadway lights don't shine bright in Southern Illinois, Tim. Your decision not to compete in the big time condemned Kerry to a second-rate career."

"Am I afraid of failing or afraid of success, Mr. Roberts? You're accusing me of both."

"They're two sides of the same coin. Though I'd say being afraid of success is the greater sin."

"Well, if we're playing amateur shrink, now it's my turn." I had had enough of this psychobabble from a dead man.

I leaned forward across the table and lowered my voice, though I had been careful to keep my face turned away from the bartender and the other customers. I didn't want the rumor spreading around the clubhouse that I was holed up in the corner of the bar, drinking myself into a stupor and blabbering away to myself after only two rounds.

"The Yale job, or my whole life for that matter, hasn't been about winning or losing. I've had my share of success, success on my terms, in my profession. You miss the point of what drives me, Cliff. I had other college offers besides Yale that would have gained me more prestige, not to mention more of a salary. But when I was nineteen years old and walked away from golf, I decided then that I wasn't going to follow my old man's path. I had seen what his endless quest for more and better and best and whatever else was out there did for him. What did he achieve? A heart attack at forty-four and death on the Metro North. That wasn't the track I wanted my life to take."

I pushed back from the small corner table and stood.

"The drinks are on me," I added, making a joke of leaving. Still I hesitated. I knew Cliff Roberts would have one last thing to say. He always did.

"We are all victims of our past, Mr. Alexander."

I nodded. I had taught enough literature to understand how writers struggled to illustrate that simple point.

"You don't want to win this golf tournament," Roberts went on. "It is rather amazing, really, to find a player with as much talent as you have who doesn't want to win the most important golf tournament in the world."

Roberts stared up at me, showing his puzzlement.

"That's your opinion, sir."

"It is not an opinion, Tim. It's obvious. Several times today you had the opportunity to separate yourself from the pack, but you played it safe, the sure shot. You didn't go for the green the way real players will. You played for a safe second. If it wasn't for me and Jimmy out there on 13, you would have never gone for the green."

"I'm low amateur going into the weekend," I reminded Roberts. "I played well enough to make the cut. That was my first objective when I arrived at Augusta."

"You could be low Rastafarian, it wouldn't make any difference."

I smiled, enjoying the thought of a Rastafarian teeing it up at Augusta National.

"There's always Charlie Smith," I reminded Roberts. "The kid had a helluva round today. Maybe you should place your bet on Charlie to win the Masters. Why waste your time on a codger like me?"

"The boy doesn't have the strength to hold up under the pressure that comes on Sunday afternoon. You're cautious and too careful, but you're mature enough to handle it. With my help you won't blow it on the back nine, or so I hope. Besides, I told you I was going to save your wife. I'll fulfill my agreement."

"Really? You're not doing so well so far," I answered angrily. "It seems her cancer has come back."

"Not if you win on Sunday."

I stared at him, trying to get a grip on what was happening. Surely what he was promising wasn't possible, even from beyond the grave. But if he could change the course of Kerry's illness; if he could make cancer just disappear, then I really had made a deal with the devil.

Saturday

31

CLIFFORD ROBERTS FOUND ME on the putting green. To be more accurate, he appeared to me on the putting green in the few minutes I used to settle myself down before teeing off. I had a 1:20 tee time and I was paired with Phil Mickelson, the three-time Masters Champ, who, with his caddie Jim Mackay, was now on the other side of the green. As he casually made putts, he talked and joked with a cluster of reporters, telling them that as usual he had stopped at the Waffle House on Washington Road for a late breakfast before arriving at the club. It was a big joke on the tour, Mickelson and his love of waffles.

I kept drilling in short putts with my borrowed hickory-shaft putter, and Clay, squatted down behind the hole, kept rolling the balls back to me. Roberts was telling me where the pin was cut on the holes. He was visibly nervous, which made him seem nicer.

I didn't reply. I was learning that in dealing with Roberts, silence was my best strategy. After a lifetime of servants who had eagerly responded to his wishes, he did not know what to do when ignored.

"Are you listening?" he finally demanded.

Instead of replying, I nodded to Clay and told him it was time. I handed my caddie the putter and balls and he hesitated and stared over at me. He had something to say. There is always a moment between a caddie and his player when it is just the two of them—without the gallery, the tournament officials, or, for that matter, their playing partners and their caddies—when they wish each other good luck and share that moment. Just two guys on a single and simple quest: to go out and play the best golf in the world. And there, on the putting green, before the ball was teed up, each believed that yes, this was their time, they would for eighteen holes play some great golf.

I shook Clay's hand and smiled, nodding that I knew what he meant and felt, and he spontaneously gave me a big bear hug and told me to go get 'em. I told him I would. I'd go get them, and at that moment, I believed that I could.

He swung my barrel bag up on his shoulder and took the path between the green ropes up to the tee, leaving me alone again with Clifford Roberts. Not until Clay was gone, and the intensity of his leaving was over, did I reply to Roberts. I told him flatly, "I want you to worry about curing my wife, not whether I can play Augusta National."

"It's a tougher course today than what you played to make the cut," he answered bluntly, focused on his task of getting me to the green jacket.

I turned and looked over at the first tee. I could see Mickelson. He was finishing up on the practice green too. It was time to go. I asked Roberts which pros he had summoned to get me around the course.

"It depends on what you'll need."

"You mean what sort of trouble I wind up in," I tossed off, heading for the tee.

"Something like that."

Without looking around for Roberts, I walked away, following the roped walkway for the players from the putting green up to the 1st tee. People were packed several deep against the rope and a few voices called my name, wishing me well. I smiled and nodded and tipped my hat and kept walking. Since arriving at Augusta National, I had been watching the pros handle the galleries. No one was allowed to seek autographs from them anywhere on the course, so there wasn't a lot of stopping and chatting with the patrons. The players moved from place to place safely away from the fans, visible as animals in the zoo, but just as untouchable.

"I'll save you a lot of strokes," Roberts added, following after me.

"Is that so?"

"You're worried because you can't get in touch with your family?" Roberts finally asked, sensing my mood.

"I worry about everything, from a downhill putt to keeping up with that guy." I nodded towards Phil Mickelson who, seeing me, approached with his hand outstretched and a wide smile on his sunny face.

"Good luck today, Tim."

"You, too, Phil," I replied, as if we were the best of friends.

I shook hands next with Jim Mackay and wished him well, and then I stepped over to the officials' table to pick up my card. Glancing around I took in the dozen green-jacket members and officials crowding the tee box and, showing my nervousness, quipped, "This looks like a convention of elevator operators."

No one laughed.

"We're proud to be members, Tim," Roberts commented, taking offense on behalf of the men who couldn't see him.

"Just joking," I said out loud, then added, "By the way, in case you need to know, I'm a forty-two regular."

They smiled, glancing at each other, and wished me luck, and one of the gray- haired officials reminded me that no amateur had ever won the Masters.

"Gee, you sure know how to put the pressure on a guy!" I grinned.

Now I had their attention, and someone, of course, mentioned Billy Joe Patton's famous run in '54, and then there was the story of Ken Venturi's collapse in '56. I wondered if the men had to pass a Masters trivia test before they were accepted as members.

I stood smiling and let them talk. They were proud of their tournament, and justly so. Most of what we see on the PGA tour today was invented at Augusta, by Roberts and Jones. I'd have to give Cliff credit.

I took my card and shook hands all around and then turned to face the tee and the first hole. It was Saturday. I had made it to the weekend. That was no small accomplishment; even with my pessimistic nature, I had to admit to that reality.

Clay brought over my driver and a new ball, and Phil, without waiting for an introduction, said hello to Clay, noting that they hadn't met. He shook Clay's hand and wished him well. He wished me well, too, though I knew he must be wondering how in the world I had managed to grab a late tee time on the Saturday afternoon of the Masters.

The twosome ahead of us reached the green, and the starter announced Phil Mickelson to the gallery. I took a deep breath and stepped closer to Clay, as if his presence might somehow calm the sudden and fierce anxiety I felt.

"You've been here before," Clay whispered.

"Not in such fast company," I whispered back   .

"We'll play our game."

"What exactly is our game?" I asked. That brought a smile to his face, and he shook his head, as if he, too, had no idea what we were doing being paired with Phil Mickelson.

Phil, hitting from the wrong side, sent his metal wood up the right side of the fairway; it cleared the bunker and gently worked its way back into the middle of the narrow fairway. He had hit his drive well beyond the bunker.

"It's showtime," Clay said, speaking up to be heard over the applause for Phil's drive.

I nodded. That's what Kerry would have told me too. It was my turn to not let down the family. If she could live through all that chemo, I could to drive off number 1 on the weekend at the Masters without making a total fool of myself.

The starter announced my name, and on cue, as if walking on stage, I teed up between the markers, managing to do it without falling over myself.

There was polite applause and a few male voices shouted out my name. I had the impression I had become the hero of the over-fifty crowd, that their hopes were pinned to my unlikely run. I tipped my cap and swung the R9. I was too terrified to look over at the gallery to see if perhaps one or two of the guys from Carbondale had actually made the trip to Augusta and gotten hold of tickets to the Masters.

"Showtime," I whispered, to encouraging myself. I took another slow swing, then mentally ran through the advice I always gave myself before playing a round. It was my way of getting in the zone. I had no psychologist on staff to teach me how to focus, no swing coach or golfing guru to guide me around the eighteen holes. All I had was Cliff Roberts, but he might be enough.

What I knew about teeing off at the Masters, or, for that matter, teeing off on any summer Sunday morning in Illinois, was what I had learned as a caddie years before, and that was on Monday mornings at the country club, when the loopers got to play. That and what Kerry had taught me from her acting classes: to pull back into myself and find my center, that place where the heart and mind are in peace with each other.

My drive split the fairway. It flew high off the metal wood and rode through the still afternoon air. It soared into the Georgia blue sky. It was the longest drive I had hit that week at Augusta National; it was the longest drive I had hit that spring; it was the longest tee shot I had hit since I was a kid coming out of the caddie yard.

If I was surprised, Clay was stunned. Even Phil glanced my way and smiled, nodding his approval as we stepped off the tee box to the cheers and shouts of the gallery. They hadn't expected the old guy from Illinois to have enough strength left in him to hit such a beauty.

Clay took back the wood and slipped on the hood. He didn't say a word. I waited him out. Maybe he was afraid to break the spell, the karma created with a perfect drive. Golfers are famously superstitious. I've known players who wouldn't let their caddie touch their clubs, others who wouldn't wash their shirts after a good round. We all knew that the wrong word at the wrong time could jinx a great round. Clay held his tongue and we walked off the tee and down the middle of the fairway toward where my ball had come to rest in the middle of the emerald green.

I hadn't out-driven Phil Mickelson, of course; he had me by twenty yards. But my ball was sitting up left of the bunker, and I could see the flag on the horizon, fluttering in the afternoon breeze. All I had was a short club to the target. The pin was cut deep and to the right side of the plateau green.

I had been here before with Clay, trying to decide what club to pull. Now it was obvious I was an amateur. A touring pro could calibrate from anywhere on any fairway the distance to the flag within a foot. And here I was, just trying to get close with my approach. I knew there was no way in the world I could score on this course unless I was within gimme range

"Hit the eight," Clay told me before I asked.

I raised my eyebrows. Ever since I'd dumped my eight into the green-side bunker on Monday morning, Clay had been pulling mid-irons for me.

I started to question him—the knee-jerk reaction of all academics—and then I just accepted his advice. The kid had gotten me this far. I pulled the eight and stepped up to the shot.

"Play it ten yards left of the flag and it will work itself to the stick. The wind is not a factor. Don't press the shot; you've got enough club." There was no hesitation in Clay's string of instructions, and his confidence was contagious. I hit a beauty. The ball came off the uphill lie high and sure. It was like Watson's 8-iron into the final green at Turnberry, but it didn't hit hard and carry over the green. My ball slammed into the shelf, checked up and came to a stop five feet below the cup. We were on in 2 and I drilled home the putt. Walking toward number 2, even I knew we were flying high. I was playing on Saturday at the Masters and 4 under par.

32

I DIDN'T GO SOUTH until the 8 hole, the hole everyone claims is not only one of the longest par 5 at Augusta National but, being uphill, also the toughest. There is an old black-and-white photograph of Bobby Jones playing the 8 hole when it was still under construction, back in 1932; he is testing his skills and strength against Alister MacKenzie's design. Bobby always wanted to build par 5s so a good player could be home in 2, but when Tiger came along the hole was lengthened by twenty yards and pros had to hit their drives at least 320 to carry the right-side bunker.

I had birdied the first hole and was 1 under on the front side, having parred my way around so far. Now I needed to make something happen before I reached the back side, and the 8, even with its length, had given up plenty of birdies in its history. Eight had been kind to me all week, so I debated about going for the green with my second shot. My drive had come up short of the right-side bunker. I was hitting from an uneven lie into a huge green, some 100 feet from front to back, with no bunkers to worry about. Jones and MacKenzie had fortified this green with large mounds on both sides; all I had to do was thread the needle with my wood. If I were playing persimmons, I might have gone with the 1-wood, but the R9 had too much mass for the tight lie. I pulled the three and told Clay I'd work the ball left to right and leave myself a long chip into the flag. It was all uphill. I couldn't reach the green, but if I got it close and made a decent chip, I'd make a birdie. The hole was cut in the front section of the green. I wasn't looking for anything better than a par.

The problem was my uneven lie. I cooked the fairway metal and hit a bullet straight at the big mound guarding the left side. I had played for my educated fade, but coming off that lie, with the ball below my feet, the shot never faded. The ball caught the far side of the mound and cascaded deep into the trees and pine straw left of the green. I was pin high, but stymied in the pines. So, instead of picking up an easy birdie, I walked off the green with my first double bogey of the weekend, and dropped to two under.

"I can't help you much if you start playing like that," Roberts said, falling into step as I walked toward 9, another of Bobby Jones's famous dogleg-left par fours. I charged ahead, ignoring him.

As we walked, Roberts started lecturing about golf management and playing smart until finally I snapped at him, "Weren't you the one telling me I couldn't win until I played aggressive? More like Eisenhower at a bridge game?" Ahead of me, Bones, Phil's caddie, and Clay glanced around.

"That's what happens when you double bogey, Bones. You start to talk to yourself," I said quickly.

"There's smart golf and dumb golf," Roberts went on, disregarding the two caddies. Mickelson moved to the markers and teed up, and Roberts kept talking, oblivious of the man, kept telling me what I was doing wrong. I could hear a note of desperation in his voice, and I was thinking that perhaps he was thinking he had picked the wrong amateur to save him from his eternity at Augusta National.

Instead of listening to the old man, I concentrated on my game, this golf course. This was another hole that favored Lefty's fade. Phil could easily cut the corner of the dogleg and hit his ball to the base of the rise, leaving him a level lie for his second shot to the green.

I stood back as Phil took his time to find the correct line on the dogleg hole. Like all big hitters, Phil had the capacity to spray a ball anywhere into the gallery. He had shown that at the Open at Winged Foot.

To distract myself, I looked toward 8 green and checked the scores. With my double bogey, my name had already slipped off the leaderboard. There were half a dozen players clustered at the top, including Tiger and Phil and Angel Cabrera. Names sprang up in red letters, then just as quickly disappeared, as mine had. I guessed by now Jim Nantz and Faldo were commenting on my double bogey. Well, as they say, one hole doesn't make a tournament. I smiled wryly at the cliché and Clay whispered, "What's so funny?"

I shook my head. I was too embarrassed to tell him I was falling back on the kind of bromides you hear on the Golf Channel early in Masters week. With Mickelson's drive, I snapped out of my daydreaming. The ball hugged the stretch of pines on the right side then curved gently into the middle of the fairway and bounced forward to find a level lie. It was as if Phil had hand-delivered it down the length of the fairway.

I followed Mickelson to the markers as the applause continued. Phil tipped his hat, looking shy and embarrassed as he always did in the face of applause.

I wasn't good at moments like this, I knew. My mind wandered. I began to think about what my playing partner had done,

how I had to match his drive. I'd think again about not making a
fool of myself, and then I'd get anxious and want to get it over
with—I'd just hit away to be off the tee. All the wrong moves for
someone playing in any tournament.

I stepped back from the markers and slowly swung the R9,
hoping to calm myself and refocus myself on my game. Under my
breath I said, "Mr. Roberts, tell me about this hole."

As I'd known he would, the old man jumped right in. He
had a story for every inch of Augusta.

"Uh, as you know, these trees are called Carolina Cherry, and
you can see what hardy evergreens they are. They bloom early
in the spring, and the flowers are so fragrant."

I shook my head. True, I had asked about the hole, but I'd been
hoping for tips on how to play it, not a lesson in horticulture.

"Excuse me," I managed to interrupt, "how about some prac-
tical advice?"

"Well, why didn't you ask?" He sounded offended. "Talk to
this man here, if that's what you want to know."

With that, he turned to the thick gallery that framed the
tee and from the midst of the living came the player everyone said was the greatest gentleman the game has ever known.

Stunned into silence, I nodded hello to Byron Nelson.

I remembered Nelson from his older years, when he commented on TV at various tournaments, but today he appeared
as the tall, rangy pro he'd been in his youth, back when he twice
won the Masters.

He smiled and said shyly, "They've been giving you lots of
advice, haven't they, son?"

I nodded, too amazed to speak, and aware, too, that I was
holding up our twosome. In another few minutes, we'd be on
the clock.

"Play away," Nelson advised, as if he had read my mind.

"Don't lay up." He was shaking his head. "Hogan did that back there on 8 against me in '42; we were in an eighteen-hole playoff, and I hit a big drive, and then my spoon into the green. Of course, the hole was shorter then; I was on in 2 and within five feet of the pin. I eagled the hole to Ben's par. That gave me the lead and Ben never could catch me."

No one would call Byron Nelson the greatest player of the game, but everyone agrees he invented the modern golf swing when the game went from hickory shafts to steel. Over six feet tall, he discovered that if he used his hips and legs and a full shoulder turn, and not the wristy method of hickory players, he could drive the ball, as he would say, a country mile.

He stepped to one side and motioned me to hit and, following his advice, I stepped up and drove off. It didn't have the distance to threaten Phil's ball, but I kept it in the fairway and, walking off the tee in stride with Lord Byron, I nodded my thanks. It couldn't get any better, I thought, than getting advice from Lord Byron himself.

33

PHIL MICKELSON WALKED with me from 13 green over to the tee at 14, both of us following our caddies, who had fallen into conversation as they led the way. Phil and I had both made par on 13 and, reading the scoreboard, I saw we were also both two shots off the lead. What caught my attention was that Chuck Smith was also in the tournament. He was a couple behind Phil and me and was playing 15.

I had seen Chuck on the range before our afternoon tee times. Watching him hit woods was an older man who I realized must be his father. And with them was Chuck's swing coach, who had his hands on Chuck's shoulders, readjusting his set up.

I studied the father, who stood back, watching the pro work on his kid. I'd half expected that Smith's old man would be a short, stocky guy, someone that Chuck would resemble, but Charles Smith Sr. was big, the size of a football lineman, and looked to be still in playing shape.

He also had a nervous energy about him. He kept pacing behind Chuck and his swing coach. He dug his hands into his linen pants pockets one moment, then folded them across his chest the next. And he kept sweeping his fingers through his short silvery hair. The man was a wreck.

But what surprised me the most about Smith Sr. was that he was wearing an Augusta National Green Jacket. I hadn't realized he was a member. That was something Chuck hadn't told his Crow's Nest roommates.

Mickelson had the honors on the tee, a carryover from the first nine. The par-4 14 favored Phil's fade. For me, it was another impossible Bobby Jones dogleg where I had to wrestle my fade against the contour of the hole. The way to play 14 was with a draw right to left around the dogleg. That would leave me a short iron into the big green. The hole had been lengthened since 2002, but it was still only 440, and it was the only hole at Augusta National without a bunker.

The difficulty with 14 came from the slope of the fairway. It ran from left to right, while the big green sloped left to right, with a ridge running across it one-third into the green.

I remember watching on television when Tiger won his first Masters in '97 and completely destroyed the short course. He hit a 3-wood off the tee, drew it around the dogleg, and the ball ran like a scared rabbit, stopping less than seventy yards from the green. Tiger chipped up within eight feet of the hole, made the putt, and went 18 under for the week, setting a new tournament record. In 2006, he came back to eagle the hole, his first on a par 4 at the Masters.

On 14, Phil gave the field a gift. He had 129 to the green after a drive of 310, but he had gone hole-hunting with his wedge and come up short. His ball didn't hold the false front, and it rolled back down the slope. That left him a pitch-and-run onto the green. When he 2-putted for a bogey, I picked up another shot on him.

We moved ahead to the long par 5 where Gene Sarazen made his double eagle 2 in the 1935 Masters and created the first legend about the tournament. Like most holes at Augusta National, this one had been lengthened over the years, from 485 to 530 yards, but still, with a helping wind, it was reachable in 2 by the pros, with their new balls and new clubs. An eagle here could turn the whole tournament around. But I couldn't get my ball to the narrow green with a cannon, let alone with two metal woods.

The fairway sloped left, and I needed to guard against pulling my drive into the pines. The best shot was to hit down the right side and draw the ball back into the middle. With the new alignment of the R9, I could hit my drive straight. But then there was the problem of the wind.

At 15, the wind always penalized the player, regardless of which way it was blowing. If it was behind me, I'd run the risk of not holding the green and running down the smooth apron into the pond on the backside. If the wind was against me, I had to worry about the pond that guarded the front of the green, which over the years had ruined more than one player's chances for a green jacket.

Clay and I looked over his yardage book. I knew what I had to do: keep the ball on the right side. I didn't worry about my second shot, since I couldn't reach the green; I hadn't even attempted that all week. Studying the yardage gave me a few extra minutes to prepare myself for the drive.

It was when I pulled my driver and stepped over to the markers that I saw her. There were spectators on both sides of the fairway, stretching down toward the hole. I tried never to look at the patrons, to keep myself from being unnecessarily self- conscious, but when I glanced up to see what the wind was doing, to see how the branches were blowing, I registered her blond hair, the slope of her shoulders, her slim body. But before I could squint to see if it was really her, the woman slipped from sight.

"You okay, sir?" Clay asked.

I nodded and told him I thought I'd seen someone I knew.

He pulled the bag away, and I teed up on the far left of the markers. I would work my ball from left to right and get out about 280 to 290, which would leave me around 250 for my second shot. I could reach the green at that distance, but not on the fly, and not with a pond of water guarding it.

I stepped behind my ball and refocused. I glanced down the fairway, found the path I wanted to take, and then I saw her again. This time she was farther away. She ducked out from the crush of spectators to look up at the tee. I stopped my preparation, and now I had everyone's attention.

It couldn't be her. She was in Illinois. I really was crazy, I told myself. Talking to dead golfers. Seeing my wife in the gallery. I turned my attention to my teed-up ball and refocused on hitting a drive that would carry to the right center of the fairway and leave me a second shot.

My drive was fine, well executed, as TV announcers are fond of saying. Nothing spectacular but safely up on the ridge. Nantz and Faldo, I imagined, were already speculating on whether I would go for the green. Back in Carbondale, at Hickory Ridge, there was a crowd in the bar waging as well. The guys in my regular weekend foursome were making bets that I'd play the percentages. They knew my game better than I knew it myself.

I stepped aside as Phil took control at the 15 tee box. When he appeared between the markers, you could feel the anticipation in the crowd. He always did something special.

He moved fast—teeing up, setting up, playing away. There was a purity to his movements and motions that mesmerized. Nothing was lost to him or by him. He drove off before I had a chance even to appreciate my own drive. I couldn't compete with him, his towering tee shots told me.

To keep myself from being distracted by the woman who resembled my wife, I walked with my head down, the way that Ben Hogan had instructed Claude Harmon years ago on how to win the Masters, telling him not to get distracted by friends in the gallery, but to stay focused on what he had to do next.

I felt Roberts beside me, though for a long moment he said nothing. Then he remarked, as if idly, "When MacKenzie laid out this hole, he said it was perfect for three shots to the green, but a skillful player could do it in two."

"He wasn't talking about me."

"You're right. He was thinking of Sarazen."

That was Roberts's lead-in comment. His way of introducing the legend.

I saw the Squire crossing the bridge over the left corner of the front pond. Even from two hundred yards away, I knew who he was, tipped off by his small size and his famous plus-fours. He was wearing the green jacket, even though when he won in '35 they weren't giving jackets to winners. I smiled. Yes, it was just like Roberts to save him for this hole.

"Sarazen," I said out loud.

"What?" asked Clay, glancing at me.

"I need to pull a Sarazen," I added, to explain my outburst.

Clay nodded, agreeing.

"Gene Sarazen made this tournament with that double eagle," Roberts said next. "Bob and I owe him a great deal."

We had arrived at my ball. I saw I had a level lie and the ball was sitting up. I was safely on the high right side of the fairway, and I had a little wind working with me. I could clear the front pond, but I might also run the risk of going long and into the backside pond.

I pulled my 5 iron. I would drive short of the front pond, chip up, go for 2 putts, and take my par safely to the next hole.

"Wait! Wait!" Roberts demanded, seeing what I was doing. "You can't reach the green with a 5-iron!" He sounded offended.

I started explaining to Clay what I was going to do. That way, Roberts would hear, too. "I'll play up to this side of the pond, then chip on."

"No!" Roberts insisted. "You can't win the Masters playing safe."

Sarazen arrived at that moment, and Roberts turned to him in exasperation.

The old pro walked over and studied my lie, then looked down the fairway at the green. He had his hands in the pockets of his gray wool plus-fours. He was wearing argyle socks and brown-and white golf shoes. Among all the pros in their fancy sponsored outfits, he was most nattily dressed player on the course.

Speaking casually, as if he had all day, he said, "When I hit that 4-wood back in '35, there were fewer than twenty-five spectators watching our group. One of them was Bobby Jones. Craig Wood had already finished and was in the clubhouse thinking he had it won. I thought he had it won, too. He had me by three shots. I was out here all alone, just trying to finish up on a cold, damp afternoon, and I needed to hit at least 230 to carry the pond, land on the green, and hold it.

"The ace in my bag was a new club. It was called a Turfrider and it had a hollow-back sole so that the club head could get into a tight lie. That club made all the difference to me; it was the reason I made that shot.

"When I addressed the ball, I played it back in my stance and toed it slightly to get more distance. And I did something else." He paused and glanced at me, then at Roberts. "When I came down on the ball, I cut across it, and that got me more loft. Bobby Jones told me later that it was the most perfect swing he had ever seen."

Sarazen pointed down the fairway. "As soon as I hit it, I knew it was a good shot, but I didn't know how good. I ran up the fairway to see if the ball had even carried the pond. After hitting into the front of the green, it had bounced left and headed straight for the hole. I couldn't see how close it was, but then this tremendous roar came back from the spectators circling the green. I knew by the cheers the ball had gone right in."

Sarazen looked at me and shook his head. "But you don't have a Turfrider. You're 240 yards to the green. You've got a little helping wind, but not enough to carry the pond. I wouldn't risk the shot, Tim. Phil will go for it. He has the ability. He'll be looking at a possible eagle, a sure birdie. But you're not Phil. More golf tournaments are lost by pros thinking they have a shot when they don't. You're not going to win trying to reach this par 5 in 2, but you'll lose it for sure by trying."

"Jesus H. Christ!" Roberts swore. He stared at the little man. "What the hell good are you?"

Across the fairway and farther ahead, I saw Phil had begun to pace around his ball. He wasn't appreciating my slowness.

"Hit your driver, Tim," Clay whispered.

I stared at Clay. All week, Clay had been careful with his club suggestions. Only in our practice round did he suggest the driver. Now he was standing up to Gene Sarazen, although of course he didn't know it.

"What?"

"You can get it off this lie with a 1-wood and you can hit your driver 250 on the fly. Cut it into that green. With the pin on the left, the ball will check up and hold, coming in high like you hit your woods."

"Listen to the kid," Roberts ordered.

"I hit a one-in-a-million shot back in '35," Sarazen interjected. "Only an amateur would try to duplicate that shot, but that's what you are, so if that's what you want to do, good luck, son." With that, he faded once again into history and left me standing in the middle of the empty fairway.

I stared at Clay a moment longer, trying to decide if I had the guts to take his suggestion. My big headed TaylorMade R9 was not Sarazen's ancient Turfrider, a club I had never even heard of. Playing off the fairway required a small shallow faced club, not a wood that needed a ball to be set up on a long tee just to be able to get under it.

"You think I can pull it off?" I asked Clay seriously. He had watched my game all week. He knew my weaknesses and strengths.

"It's the right distance. You can't back down. You can win this thing."

I pulled the head cover and took out the driver. The spectators standing closest saw me switch clubs, saw me go with the wood, caught the significance of the club selection, and realized I was going for the green. A roar went up from them sweeping like a wave down the long line of patrons along the fairway. I stepped behind the ball once more, getting my angle on the target. I would aim for the left edge of the green and let the ball fade toward the flag stick. All I had to do was clear the water hazard and avoid coming into the green too hot. I had to keep it from hitting hard and bouncing high, as Gary Player's ball had done decades before. Now, thanks to the rules imposed decades ago by Cliff Roberts, there were no spectators ringing the green and ready to snag a wayward shot and bat it back onto the putting surface as they did with Player's ball.

"Nice and slow, Tim," Clay reminded me. "Let the ball have its way, and it will find its way."

The ball came out with a low trajectory. It wasn't helped much by the following wind, but my natural fade worked the ball right; it hit short of the green but bounced on, checked up, and curled toward the flag.

I hadn't duplicated Gene Sarazen's famous double-eagle. My ball was short of the pin, and below the cup. But I was on in 2 and I was putting for an eagle.

34

THE CHEERS OF THE CROWD followed me down the slope to the green. The spectators only fell silent when Phil played his mid-iron to the 15th. His ball was inside mine, and he too would be putting for eagle on the long par 5. Phil was cheered as he caught up with me and we walked across the bridge together. He complimented my shot and asked if it had been the driver. I nodded and he shook his head, saying, "You guys who play public courses. You can hit off tarmac." I caught a slight edge in his voice. My hanging in was getting to him. He must have been thinking, "Who is this guy?"

"Hell, that's all we play on!" I tossed off. "Tarmac!"

But Phil had done his homework. "Hickory Ridge is a top-rated course. You're not playing on some cow pasture."

Applause rose from the observation stand as we stepped off Sarazen Bridge. Mickelson tipped his hat and continued onto the green. I saw up on the leaderboard that I had made it back into the top ten. And two shots behind me was Chuck

Smith, who must have bogied a hole. The amateurs were putting on a show for the Masters. And Tiger had all of us—Mickelson, McDowell from Northern Ireland, and Ian Poulter from England—by four shots. He had picked up two birdies. He wasn't going to let me, or anyone else, walk away with the win, not after what he had been through in the last years.

Clay handed me the ball, saying, "What do we have to remember with this putt?"

"The green break towards Rae's Creek."

He grinned and stepped away. I leaned over and carefully replaced my ball, aware that there were CBS cameras everywhere and that all my moves were live on television. One small violation of the most obscure rule of golf would generate emails and telephone calls from around the world.

I crouched down to get a read on the putt. In the afternoon shadows that crossed the green stood several of my ghostly coaches. I wondered if Roberts was running out of pros to help me. I knew I was running out of holes.

I stepped over to the shadows, as if I were stalking the putt, and asked Bobby Locke in a whisper for any words of wisdom. I had a ten-footer left. I was below and to the left of the cup, which was tucked into the narrow neck on the far left.

My question started a quick exchange and disagreement among them as Nelson and Demaret recalled putts made and missed on this green. It was as fast as a billiard table, they agreed. Only Hogan kept silent.

Then Locke spoke up and silenced the others. They all deferred to the South African when it came to putting.

"There is only one thing to remember, laddie, when you play Augusta late in the day: The grain on the green always goes the opposite way of your shadow. That putt of yours is due north, so give yourself a half hole to the right of the cup. Stroke it harder than you would earlier in the day and spin the putt, cut it with your follow-through." He pointed to the hickory club and his muffin face brightened. "Swing your putter like your driver, inside back and square at impact. It will get the ball rolling smoothly."

I nodded my thanks and circled back to stand behind my ball. Carrying the flag, Clay came over and advised, "You better plum-bob this one, Tim."

Agreeing, I moved behind the ball, stood and held the hickory putter at arm's length and straight out in front of me with my thumb and forefinger so the putter hung down vertically. Then I moved the putter so that the lower part of the shaft covered the ball. I closed my non-dominant left eye. This, I knew, wasn't something that Bobby Locke or any of the others had ever done on a golf course in their day.

Plum-bobbing was simple enough. If the shaft covered the hole, I knew I had a straight putt. When I closed my left eye, I saw the shaft was to the right of the hole which meant my putt would break from right to left.

It wasn't long enough to be a lag putt, but I played it that way, taking no chances. I just wanted to get close enough for a tap in. I had arrived at Augusta determined not to leave anything short, to charge every putt, and I wasn't going to leave Augusta with the reputation of a player who was afraid to get it up and down.

I stepped over and settled into my routine. I shook my arms and relaxed my shoulders. I lightly gripped the old hickory stick and took two careful practice strokes, regaining the feel of the thin blade and mentally repeating Locke's instructions on how to swing.

I took another half step closer, then settled down again with my eyes directly over the ball. I glanced once at the hole and tracked back to the ball the line I wanted. I froze out everything and everyone but that moment and that putt and I stroked the ball.

As soon as it started to move, I watched that ball as if I

were witnessing my whole life, all the putts I had ever made, all the matches played and won. The ball inched toward the cup and I realized there was no way it was going in. And yet it kept moving. I was disbelieving until the moment I heard the final click as the ball dropped into the plastic cup. The roar of the crowd assaulted my ears and for a moment I couldn't breathe.

I wanted to step over and nonchalantly lift the ball from the cup, then nod and tip my cap to the gallery. I wanted to walk off the green as if I had been making putts at Augusta National all my life, but I couldn't move. My legs were locked, my hands were trembling.

Out of the corner of my eye, I saw Clay hand the flag to Bones, look my way, then walk over and lift the ball from the cup and come over to me. Without a word, he took the hickory putter from my hands, and gently slipped his hand under my elbow as if to lead me off the green. I knew from thousands of hours of watching golf on TV that there was a camera focused on me, that all my reactions and expressions were being followed by millions around the world. I was now back to four under, two behind Tiger.

Hogan stepped to my side and smiled. He nodded approvingly, saying, "You remind me of myself in my day."

Remembering the cameras, I didn't speak, just arched an inquisitive eyebrow.

"They always said that about me when I played, that I had ice in my veins. You can't teach that. It's a gift. I had it, and then I lost it. You have the gift."

I nodded, thinking I didn't feel as if I did.

"Nothing lasts, Tim," said Hogan. "Do the best you can with your life while you can. You'll be dead for a long time. Trust me." He smiled wryly, but the pain registered in his steel-gray eyes had been there forever.

Sunday

35

IT WAS WELL AFTER MIDNIGHT when I woke to hear Chuck Smith sobbing in his cubicle. Like all parents, I was schooled because of my kids to children's after-hours traumas, and I instantly came fully awake.

I sat up and swung my feet over the side of the narrow bed and listened. Chuck and I had not spoken to each other earlier. When I reached the Crow's Nest after my round and another interview at the press center, Chuck had already showered and changed and left the clubhouse, leaving me a note that he was eating dinner in town with his family. Our roommates had left Augusta National on Friday, after not making the cut.

Chuck didn't say anything about how his game had gone south on the back side, but I had read his score on the main board on my way to the press center. I had him by four shots going into Sunday's final round. From what Smith had said about his father at breakfast, and remembering the look on the man's face from the range that morning, I knew their dinner would not be a happy hour.

As quietly as I could, I crossed the Crow's Nest to the bathroom. I didn't turn on the lights, but made my way with the benefit of a bright Georgia moon pouring beams of light through the high cupola.

When I walked back into the sitting room, Chuck was up and sprawled in one of the deep upholstered chairs. All I saw of him was his bulky frame and the glow of his cigarette. He was wearing boxer shorts and a tee shirt. Before I said anything, he spoke up, saying he was sorry to have woken me. He congratulated me on my round and wished me good luck on Sunday. He also told me that he wasn't going to play his final eighteen. He was going to WD and split from Augusta National once it was daylight and he could get a ride from the club to the airport.

He said it very calmly, having thought it all out, but I had dealt with enough emotional teenagers as a professor and as a parent to know he was operating more on rage and self-pity than common sense.

I slipped down into the other deep chair and nodded okay, agreeing with him. If he had expected a fight, he wasn't going to get it from me. I didn't turn on a light. There was a certain comfort in the moonlit shadows. I let the boy talk. When it comes to a crisis, there is nothing quite as satisfying as unburdening oneself to a stranger. Getting my approval for what he wanted to do would give him enough courage to quit Augusta early.

He gave me chapter and verse on how he had played the last four holes of Saturday's round, more or less as if he were confessing to a crime.

When he finished, I didn't express agreement with his assessment but instead caught him off guard by remarking, "So, your old man's a member of Augusta National." Chuck reached over to butt out his cigarette in the ash tray. My comment wasn't what he'd wanted to hear.

"Yeah, not that it did me much good today. I've only played here a few times before this week. My dad's got this working-class ethic that I've got to earn my way to play his club. He made his own success, and he wants his kid to prove himself too. You know, there's no free lunch in life, that sort of bullshit."

"What does your dad do?"

"He buys and sells scrap iron. He started out working in a yard at fifteen and now he's the scrap metal king of the west coast. Some magazine actually called him that." Chuck leaned back in his chair and sighed, weary of his life as the scrap metal prince.

"So on fifteen you went for the pin and didn't play it safe and knocked it into the pond," I said, going back to his round.

"Something like that."

"What happened?"

Chuck was silent for a moment, collecting his thoughts and also, I guess, deciding how much to actually confess. But in the end, the safety of the shadows won out and he told me the truth: that when he walked up to his ball he saw his old man in the gallery, standing there growling at him for not keeping the ball right, and he rushed his recovery shot; he didn't get it up high enough on the steep ridge, and the ball came down off the green.

"I had a forty-footer and I 3-putted. I lost it. I couldn't concentrate. That look on my old man's face. It put a knife straight through me." Chuck let his anger register in the word "knife," and then he shook his head and fell silent; he had nothing more to say.

I had two possible courses of action. The first was that I could wish the boy goodbye and good luck, shake hands and go off to bed. We were in competition and I was winning; the Amateur Bowl was mine regardless of what I shot on Sunday. And Charlie Smith wasn't my son; his fate was none of my concern.

Of course, that first choice wasn't a real possibility for me. It wasn't by chance that when I walked away from golf, I turned to teaching.

I let a few moments pass to clear the air of Chuck's emotional rant. I knew boys. They often wanted advice, but would never ask for it. With Chuck, as in certain games of golf, I'd have to find a whole new way to play the course.

I got up and walked to the door of my room, suggesting I was done with him and heading off to bed   .

I put my hand on the swinging door, ready to push it open and disappear for the rest of the night, and then I paused, as if I suddenly had another question. Turning to Chuck, I asked quizzically, "Do you mind me asking, what are you trying to prove?"

"What am I trying to prove?" he asked, sounding annoyed. "What are you talking about?"

"Well," I said, "you could be trying to prove you're your own man, that you can walk away from this tournament at your father's golf course. Of course, not everyone will think you've proved that. Some people might say that walking away means Augusta National is too tough for the likes of you, an amateur who's only won one major tournament."

"Look, why shouldn't I walk away from golf?" he snapped. "You did!"

I stepped back into the room and sat on the arm of the other chair.

"Don't do what I did," I told him. "Quitting golf was the worst mistake I ever made."

Chuck shrugged; at the moment, getting back at his father was worth sacrificing just about anything.

"You've got a lot of talent, Chuck," I said, and stopped. That was the wrong approach. I couldn't patronize him. Golf came easy to the boy. He was like a pretty young girl who thinks her looks will last forever.

"Golf isn't a metaphor for your problems," I said next.

"What the hell are you talking about?" Now I had his attention, which was a start.

"Quitting won't solve your problems with your old man. Quitting is never the answer. I know that from my own life. To this day, I still think of my father dead on that Metro North train. I never had the chance to come to terms with him. That's the reason I quit the game. I was using it as a weapon against him, and when he died I didn't need a weapon. And then I had nothing."

"What would you have told him?"

I could hear curiosity in his voice, a sense that perhaps my answer might enlighten him about his own old man.

"I think I would have told him that all I ever wanted was his attention. He never gave me that. He was on his own journey to become a great financial success. He was wrestling with his own demons. He was showing off with the money he made. Buying bigger and bigger houses. He was proving something to himself. What he was doing had nothing to do with me. I might have needed him, but he didn't need me."

"I'm not trying to get my old man's attention with my game," said Chuck. "He's the one who's all over me. He's pissed at me for letting you get four shots up. You should have heard him last night. You'd swear I had murdered a kindergarten class. It's because he's a member. If I win the Amateur Bowl, he can strut around this clubhouse wearing his green jacket with his chest all puffed out."

"What if you did win?" I asked.

"There's no way in hell that happens. Hell, you threw up a 70. You got those TV people talking about how you could win the whole tournament. They're saying you're another Venturi."

"What if I said you could win the Masters?"

"I'd say you've been talking to that crazy old guy you saw last Sunday, the one who claimed an amateur was going to win. I don't know if you looked at the board lately, but Tiger has the lead. There's no way he's going to let anyone take this win away from him! Not now, not after everything that he' been through. He's out to prove he's the greatest golfer that ever lived. Ever!"

Chuck exhaled a cloud of smoke. Then he said, as if these were his last words on the subject, "I'm out of here. I'm WD. I had no real business being here in the first place; all I did was win a tournament on my home course."

"None of us have any business playing in the Masters, Chuck. It's a gift. So why don't you show a little more respect for the opportunity you've been given? Half the golfers in the world would cut off their right arm just for the chance to tee it up once on this golf course."

"Yeah, yeah…" Chuck was shaking his head, annoyed by my lecture. Now I really was sounding like his old man. I paused and decided to try another tack.

"Where will you go after you leave?"

"Las Vegas and shoot craps. Play golf and hustle some hackers. Those guys see someone like me, a short fat kid, and they think they can take me to the cleaners. I can make enough hustling hackers and shooting craps to get by. Like you, I don't have to ask my old man for anything."

"Tell you what," I said, concocting another scheme on the spot. "I'll bet you a thousand bucks that if you tee up this morning and play the final round, you'll win the Amateur Cup."

Chuck stared at me for a moment, and then he grinned good-naturedly, as if this were the dumbest offer he had ever heard. "Mr. Alexander, you've been out in the sun too long."

"I'm dead serious. Play and win, I owe you a grand."

"I'm four shots behind you."

"You don't remember Norman back in '96. He had Nick Faldo by six shots going into Sunday's round and finished second, lost to Faldo by five, a swing of eleven shots. Anything can happen at the Masters."

"What's with you, Alexander?" Chuck asked bluntly. "You're a teacher, not an investment banker. You can't afford a grand. Why are you pushing me to play?"

"I don't want you walking away from Augusta with a WD."

"That's my business. Thanks, but no thanks."

Charlie Smith was done with me. It was obvious in the tone of his voice. He lit another cigarette, as if to end the conversation.

"Let me tell you one more thing," I said.

"Jesus, you never quit!" He laughed, shaking his head and sighing. "You're actually worse than my old man." Now he was more amused than angry.

"If you want me to shut up, get your head out of your ass and listen." This really was my last shot. It was two A.M. and I had eighteen holes to play without a good night's sleep.

"Don't flatter yourself by thinking that by quitting the Masters you're punishing your old man. All you'll demonstrate with a WD is that you don't have the balls to come back after a bad round. That is something I don't believe about you, Chuck. If you were that kind of player, you wouldn't have made it to Augusta."

With that, I turned away from him and pushed open the half door of the cubicle. It was time to get some sleep.

"What about your bet? The grand?"

"Forget it. I'm not so sure you're a good bet. You said it yourself, you're too far off the lead." I was in my cubicle, the door swinging behind me, but Chuck kept talking.

"I'll throw up a low number and be in the clubhouse before you, and we'll see who's talking." He answered, challenging me. "A grand if I win the amateur cup. Is that a bet?"

"We'll see about that," I answered. I was back in the narrow bed and I was smiling. The kid had done a three-sixty. Now all I had to do was talk Charles DeClifford Roberts, Jr. into making sure the kid won it all.

36

"WHAT?" ROBERTS ROARED. Chuck had left for the range and we were alone in the Crow's Nest. I was packing my gear, getting ready to leave after my Sunday round. It wasn't yet eleven, so I still had plenty of time before my late-afternoon start time. I was paired with Tiger. We were the last twosome to tee off.

"All you need is for an amateur to win. Right? Chuck's an amateur, and better still, his old man is a member."

Roberts shook his head so hard his jowls shook.

"The boy's too young. It's one thing to win the amateur cup; another to win the Masters. You're the only one. You have the experience to stand up to the pressure. He won't be able to put a sub-par round together. Besides, having you win is just the sort of victory that makes the Masters what it is."

"If a brash young kid with no experience is the winner, that'll be just as good," I shot back and kept packing. For a week

I had dealt with Roberts's comings and goings, his pronouncements and demands. Now it was my time to have my say.

"Why in God's name are you so against winning this tournament?"

I sat down on the bed and confronted him. "We made a deal,
right?"

I waited for him to nod before continuing, "You said you'd
see that my wife was cured of her cancer...."

"And I will...if you win the Masters."

"If an amateur wins the Masters...Charles Jacob Smith of
San Diego is that amateur." I stood up again to finish packing.

"He's a boy."

"Your Bobby Jones was younger than Smith when he won
his first U.S. Amateur."

For the moment Roberts fell silent. I didn't know if he was
mulling over my proposition or seeking some other way to rebut
it. I zipped up my single piece of luggage and carried it into
the common room.

Roberts followed me, working on his cigar, saying, "The
boy doesn't have the gravitas."

"Now I've heard it all. Gravitas?"

"If Hogan or Locke or any of the others were to come out
of the pine woods and appear to the boy, he'd piss in his pants."

"I didn't piss in my pants. And don't go telling me it was
because I have gravitas!"

"You've had enough life experience to know that reality isn't
always what it appears to be. Besides, it's too much ground to
make up. Tiger has him by seven shots."

"Tiger has me by four."

"You can catch Tiger."

"Look, this is my deal. I want the boy to win the Masters—not
just the amateur title, the green jacket."

"Tim, I'm handing you the tournament!" Roberts stared at me, his cold face perplexed by my demand.

"When I came to Augusta all I wanted was to make the cut. It was my bargain with my wife, to show her that if I could come back to the game, she could lick her cancer. And then you came along with your deal: my win for her cure. You were offering a starving man a morsel of food. I took it. I made a deal with the devil—no offense, Cliff.

"But then something gets added to the mix: this young, confused kid who is going through what I experienced with my old man more than twenty years ago. Last night I saw I could somehow repay the golfing gods by giving Chuck the victory, letting Charles Jacob Smith win the Masters at his father's club. I'd show him that he is a worthwhile human being, which he doesn't think he is. His old man has his thumb pressed down hard on this kid's ego. A green jacket, Clifford—and you know this better than most—will change Charles Smith's life forever.

"You have the opportunity, Cliff, to make one last positive gesture, not for me or Chuck Smith, but for yourself. You can wipe away decades of bad karma. Help the boy win, Cliff. I don't need a green jacket to live happily ever after, but Chuck does. All I want is for you to keep your promise and give Kerry back to me."

I'd had my say, and for a moment Roberts did not reply. He stood in the middle of the small room, his legs apart, his left hand holding the thick cigar, his right hand in the pocket of his linen trousers.

I kept silent. I knew when it was best not to rush a person. Finally, driven to it, he told me the truth.

"I can't just make this person or that one win the Masters, Tim. It doesn't work that way. I'm only human, or at least I used to be." With that he permitted himself a wry smile. Then he said thoughtfully, as befitted the man who had created the Masters and seen it become the most important golf tournament in the world, "If I'd had that ability I would have done it years ago with this young player or that. With Tiger Woods, for one!" He stared at me, choosing his words, as always, with great deliberation.

"To win the Masters, especially someone like yourself, a rank amateur, you have to have a great need in your psyche, a great desire, a lament or longing. That's what you had coming into Augusta National. You couldn't stop your wife's cancer, and it was killing you.

"We know enough about golf to know that it is a game of the mind. Players win and lose tournaments in their minds, not in the way they swing a golf club or how far they might hit a King Cobra.

"Even before you arrived, I knew you were the one. You had the skills, the need to do it, and with the help of the greatest players who ever won at Augusta, the ability. That's why I asked you to meet me at Amen Corner."

He stopped speaking and waited for a response. Instead of answering, I asked a question that had been on my mind since Saturday's round.

"Was that my wife in the gallery yesterday? I called home twice last night and there was no answer."

"Yes, it was Kerry."

"How did that happen?"

"It's a prerogative of the chairman to invite his own guests to the tournament, so I took the liberty of sending your wife a plane ticket to Augusta and an honorary guest pass to the tournament. She was told we were hoping to surprise you, so she agreed not to contact you until after today's round."

"You appeared to my wife?"

"No. It was all done by phone calls, emails, and FedEx." He smiled, pleased with his cunning.

"And does Billy Payne know you usurped his prerogative?"

"He will soon enough, once he gets the bill for her airline ticket and hotel. Mrs. Alexander is staying at the Doubletree." Roberts smiled.

"Is she all right?" I asked. "Has she been cured?" It was the single most important question of my life.

"Win the Masters," Roberts replied coolly.

"You bastard."

"You wouldn't be the first to call me that, Mr. Alexander. I'm a damned man, loathed by many during my life, forgotten by most after my death." He smiled again and added, "You're my last hope, Tim. You are my only hope. Win the Masters. Free me from this prison, and your wife will be cured."

At that, without a goodbye, he turned away and vanished.

Alone again in the Crow's Nest, I heard the distant sounds of the Masters Tournament on the warm April-morning breezes: the voice of the starter announcing with great solemnity the names of the players teeing off, the respectful applause, and, from farther away, the occasional sudden roar as another miraculous shot was made, another birdie recorded, as some player on the backside made his own run for the green jacket.

It was pleasant in the quiet Crow's Nest, where I was safely shielded from my responsibility of playing well and winning. But I couldn't hold back the day. I stood, picked up my golf shoes, and swung onto my shoulder the barrel bag Kerry had given me so I would look like a real golfer when I arrived in Georgia. Then I left the Crow's Nest to face, like Jack Burden in *All the King's Men*, my own existential moment, to play out on Augusta National the awesome responsibilities of time.

37

WE CAME UP THROUGH THE CROWD behind 9 green and headed for 10 tee. I was following Tiger Woods onto the back side, where, as the golf writer Dan Jenkins said years ago, the Masters Tournament really begins: the final nine at Augusta National late on Sunday afternoon.

The gallery was cheering as I walked through on the roped path that separated the patrons from the players and caddies. I tipped my hat to the fans, most of whom had been there for hours, having staked their claim on 10 tee and waited patiently through the long, warm day just to be there when the tournament leaders teed off on the final nine.

Making the putt on 9 had pulled me even with Mickelson, and we were both one shot behind Tiger's lead. It had also sent a roar through the crowd that echoed across the course, ran the lengths of the fairways, and bounced off the trees that shielded Augusta National from the outside world. Anything could happen next, and I could feel the gallery's excitement streak like a bolt of summer lightning through the pines.

When I reached the high tee box I glanced over at the leaderboard and saw Charlie Smith was on 14 and burning up the course. All he had to do now was get a couple more birdies and he'd be the leader in the clubhouse. I walked over to Clay. He had his yardage book out and was reviewing how we had played 10 that week. Tiger and his caddie, Stevie, had stepped to the right of the markers and were waiting for me to play away.

I stood on the tee, staring down the cascading fairway. My eyes were blurry with fear. I knew I had to reach into my mind and find that place that long ago the British pro J. H. Taylor had called "courageous timidity."

Fear on the golf course is a funny thing. It begins in the recesses of the mind and percolates. At that moment, with Tiger just yards away and people watching our round from everywhere on earth, I couldn't feel my fingers. I took another deep breath, thinking there wasn't enough oxygen on this golf course to fill my lungs. To calm myself I concentrated on the geography of Camellia. The 10th fell gracefully away from the tee, a breathtakingly beautiful hole.

From the tee to the dogleg, it was lined with people. Spectators stood two and three deep on the left side, pressed against the green rope that stretched the length of the fairway; more fans filled the woods beyond the right-side second cut. Spectators were streaming through the trees to follow us for the last nine holes.

I pulled the R9 and took several swings, reminding myself each time to let the club do the work. I moved over beside Clay and wiped the face of the driver, stalling for more time. Ahead of us the twosome Poulter and Mickelson cleared the corner and disappeared. A marshal at the edge of the dogleg signaled that I could play away.

"Nine to go," I said softly.

"We're doing great," Clay answered, as if we were Little League players pumping each other up on some sandlot instead of an amateur and his caddie standing alone on the 10th tee at the epicenter of golf in America.

At the moment, on the same hole as Tiger Woods, I could not have been in further over my head. Tiger had outdriven me on every hole on the front side. I had made a few putts and one great chip on number 4 for a birdie; they were the only reason I was still in contention, up there on the leaderboard with Woods and Mickelson and now young Charlie Smith, who, unbelievably, was putting together a 6-under final round.

I walked back to the markers and glanced around for a firm place to stand. Playing in the last group on Sunday meant that most of the grass in the box had been chewed up by earlier players. On the other hand, playing last in a stroke tournament wasn't something I often experienced, and that amused and even strangely relaxed me.

I focused on where I wanted to place my drive, visualized hugging the left side and hitting to the edge of the avenue of pines, giving myself a chance of catching the steep fairway incline, which would gain me around thirty yards. What I didn't want to do was get greedy and overpower the shot, catch the left-side second cut the way Ballesteros did back in '89, leaving himself a blind shot to the green. Just as bad would be to go too far right, hit the wrong side of the ridge, and scoot down to the low end of the fairway. That would leave me a long iron into the green.

I followed my drive in flight as it split the fairway, and just before the dogleg, it caught the slope and ran. As I stepped away, Tiger moved forward, nodded his approval, and teed up his Nike.

I slipped my driver into the bag, winked at Clay, and moved to one side. I was conscious that everyone was watching me, then glancing at Tiger, then turning to see what I was doing, ready to catch any reaction to indicate whether I was cracking under the pressure. I took a deep breath and sighed. I had safely driven off number 10.

Tiger hit a beauty. It was one of his patented drives that climbed into the sky, hung up there forever, then rode the wind to land a good thirty yards beyond where my ball had come to rest. Tiger was 335 down the left side; he had at most 155 to the elevated green.

He charged off with Stevie in stride beside him. I was tempted to keep up, to match his pace as if to demonstrate to Tiger and the gallery that I had the resilience to compete with the best. But long ago I had read that when Byron Nelson was first starting out on the tour and the gallery walked beside the players from shot to shot, he had taught himself not to get caught up in their excitement, but to set his own comfortable pace from tee to green. I followed that advice.

Besides, I didn't have the leg strength to keep pace with Tiger and Stevie. I had been playing golf for seven days, the longest straight stretch since I was a kid at Wake Forest. I wasn't sure how many good swings I had left in my bag.

My tee shot on 10 had finished on the level fairway, as I'd hoped, but I was still away. Still it was the closest I had been to Tiger all day, thanks to the long roll off the ridge.

I was hitting into an enormous green that favored my fade. All I had to do was keep the ball below the hole and not catch the right green-side bunker. The real problem was that this green is in deep shadows much of the day, and so the grass is thinner than on most of the Augusta holes. It was a hard green to putt. Having kept my ball out the woods with my big drive, what I had to do now was get my approach close enough to the pin to avoid 3-putting.

"The grain runs toward the 11 tee box," Clay reminded me. "Four?"

"Okay. Don't force the club; you won't get your fade," Clay cautioned.

I wished now that Roberts would appear with one of his legends; I could use their help to club me on this final nine. I wondered if perhaps Cliff was off helping Chuck as I had asked. Or was Chuck having all this success on his own?

I pulled the 4-iron.

"Be committed," Clay said, moving the barrel bag.

I nodded. The trouble with being torn between clubs is not having faith in the one you pull from the bag. It would have been reassuring to have one of the old pros verify my decision. I was worried, too, about the winds in that far southeast corner of the course, and remembering what had happened to young Senese on Friday afternoon. But if I was going to miss, I wanted to miss left and still have a putt going against the grain, and going uphill. I hadn't canned any forty-footers yet, but my ball had been close on several monster putts. It was only a matter of time, I kept telling myself.

I didn't jump all over my 4-iron. It came in low and fading onto the big green and caught the front left fringe, bounced hard, and kicked onto the putting surface. I was on, though well short of the hole, which was cut on the front left. I felt instant relief, then disappointment at myself for not getting closer. Golfers are never satisfied.

Tiger took his club and set himself to play. Clay and I fell as silent as the gallery, the thousands of patrons who lined the fairway and circled the green. All eyes were on Tiger playing up with a short iron. The right-side bunker was not a problem, nor was the wide amoeba-shaped bunker carved into the fairway by MacKenzie when he built the course. When the 10th was lengthened by Perry Maxwell back in 1937, it left the bunker well short of the new green set high on the rise and framed with Georgia pines.

Tiger's high approach, however, got caught up in the swirling winds at that south corner of the course and came up long, leaving him a downhill putt to the front quadrant. He missed it, then tapped in for a par and stepped off the green, leaving me to survey a twenty-footer for a possible birdie.

Reading the green was difficult, given that it was shrouded in late-afternoon shadows. It wasn't surprising that more Masters had been lost on this hole than on any other.

"I want it close," I whispered to Clay as we crouched to study the putt. I could see the break from left to right, and although I was putting uphill, and against the grain, I also knew, from playing all week, that the green was fast. I didn't want to be beyond the hole and have to come downhill to save par. All I wanted was a lag putt that would be close enough for a tap in.

I got it. I hit the ball too hard, but it nevertheless took the break and hit the cup dead center, bounced high, and dropped down five inches below the pin. I stepped up and tapped in the short putt for my par. Heading for Amen Corner, I was still hanging onto second and a shot behind Tiger.

38

WALKING OFF 10 GREEN, I glanced at the huge scoreboard. Mickelson had made par on the hole ahead of us and was keeping pace with me, but more importantly, I saw Charlie Smith had birdied 15.

I wondered if Roberts was helping the kid, if he had brought out his big guns to get Chuck to 7 under. But at the moment, I had other questions to answer. I was on the tee again at 11 with the honors and playing the first, and toughest, of the three holes at Amen Corner, the par-4 505-yard hole called White Dogwood.

All I wanted was par. I'd hit my drive down the right side, play up short, as Hogan always did, and settle for two putts. Unlike Tiger, I wouldn't be trying to reach the green in two. Woods could pull off a run of birdies and it would be up to me to stop him. I couldn't keep up with him off the tee, or match his length. I would have to win the Masters some other way.

I teed up, thinking again how Clay had changed my chances

for a green jacket by getting me to readjust my R9. Having faith in my metal wood off the tee took a lot of tension out of my swing. It was usually on the back side, late in the day, that my age began to catch up with me and I started to press.

The answer for me off the tee was to slow down the arc, feel the club head gain speed as it approached the ball. I took my time. I counted to three. And then I hit a high, arcing drive that rode the right side of the fairway, keeping away from the new pines planted to narrow the chute. The ball didn't fade into the second cut or the tall pines. It disappeared, but I knew it was safely somewhere down the fairway.

Woods went left with his drive, not into the trees but down the left side of the par 4. With his length, the ball would bounce off the fairway ridge and pick up an extra dozen yards. He didn't have to worry about the small pond fronting the green or Rae's Creek circling behind it. Not the way he could work his irons.

Stepping off the tee, I scanned the gallery that had gathered in clusters behind the green ropes; I was looking for Kerry. I had been searching for her all morning, since Roberts admitted he had sent her a plane ticket. It was just like her to stay out of the way; now that I was in contention, she wouldn't want to throw off my game. But she would be following me for the round; she wouldn't be camped out in one of the observation stands waiting for my twosome to play through. Kerry didn't care about golf; she only cared about me.

But finding her wouldn't be easy. My guess was that she was disguising herself in some kind of costume. She had a talent for concealment. Often when she played a role I couldn't tell which actor up on the stage was my wife.

Clay fell into stride beside me as we walked up the rise to the wide-open fairway. Unlike some of the famous loopers at

Augusta National, he didn't try to charm me with conversation or pump me up with words of encouragement.

"How we doing?" I finally asked, breaking the silence.

"We're hanging in there," he answered carefully .

"Hanging is the word, all right."

Clay laughed, then replied, "This is something, really."

I could hear the wonder in his voice.

"I mean, being in the final twosome, playing with Tiger, one shot off the lead." He shook his head.

"Let's not count the putts before they're made."

"Thanks for letting me be your caddie," Clay said next, out of the blue.

He was staring at the ground as he walked, his body hunched slightly forward. My barrel bag rode the small of his back. I tapped him lightly on the shoulder and told him I was the lucky one to have him looping for me.

"You made my mom really happy," he said next, glancing over. I could see a glitter of tears in his blue eyes. "My Dad, he would have been really proud."

I reached over and wrapped my arm around his shoulder, then briefly scrubbed the back of his head with my hand. I didn't know what to say. His burst of affection brought a lump to my throat. I had been so wrapped up in my challenge, I had forgotten that Clay Weaver was living out his own dream. At the Masters there is always more than one drama being played out.

"We're going to be okay, Clay," I told him, "the two of us." I spoke with more buoyancy than confidence, stirred by the raw emotion of the moment. "Let's win this one! Okay?"

Now, beneath the shadow of his cap, I saw a trail of tears on his sunburned face. He nodded and grinned and then he stopped walking, swung my big bag off his shoulder and set it down. We had reached my ball in the middle of the emerald-green silkiness of the fairway. And I was away.

For once, my club selection was a no-brainer. On my second shot I wasn't going for the green. I would play to the pond, chip up, get a safe 4, and walk away. I wasn't going to challenge the next two holes either. This end of Augusta National wasn't called Amen Corner for nothing.

39

HALVING 11 WITH TIGER, we walked off the green together and headed for 12. As we crossed to Golden Bell, the cheers and applause came toward us, one wave after the next. Tiger was striding fast, and I could see the man pulled back into himself when there was a match to be won, when he could sense that something was happening that had nothing to do with his game. I was a person who had to be dealt with, like an irritating itch in the small of his back.

Tiger and Stevie stepped to one side to consult their yardage books, developed over their long history at the Masters. They were standing close, whispering fast. Both of them knew from experience where the pin was placed on Sunday afternoon. They knew the shot to be played; it was just a question of what club, given the wind, the atmosphere, and how strong Tiger was feeling at that moment.

I could see the flag stick on the right side of the shallow green,

six paces from the fringe. I glanced at Clay, and he slipped his
fingers around the wedge but didn't pull it from the bag or say anything. It was an old caddie trick in case Tiger or Stevie was waiting
to see what we were playing, but Tiger already had a wedge in his
hand, though I wasn't sure what degree it was. I knew he carried
three and that he could hit a pitching wedge as far as I hit my 9.

I was thinking of what Roberts had said earlier in the week, that
I had to play my own game and ignore what Tiger was doing. The
problem was, Tiger was so great, I couldn't keep from watching.
Most of the pros on tour were spectators when he was around.

Tiger saw the shot he had to make, knew where he wanted the
ball to land and how he wanted it to behave on the green. With
Tiger there was no hitting and hoping. There was no hesitation.
Occasionally something would go wrong, but only occasionally.
In his personal life a lot had gone wrong, but his golf game
was under control.

I kept staring up at the green as if I might find in the distance the answer to how to play the hole, but I didn't know
what to do. My irons might as well have been a grab bag; I had
no idea which club to pull. Still, with the cup cut on the right
side, I knew I was looking at one club longer for the yardage.

"Check the pines," Clay nodded towards the trees left of
Hogan Bridge. The tall pines were the key down at that end of
the course, and the late afternoon breeze was helping as well
as hurting. I didn't want to be over on this green. If I was anywhere on this par 3, I wanted to be short.

"Nine?"

"It's got to be soft," Clay advised. He, too, knew the trouble I
could be in if I caught one of the back bunkers. It was a narrow
green, and the grain ran toward Rae's Creek. "Hit the wedge."

The front bunker was easier to handle and it might not be a bad
idea to play it safe with a wedge and take my chances from the sand.

Still, if I was going to keep pace with Tiger, I had to be putting for birdie, and this was one of the few flat greens on the course.

Pulling the wedge and stepping up between the markers, I felt the breeze again off my left shoulder and remembered what "the Book had said: Don't pay any attention to the breeze over your left shoulder. That wind is coming down Rae's Creek, around those pines, and comes back over your shoulder. Always play it long on 12, or you'll be in the creek.

The cup was cut on the right side, giving me even a smaller target.

"Not enough," a voice beside me said softly. "Hit the nine." His voice was firm.

I glanced over at Hogan. He was staring up at the green. His arms were crossed and he was slowly, thoughtfully smoking a cigarette. He never once looked my way.

I stepped away from Ben without responding, walked back to my bag, and pulled the 9, not looking at Clay. He didn't say a word. I was afraid of the creek. I was also afraid of going long. This hole and the par-5 13 finished off more potential winners than any other holes on the course. Back in '37, Nelson picked up six shots on 12 and 13 to beat Ralph Guldahl and win the Masters. Twelve was a hole that took away; it didn't give. If I had to be wrong on this hole, I'd rather be wrong going long than leaving it in the creek.

I stepped back and re-teed my ball and, as if on cue, Roberts appeared, telling me how this was the easiest hole at Augusta to build. He sounded like a real estate agent trying to make a sale, chatting away and disregarding my apprehensions.

"We spent some money on the green, leveling that ledge, and up here, of course, making this tee. But there was one problem." He stopped dramatically and I glanced his way. That was his ploy. "Indians," he whispered, and nodded knowingly. "When constructing the site, we discovered that the spot where we were building the green had once been an Indian burial ground. Members to this day blame their bad shots on Indian spirits who are upset by the way their final resting place is being disturbed." Roberts smiled, enjoying his moment. "But what would I know about a final resting spot?" And with that he slipped out of sight.

I was staring blindly into space and realized only then that I was looking directly at Tiger Woods, who crossed and re-crossed his legs, demonstrating his frustration at my slow play.

I took one more easy swing and stepped up to the ball. From this angle the green looked like an enlarged shoe print with the toes, the narrow instep, and then the heel. I was aiming for a spot six yards in from the right edge on the wide one-hundred-foot green, above the heel of the foot.

It wasn't the percentage shot, going for the flag. More than one touring pro had lost the Masters at 12 by aiming at the pin tucked into the heel of the footprint. Ballesteros had an eight-shot lead in 1980 when he double-bogeyed the hole; Sandy Lyle also double-bogeyed 12 in '88, but saved his win by making a birdie at 18.

I wasn't going to win by playing safe, not against Tiger. We were playing match now. I couldn't afford to give him this hole. He could get it in from anywhere, as he had in '97, chipping in from ten feet off the green and shooting 30 on the backside.

All I knew was that I didn't want to be short and hit into the bank and have the ball roll down the slope and into the creek, nor did I want to go long and find the back bunker. That was enough to worry about. I didn't need to think about burial grounds and the Indian spirits.

But I forgot about the mystical swirling winds. As soon as I hit the 9, I felt the breeze on my face. It was crossing the shallow valley, spinning the tops of the pines. My ball stalled in mid-air, then dropped straight down, not into Rae's Creek, but still into trouble. It landed in the narrow front green-side bunker. The only saving grace, I could see, was that I wasn't plugged in the golden sand. I was safe. And Ben Hogan had been right about the wedge. My ball would have caught the water.

Tiger's wedge didn't work for him either. He should have found the green, but in the swirling wind his ball carried the green and stayed perched on the back fringe. It would be a tricky putt, but at least he had a putt. I needed a sand save.

A hundred different things can happen to any player in the sand, but if you play enough golf, coming out of sand is the easiest shot in the game. My trouble was, I didn't play enough golf. And the sand I played in wasn't the golden sand of Augusta National. Every bunker at Augusta National was a perfect sandbox, nothing at all like the public course bunkers in southern Illinois.

Crossing Hogan Bridge and reaching the green, I stood up on the fringe and studied the shot I had to make. The grain was against me, but the green wasn't. I could hit into the five-foot rise and let the slope function like a backboard. I told as much to Clay and told him to pull the stick.

"What?" Clay asked.

"Yeah, let's have a little fun."

"You think you can make it?"

"Why not?"

Clay kept shaking his head.

"Pull it, Clay," I said, and stepped into the sand, moving around behind the ball to get my angle to the cup. The galleries were away from the green, back up on the tee, and it was a moment before they realized what I was doing: having my caddie pull the flag. The cheers came across the hollow of the hole and echoed in the forest of pine trees that framed the 12th green.

I didn't look away from the cup as Clay removed the pin. I couldn't see the hole now, down in the bunker, but I knew the spot on the horizon of the green. It was all showmanship.

Later, Kerry would liken it, not to any great shot by Seve Ballesteros but to something more like a Hollywood movie, some western lone ranger coming into town to clean up Dodge.

I wanted to be close, wanted a gimme. A par would save me from looking like a complete fool. I could just imagine the shouts going on back home as the gang gathered in the bar at Hickory Ridge to follow my round live from the Masters.

This wasn't my way. I had more sense than to pull a flag when it was pointless, when I might need the flag to knock down the ball if I hit it too hard.

I took a few practice swings, getting the feel, burying my shoes in the warm sand, making sure the clubface was open, measuring the distance in my mind, telling myself to keep accelerating my hands on the downswing, keep accelerating them toward the target until well after the ball was gone. I wanted to be left of the cup, high on the slope. The ball would hold and spin back if I did it right, if I kept it simple and made all the basic moves.

And I did.

40

ON THE TEE AT 13 Clay pulled my driver and reminded me to hit it nice and easy. It was his code phrase for keeping me calm. He could see that sinking my bunker approach to birdie 12 and picking up a stroke to tie Tiger had sent a bolt of electricity through my system.

"Easy," he whispered.

I stared down the length of the hole, letting the lovely contour of the dogleg settle my nerves. There was only one way to score on this hole: I had to do what I'd done on Friday: lace my drive tight down the left side and hit it far enough to clear the dogleg. Then I'd have a second shot of 200 into the target.

That is what Clay wanted me to do, what I had done before, with Demaret's help. But Jimmy wasn't there now; I was on my own.

I was sure the television audience across America was listening to Nantz and Faldo discussing my percentages, whether it would be worth the gamble. One or the other would mention that I was running out of holes. Faldo, naturally, being a player, would point out that I hit a natural fade. Nantz would answer something like, "Yes, but he's been driving the ball straight all afternoon." I wished I was up in the tower. Commenting on a tournament was a lot easier than playing in one.

I knew Tiger would be home in 2. So how could the Cinderella Man make it a match? Not by trying to pit myself against the champ. Friday's wood had been a fluke, my getting on in 2. As Faldo knew, I needed to play the percentages, and for me that was to drive safely. I couldn't pull off another wonder shot, not now, not with Cliff and his pals nowhere in sight.

So that's what I did. I played safe. I aimed at the right side cypress trees and hit my drive 287 into the center of the wide, inviting fairway. I would have a long second shot to the green. I couldn't get home in 2, but my ball hit hard into the sloping fairway, kicked left, and picked up a few yards. I'd be playing off an uneven, sidehill lie, but at least I didn't have tree trouble. I stepped over beside Clay and watched Tiger tee off.

The speed of his swing and the whack at impact silenced all of us. I followed the flight of the ball, watched his Nike ride the left side. It wasn't hooking. It wasn't fading. He drove the ball 290 yards on the fly. The ball landed safely, kicked left, and took the slope, leaving him 178 to the 510-yard par 5.

"Nice," I said, as I walked off the tee. Tiger smiled. He knew just how good that drive was. We both knew he had put me in my place.

When I reached my ball, Clay asked if I was going for it and I shook my head.

Looking at the lie, I saw the ball was a good four inches higher than my stance. I'd have to shorten my swing and play a big hook.

I wouldn't get my normal distance, but the ball would come in hot with overspin. It was a big green, nearly forty yards wide and deep, and while the grain ran against me, a hook wouldn't hold, and beyond the green were bunkers. No, going for it wasn't the percentage shot. I didn't need anyone, not even Faldo, to tell me that.

"You need to go for it," Roberts declared, and I jumped at his sudden arrival. Unperturbed, Roberts continued.

"Your boy Smith bogeyed 18. He drove it in the fairway bunker, came up way left of the green with his second, and couldn't get down." He nodded toward Tiger. "Tiger is going to birdie one or more of these holes coming home. You're the only one keeping up with Woods."

My body sank with this news. I was hoping Chuck could post a number and take the pressure off me. But I wasn't that surprised he faded in the stretch. He wasn't the first player to lose the Masters on 18 on Sunday afternoon.

"It's up to you, Tim." I could hear the desperation in the old man's voice.

I stepped away from Clay and Roberts, giving myself distance and time to think. I let my eyes sweep the forest of azaleas that ran from tee to green, well over fifteen hundred of them. It was another beautiful spot at Augusta National, and I knew that when MacKenzie first saw it, he'd thought it was the most natural golf hole he had ever seen. But now, to me, it was a booby-trap waiting to destroy my round.

Tiger would go for the green; that was obvious. He'd make a birdie or even an eagle. I could play safe, get my par, and be a shot off the lead, but now that wasn't enough.

Again I did the math of what I needed to score to beat Tiger. It was like being in school studying for my SATs.

I returned to my ball and asked Clay what he thought.

"You need a birdie," Roberts answered as if I was talking to him. "Tiger will be on in two."

Clay said, "Three. What do we have to lose?"

What Clay didn't know was that I had everything to lose. This was more than a golf tournament. More than the Masters.

I pulled the 3 fairway metal wood, and on the near side of the fairway, the gallery burst into applause, seeing I was going for it.

"Just carry the creek," Clay instructed. "You've got plenty of green. You've done this before."

Of course it wasn't the same shot. You never hit the same shot the same way twice, and no two rounds of golf are ever alike. Golf is always a game of firsts, no matter how many rounds you play.

Off the side-hill lie, I choked three inches down on the grip and played the ball forward, looking for a big hook. I moved my left hand over the shaft and dropped my right foot back to close my stance. I had to hit the ball further than I had played the hybrid on Friday morning, but coming off this lie, the ball would have a lower trajectory and gain distance. It would come in hot to the green.

The ball looked good coming off the face of the metal-wood. It came off higher than I had expected, fought the wind, and carried to the green where it hit hard and rolled past the cup and onto the ridge way behind the pin. I was on in two, but barely. I'd need to grab a taxi to get back to the cup.

41

I DIDN'T GET A TAXI. It took me two putts, but I matched birdies with Tiger and we went to 14 still all even. And when I reached the tee, I focused first on the scoreboard and studied the leaders. There were five of us, all within three shots of each other: Woods, Mickelson, Steve Stricker, Cabrera, and myself. Chuck was in with his 288, but there was no way that score would hold up, not with the talent still on the course. That final bogey had been his death knell.

"This is your hole, Tim," Clay said. "There's nothing to worry about. No bunkers. Just keep it in the fairway."

"You want me to smoke it?" I pulled the driver.

"It's wide open." He pointed down the fairway.

What Clay said was true. It was another of Mackenzie's adaptations of St. Andrews in Scotland. This hole was patterned after the Old Course's 6. Both holes were built for players who could work the ball from right to left, so long as they didn't get too eager. That was what Freddy Couples did back in '98 when he hooked his drive into the woods.

A week at the Masters had also taught me something else: that Augusta National wasn't originally designed for long hitters or great putters. Jones and MacKenzie built their course for players who could place their drives on the wide fairways. A hole that needed a draw one day might need a fade the next. The greens were set to be played with run-ups, not as targets. It was a different game than what we see on the Golf Channel.

"Play away from trouble," Clay advised, pulling my mind back to the present and the hole I had to play now. Fourteen was 440 yards from the tournament tee, and it favored my fade. I could aim down the left side and let the ball work back into the center of the fairway. Still, with my readjusted R9, I could also hit the ball to the right side and it would catch the crest of the hill and run. All week, I had been hitting mid-irons into the target. As with all the holes of Augusta National, it was the second shot that mattered the most.

What also favored my game, and kept surprising me after three rounds, was that my fade worked to my advantage on my approach shots. Any ball that came into the green on a draw wouldn't hold. A high, soft fade checked up, but this green, unfortunately, terraced down from left to right.

I teed up and stepped behind the ball. The gallery was stretched from the tee down the right side of the fairway, waiting and watching me. There were close to five thousand patrons. They stood silently in the afternoon sunlight, three and four deep; they stretched away in a tight band of color to where the dogleg bent left and the fairway disappeared. I scanned the gallery, looking down the left side, then the right. I didn't see Kerry.

Thinking of her, I did my pre-shot routine, wondering if she could see me standing behind the ball, patiently swinging my club while visualizing where I wanted to place my drive.

What I did next wasn't spectacular. It wasn't a John Daly drive or a Tiger Woods bomb. It wasn't a drive you'd find on the Champions Tour, but it was enough to reach the ridge and land safely in the fairway. Applause rose from the gallery, more for me than for the drive, which carried, at best, 285.

I picked up my long tee, tipped my cap in recognition of the applause, and moved aside. I knew the surge of cheers was all about my being the underdog, the outsider.

Every player in America could derive hope from my unlikely challenge of Tiger, Phil, and sixty of the other great golfers in the world. I hadn't backed off. I was on the back nine at Augusta late on Sunday afternoon. It was a movie script; it was an eye-moistening moment like Hogan's final-nine 30 back in '67, or Nicklaus winning in '86. But I needed more than a movie script. I still needed to win for Kerry.

After Tiger drove we stepped off the tee together and fell into step.

"You're a college professor, Tim?" Tiger asked, sounding genuinely curious.

I nodded. "I teach everything from a freshman survey to graduate courses. When I started out, my subject was English and now I teach communications, whatever that is."

"You've gone from persimmon woods to titanium-and-graphite drivers," he answered, a grin lighting up his face. Then, getting serious, he asked, "You play a lot of golf?"

"On weekends, mostly, in the spring and summer. Southern Illinois isn't Florida. Some days we play in the snow."

Tiger shook his head, "You're a helluva player, Tim, even if you're not playing in snow."

I could tell by his tone that he meant it. My being in contention impressed him. I had no history on the tour, no pedigree as a player. Of course, Tiger didn't know about the cast of characters Cliff Roberts had produced for me. And being Tiger, he didn't believe the round I was putting together could stop him. He might be magnanimous, but Tiger knew—as did everyone else—that whenever he stepped onto the first tee in any tournament in the world, he was the man to beat.

I reached my ball, and Tiger still had yards to walk. The discrepancy between our drives was impressive. Tiger might as well have been playing alone. He couldn't learn anything from my game.

"Don't talk to Tiger," Roberts declared, materializing again by my side. "He's trying to break your concentration."

"Well, you're doing a good job of that yourself, Mr. Roberts."

I stared down at 14 green, the toughest green at Augusta National. Everything hit short would come off the green and cascade back down the fairway. Hitting long produced even more trouble. Nothing held on the quick bentgrass. That's why Tiger had the advantage. His distance off the tee left him a lofty wedge with plenty of backspin to get it close to the pin.

"We've got 146 to the front edge. The hole is cut six yards from the mound," Clay informed me, returning to the bag.

"What number?"

"Seven, I'd say. You have plus-20 from the fringe."

"Hit the eight." I knew from the voice that it was Hogan. Again, he wasn't looking at me. He was staring with his hawk-like eyes at the green and slowly, carefully working away on a cigarette. He said, "What you want to do is come in high and land beyond the pin. You want to stay ten feet left of the flag. Play your ball off the ridge that cuts across the middle of the green. If you catch the ridge, the ball will filter back to the hole. You'll have nothing left but a short putt."

What he was telling me was true enough, but I knew he was thinking of the years when he played at the Masters, when the hole was 35 yards shorter.

I pulled "The Book" from my back pocket and flipped open to the 14th hole.

"Put that away," Roberts told me, swooping down from the other side. "You've got one of the greatest golfers in the world here—you don't need a caddie yardage book."

One could chew a meal on the disdain in his voice.

Behind me, Ben Hogan said flatly, "Go with the club you believe in, Tim."

I pulled the 7.

"Goddammit," Cliff Roberts swore.

Clay moved my bag away.

"It's a seven," answering Hogan and Roberts.

I closed out the world around me. I set the face of the club behind the ball, positioning it on the line of flight I wanted. Then I stepped around and set myself with a slightly open stance and gripped the seven with both hands, not squeezing the club, but keeping my hands and arms and whole body relaxed and ready.

"Imagine yourself as Paul Newman in Cool Hand Luke or Clint Eastwood in The Good, The Bad and the Ugly," Kerry had instructed me. "Imagine yourself as the cutest guy on campus walking across the quad that September afternoon when you first saw me at SLU and were totally smitten by my drop-dead good looks."

She was smiling, remembering our chance meeting, the luckiest moment in my life. I had gone up to her, bolder than I had been with any girl, and said hello. I told her my name and said I was a grad student in English from New York. Then I asked her, without hesitation or stammering or any doubt that it would all work out between us, if we could get a cup of coffee at the Campus Club.

"That's the confidence you need in your swing," Kerry had instructed. "I knew then, just by the way you handled yourself with me that first time we met, that regardless of whatever else happened in our lives, you would always be there. That was all I needed to fall in love with you. That is the confidence you need when you play."

I took one easy swing to find my tempo, then hit the seven, feeling the clubface against the ball, registering the smooth, clean impact. I finished my follow-through as the thick divot flew twenty yards ahead of me. I kept watching the ball as Clay left the bag and went to retrieve the clump of fairway grass. He too was following the flight, and we both saw the ball hit to the left of the cup, high on the ridge and check up, then spin back. It wasn't too much club. It was enough to get me up on the green and over the false front that had been a black hole for players in the long history of Augusta National. The ball came slowly down the slope toward the pin. I had less than two feet for a birdie. And it was an uphill putt.

"How's that!" I said to Roberts, knowing he wouldn't show his face.

The silence, as they say, was golden.

42

I DIDN'T MATCH my Saturday eagle on 15, but I stayed out of trouble, I equaled Tiger's birdie to stay even with him, and we both kept ahead of Mickelson and Stricker. I liked Stricker, and if I'd been at home in Carbondale watching this final round, I'd have been pulling for him. He was a Midwestern kid from a small town, and I remembered when he first came out on tour with his wife as his caddie, two young kids trying to live out their dream.

On the 16th tee, a long, green metal bleacher stretched down to the front edge of the short par-3 water hole, making it look like nothing so much as a basketball seat in a high school gym. Cheers were bouncing off the trees from other fairways and greens, but it wasn't the deafening roar that follows a hole in one. This was the famous Masters gallery which recognized golf well played.

I stepped up onto the tee box. The hole was only 170 yards, and the shot was over water to a green shaped like the continent of Africa, and concave and bunkered. The entire hole was encased with patrons so it felt as if you were playing golf inside an amphitheater. It was, as least according to Jack Nicklaus, the most exciting place to be at the Masters.

The challenge of the innocent-looking hole was not the water or the sand but the green and its ridge, which divided the putting surface into two halves, one more difficult than the other. I hadn't been close all week. The only sure way to succeed was to ace the drive. I had never made a hole-in-one in my life and I wasn't about to make one now, in the final round of the Masters.

I tried to block out the gallery in the stands left of the tee and sitting on the hillside left of the green. There were always crowds at 16; earlier in the week, during practice rounds, players had entertained patrons by skipping balls across the water and onto the green, a tradition Trevino started back in the '70s.

I could see the cup was cut in the back left quad. The ideal play was a slight draw that would leave the ball below the hole. I needed to cut it over the left front bunker and left of the ridge. Then the ball would trickle down to the pin at the back section of the green, just as Tiger had done in '05 when he made the phenomenal chip endlessly memorialized in TV commercials.

"Six iron?" I said out loud.

Clay shook his head. "Seven. You're pumped up. You'll hit that seven as far as you would a six."

I had pulled the 7 and started toward the markers when Clay whispered, "Your cell phone is ringing."

"I shut it off." I had forgotten I had slipped it into my bag when I had my clubs up in the Crow's Nest.

"You must have put it on vibrate. I can feel it."

I shook my head. There was no way I was going to answer a cell phone in the midst of the round, in the midst of the Masters, in the midst of all those green-jacketed members.

I stepped between the markers set way in the back of the

box, 170 to the left side where the cup was cut. I had to clear the water, clear the bunker, and cut the ball into the shallow left side, below the ridge that bisected the green like a backbone.

I smiled. I couldn't make it any more difficult for myself. As I teed up, Roberts commented, "You don't have enough club."

I glanced over and saw he wasn't alone. Locke, Demaret, Sarazen, Nelson, and Hogan had gathered with Charles DeClifford Roberts, Jr. They had all come back to watch me play my final holes.

"Don't leave it short the way I did in '42," Hogan spoke up. It was the hole that had cost him a green jacket.

"Listen to Ben," Roberts lectured.

I walked back to Clay and slipped the seven into the bag. Woods was standing to the right side with Stevie. They were watching the scenario between my caddie and myself.

"No!" Clay declared. He had clamped his hand on the top of the six. He was shaking his head. "Too much club," he showed a flash of anger.

I wanted to turn him around and point to the pros, to say, "Look! I've got a half dozen of the greatest players in history telling me to hit a six."

"Why are you so sure?" I asked, keeping calm.

"I know your game, Tim," he said simply. "I know what you can do."

I looked at him for a moment, then pulled the seven again and walked back to the tee. I disregarded Roberts and the others. I was all motion, all determination. I just focused on where I wanted to start my iron. How it worked out had more to do with fate than good luck or good golf. It had to do with what my caddie thought was right.

I rose to the occasion, I have to admit. I didn't cook the iron. I didn't leave it in the front-side bunker. I didn't over-swing. I cut it as neatly as if I were slicing bread onto the back lower half of the green and left of the flag. Tiger would have to hit another of his patented great short irons to get inside of my dead-solid, perfect 7-iron to the green.

Which, of course, he did. The cheers followed us from the long bleachers and packed hillside. Walking around the water, feeling great about my 7-iron, I decided to check my cell phone, knowing it had to be from home. I took it from Clay and saw the call was from Kerry.

Cell phones weren't allowed on the grounds of Augusta National. But this was Kerry, and there was no way I wasn't going to answer her call.

43

"WHERE ARE YOU?" I asked.

"I'm here; I'm here." She sounded overjoyed.

"Where?" I spun around and scanned the hillside where spectators were sitting on the grass as if out for an afternoon picnic.

"I'm watching you. You're wearing your good-luck Greg Norman blue shirt and your gray slacks and those heavy brown golf shoes I don't like." She sounded absolutely pleased with herself. I grinned at her cocky rejoinder and kept walking as I searched for her.

"I'm standing on the hillside, up by these beautiful white woodbine. The golf course is so gorgeous."

"Wave," I asked. The hillside, left of 16 green, was a blanket of people and flowers. Then I saw my wife. She was at the very crest of the rise, silhouetted against the bright-blue Georgia sky. Her hair glowed in the sunlight. She looked radiant. From a hundred yards away, I could see her smile.

I stopped walking. Clay was already at my ball waiting for my arrival. Tiger had marked his and tossed it to Stevie.

"I've got to go," I said to Kerry.

"I know. Go make that birdie. I'll be here. I'm not leaving you," she whispered.

I flipped the cell phone closed and slipped it into my back pocket with my yardage book and score card. Then I stepped onto the green. The cheering had subsided with our arrival and the gallery had settled down. Kerry would appreciate that, I thought, how the audience became quiet when the drama on the green began.

I marked my ball and tossed it to Clay and then walked around to study the putt. It was longer than I'd thought, closer to eight feet than six, and my heart sank as I realized I was on the ridge. I would be putting down the slope.

I took the ball back from Clay without even looking at him. I was consumed by how I might play the putt. There was a big break, but there was always a break on Augusta greens.

Clay didn't say anything. He kept watching me until I asked what he thought.

"The putt is slower than you think. The grain looks like it's going downhill, but it's not."

"What do you mean? It's not bent toward the water?" This was the most elementary rule in putting. The grain always grew towards the water, or the mountains.

I stared at the putt. I had no idea how to play it. I looked up and spotted Roberts. He was standing alone on the fringe of the green and, when I glanced his way, he took it as an invitation to join me. He and the others had gathered together on the fringe below the hole.

I crouched down again and took another look at the line. Tiger had begun to pace at the edge of the green. Good, I thought, at least I was getting to him.

"Tim, I have someone who can help you on these last holes."

I stood up and there he was, the one legend of the past I had been waiting to meet.

"Hello, Tim. It's nice to meet you."

"Hello, Mr. Jones. It's my pleasure."

"Please call me Bob," he asked, smiling.

He was smaller than I expected from seeing him in old black-and-white photographs—only five foot nine and 170 pounds. The perfect size for playing golf with hickory clubs. He was as handsome as he had been in real life, an old-fashioned Southern gentleman lawyer with a sweet smile, a soft drawl, and short, fine brown hair combed straight back and parted down the middle.

"We don't want to be called for slow play," Roberts spoke up, glancing at the officials huddled on the fringe.

I turned to Jones and asked him what he thought.

Jones gestured toward the putt. "It matters more what you think. Putting is not a science, Tim. It's an art. Two players can read a putt two different ways, and both can make their putts. Just because a putt will break right doesn't mean that every player will play for the same amount of break. A lot depends on the pace, how hard we stroke the ball."

I held up Bobby Locke's putter and said, "I'm using a hickory blade like your old Calamity Jane."

Jones took a deep drag on his cigarette and smiled wryly, shaking his head.

"A golfer doesn't win with clubs, Tim. They're just the tools of the trade. Golf is played in your mind. You have to think clearly and manage your emotions. I had to quit tournament play when I was in my twenties because I couldn't take the pressure. My nerves were eating away at me every time I teed up in a tournament."

He turned and moved toward the apron, then hesitated once

again and summed up, "The best advice any of us can give you is to listen to your caddie. The boy has the eyes of an eagle."

And then Bobby Jones was gone.

To mask my surprise, I knelt down again and took another long look at the tricky slope and nodded to Clay to step over behind me.

"Okay," I asked, "what do we do?"

"Well, I could load your ball," he replied, making a joke of my dilemma.

It was an old caddie trick at Augusta to leave spit on a ball when cleaning it so that the saliva would curtail the speed of the ball and give a putt a chance when the greens were slick.

Clay pointed to a dip on the manicured green and told me to putt to that spot. "A straight putt of three feet," he explained. "From there the ball will take the slope and fall straight down to catch the cup."

I did exactly what Clay told me to do. I used his young eyes to read the treacherous green and tapped the ball gently enough to roll to the edge of the ridge a yard from my feet. In the silence of that natural amphitheater, the soft, muffled click of my hickory blade putter on the ball must have been heard by the thousands surrounding the hole. I wondered if they too were holding their breath as we watched the ball traverse 16 green.

Millions of TV watchers must have watched the Titleist tumble into the cup, giving me a one-shot lead for the first time at the Masters when Tiger missed his putt.

44

"THERE'S YOUR WIFE," Clay told me when we reached the tee. He nodded down the 17th fairway, looking toward the left-side rough where the gallery stretched the length of the hole.

"How do you know?" I asked, surprised that he knew who Kerry was and thinking, also, that he was trying to calm me down after my birdie putt.

"She introduced herself to me this morning," he answered, looking guilty. He spoke in a whisper. "She told me not to say anything. She didn't want you getting upset, her being here." He shrugged.

I saw Kerry now. She was less than two hundred yards away, standing to the left of the Eisenhower tree, the tall pine that stood like a silent sentry blocking the view to the green.

I hit him playfully on the shoulder so he'd know it was okay between us. Everything was okay. Kerry was okay. She was here. It was as if I was out playing a practice round.

But of course nothing was normal. I was paired with Tiger
Woods at the Masters, and I was talking to dead people.

I teed up and looked down the fairway. Kerry had disappeared.

"She's gone," I whispered to Clay.

"I can still see her."

Of course he could, having better eyesight.

I took a few more slow practice swings, focusing on my drive,
and stared down the fairway. The hole was famous mostly for
Eisenhower's Georgia pine. When Ike was a member he had
wanted the left-side fairway tree cut down because it always
caught his slicing drive, but when Ike's request was scheduled
to go before the Grounds Committee, Roberts adjourned the
meeting. Since then the tee had been moved back twice and the
big pine was now close to 210 from the tee.

I wasn't concerned about Ike's tree. I needed to drive to
the right side of the fairway and keep my ball left of a mound
and two pines at the crest of the rise. This would give me a
short approach. I had learned early in the week that the right side
gave me the best angle to the target.

The pin was cut close to the front of the green. With any
kind of a drive, I'd have around 150 left. I could hit a high
8-iron. The only trouble was that this green was harder than the
others. I had to hit high enough to spin the ball back to the flag.

But I was getting ahead of myself. I hadn't yet driven off.

I took another swing, and Clay moved to give me room.
I stepped up to the ball and paused. Bobby Jones stepped out
from behind the Eisenhower pine. He was walking leisurely across
the wide-open, empty fairway.

"What's he doing?" I said out loud, guessing Roberts was by
my side.

"Bob is showing you where to aim, Tim." Roberts answered.
I could hear a smile in his voice.

I smiled, too.

"Okay," I said, but only to myself. I would do what Bobby Jones was telling me. I couldn't ask for a better guide at Augusta National.

I drove away, thinking as I aimed my drive at Bobby Jones that if my ball took its natural fade, it would disappear into the length of pines that guarded the right side of the fairway. But my drive did not fade. I saw Bobby Jones gesture to the ball in flight and it turned with his guidance. Perhaps it was just my imagination, or the work Ed Mitchell had done on the driver. Whatever it was, the ball came safely into the middle of the fairway and disappeared beyond Eisenhower's tree.

From deep down the length of the hole, I heard the spectators sighing with relief. They were pulling for the impossible—to have an amateur win at Augusta. I plucked my tee off the ground. I felt like Silky Sullivan, that old Kentucky race horse, coming from far off the pace and trying to catch Tiger Woods in the home stretch.

"I think we got his attention," Clay commented, catching up to me.

There was a certain calmness in the wake of Tiger, as if we were in the eye of the storm. I felt totally alone out there in the middle of the fairway, and it was only then that I realized I was crying. There were tears on my cheeks. They came from deep inside me. It was just possible that Kerry was going to be okay. And even as I cried I did not break stride. I did not stop moving. The miracle was so close I could taste it—but I had to keep moving. I still had two more holes to play.

"It's okay," Clay said, "back in '86 after Jack Nicklaus birdied 16 and took the lead for the first time, he started to cry walking down this hole."

I reached out and briefly hugged Clay and told him I was okay. I asked him if he saw Kerry. He glanced around, checked the press of spectators on both sides of the fairway, and shook his head.

My guess was that Kerry had walked ahead to the green where she could watch me putt out. I pulled out my Day-Glo yardage book and studied the stats for the 17th hole, checked where I was and what I had left to the green.

Clay was doing the same, studying his homemade caddie book.

"You've got 148 to the left side; 157 on the right," he told me.

The cup was cut on the right, tucked behind the bunker. I knew I wanted to fly it over the bunker, over the flag, and spin it back to the cup as if I was pulling the string of a child's toy. An easy shot. I had made it a dozen times just this week, hitting into the high greens. I was forgetting, however, there are no easy shots in golf, regardless of the course. Golf isn't a game of easy.

I took a deep breath and placed my left glove hand on the top of the irons and just stood there, staring at my sticks. I couldn't move. My legs crumbled under the weight and I leaned forward, clutching the barrel bag, telling myself as I did that I had to pull myself together, I couldn't break down like some golf version of Jimmy Piersall.

"Tim? You okay?"

I nodded yes, but I wasn't okay. I pulled the 8-iron and used the club to steady myself.

Clay took charge. He began telling me what I had to do, going through a laundry list of where I wanted to aim, what I was trying to do with the short iron. He talked fast. All I needed was a par, he said. The 17th everyone knew, didn't give up birdies.

I didn't bother reminding him that Gary Player had birdied this hole twice to win two of his three Masters.

I took one practice swing and then another and another. It was, as always, my way of calming down, of gaining control of my life. For me, the simple physical routine of swinging a club worked the way benzodiazepines are used by half the world, and yoga by the other half.

I felt my tension slip down and out the club shaft. I stopped swinging and glanced over at Clay. With him, but oblivious to him, were Roberts and Bobby Jones and the other legendary players who'd shown up to help me out.

"Go ahead, Timmy, make us all proud of you," Bobby Jones said, his voice full of southern charm. "Stay eight feet left of the flag, Tim," Jones advised next, gesturing up the hill, "with your fade you'll be in fine shape." He had all the confidence in the world that I had the ability to pull off the approach.

I addressed the ball that was slightly above my feet, gripping down a half inch on the shaft to compensate my stance, and said out loud to Clay and all the others, "Well, here goes the ball game."

As soon as I hit it, I knew I was in trouble. It was too much club. A solid nine would have been enough. The ball was going to carry deep into the green, hit up on the ridge and run over the green.

"Come down!" I shouted after the ball.

"It will," Bobby Jones answered softly. He stepped to my side and raised his arm, gesturing to the high-arcing Titleist. Whether it was Bobby Jones or whatever wind there was swirling around the green, the ball hit short of the ridge, jumped back and came down the slope to the cup. I was safely home in two with another birdie opportunity.

45

TIGER WOODS DID NOT HAVE Bobby Jones or any other phantom legends helping him with his wedge into the 17th green, but nevertheless he was able to answer my birdie with one of his own and together we walked over to 18 tee, and the last hole at Augusta National.

Walking with Tiger, I glanced over at the leaderboard and saw that no one had caught us. Ahead, walking up eighteen fairway, was Mickelson, but this year he had shot himself out of the tournament—there were no miraculous eagles on the backside as there had been on the Saturday afternoon in 2010, the year he won his third Green Jacket.

So it was up to Tiger and me to decide it all on 18. For decades, the pros had considered this finishing hole a piece of cake; then, in 2001, when Tiger demolished Augusta National with a record score, the hole was lengthened by 60 yards. The tee box was pushed back and moved to the right to create a tighter dogleg.

The two bunkers on the left side of the fairway were enlarged to catch any drive that didn't fade.

As I stepped to the tee, I heard Byron Nelson ask Hogan if he remembered their final round in '42, when Nelson had bogeyed 17, which tied him with Ben, and then he had driven into the pines that ran down the right side of the fairway.

I glanced over at Hogan. He was smiling shyly, nodding that he remembered. All these years later, the old pros could finally take in stride an afternoon when they'd battled it out.

"That was a helluva shot out of the pines," Hogan said, remembering.

"One of the great shots of my life," answered Byron. He went on to explain how he had kept it under the branches, and while the ball had landed short, it had run on the hard, dry fairway up and onto the green. "I 2 putted to tie and won the playoff the next day." He grinned broadly at the long-ago memory. Then, catching my eye, he gestured at Hogan, with whom he had caddied in their boyhood days in Texas. "But nothing I did could match what the little man did here back in '67."

The circle of players acknowledged Hogan's achievement. On the last green, he had holed a 25-foot breaking putt for a record-tying 30 on the back side, finishing off one of the great rounds of golf at Augusta. At the age of 54, he'd shot a 66. The old players fell silent remembering Hogan in his last major tournament—how, on his bad legs, he had slowly climbed the rise to 18 green, to be greeted by the emotional cheers of the huge gallery encasing the hole.

Remembering Hogan's triumph settled my nerves. Whatever I had to do was nothing compared to what Hogan had achieved on his busted legs in his lifetime. I stepped up between the markers and teed up.

Aiming for the bunker, I let it fly. My drive carried 287, landing safely. I had a mid-iron to the green. Tiger pounded his metal wood straight for the left-side bunkers, but when the ball cleared the tight corridor of trees, it worked right and bounced safely out of trouble. We were both in the fairway, but Tiger had only a wedge left to the elevated green.

We stepped off the tee and uphill to our second shots through the avenue of pines. It was oddly silent and peaceful inside the corridor and away from the press of people. Even the officials with us were leaving us alone. They, too, were acutely aware of this moment, the two of us dueling for the green jacket.

Tiger didn't speak. He had that look of frozen concentration I recognized from watching him on television. He knew that, unlikely as it seemed, he was still in a match and a mistake on the last hole meant he would lose to the most unlikely player in the field. I hadn't broken under the pressure. Noticing that, for some reason, made me feel immensely better. I took another deep breath.

Clay, twenty yards ahead on the fairway, reached my ball and, setting down the bag, pulled out his book to check the distance. When I reached him, he gestured to where my ball had come to rest. It had found one of the few scars on the immaculate 18th hole. Some caddie had not replaced the turf earlier that day.

"It happened to Immelman," Clay said. "Remember? On this hole!"

All week my ball had been sitting up on the velvet green fairways and only now did it find a divot. Not only was the ball in a divot mark, but I also had an uphill lie to an elevated green, the hardest shot in golf. Even the best players would stay back on their downswing to try to lift the ball. If I did that I'd hit it fat.

What I had going for me was that I faded the ball and it was most likely that I would do so now from this divot. The ball would come out with a lower trajectory, I thought next, going through a litany of what might happen playing from this uneven lie.

Eighteen green was two-tiered, fifty feet wide and a hundred feet deep. It had been a big target and an easy shot earlier in the week, but now the hole was cut on the front half, as it always was on the last day of the Masters—another decree of Cliff Roberts. He had made that decision so the gallery framing the green could see the final putts of the tournament. What I had to do was hit past the pin and use the slope as a backboard to spin the ball back to the flag.

From deep down in the fairway, I saw the top of the flag tucked in behind the front left bunker. I was far enough to the right side of the fairway to have the angle on where the cup was cut, but I still had to fly it to the ridge and let the ball spin down to the hole. I turned to Clay and raised my eyebrows, waiting for his suggestion. Without hesitating, he pulled the 6-iron.

I didn't know if I had the strength to play the mid-iron. My whole body was feeling the weight of this incredible day. Could I manage one last crucial swing?

"Make sure you align your shoulders with the slope and shift your weight to your left side," Nelson instructed, speaking up as if he were my father. "Let your fade work its magic." The other pros nodded agreement, as if they were a Greek chorus.

I stepped behind the ball to get the alignment. Down the length of fairway and encircling the green the gallery had gathered. The colors of their clothes on the bright afternoon were more spectacular than the flowering azaleas.

I felt a cool breeze wash across my face, and I looked toward the clubhouse to study the flags to see which way the wind was blowing, and how strong.

I glanced over at the pros and saw that Bobby Jones had joined Roberts and the others at the edge of the fairway. Beside them, all clustered together, were the tournament officials, the state police guarding Tiger, a handful of CBS technicians, and David Feherty, the CBS commentator. He was whispering into his microphone and I had to resist the urge to walk over to him and eavesdrop.

Tiger was waiting off to my left. I took a few easy swings of the 6-iron and said, "Thanks, Clay, for everything."

He smiled and looked embarrassed, as if he hadn't done anything at all.

"Go ahead, Tim," he said. "This is your time at Augusta."

A good caddie, I thought, encouraging me and without any doubts in the world.

I stared one final time at the green high on the horizon and encased with gallery. And then, unexpectedly, surprisingly, I heard a soft roll of applause from behind the green, and saw the patrons who made up the enormous gallery begin to applaud, and as one, rise from their green chairs and the metal bleachers encasing the hole and rally around me to make my approach shot to eighteen.

I stepped away from my ball and touched my cap, then raised my arm and waved, nodding my thanks to both sides of the fairway. The phantom pros were applauding, too, as were the Augusta officials and, standing with Stevie Williams, Tiger joined in and smiled at me from across the fairway as he, too, acknowledged the round I had just played, regardless of the outcome.

I turned to Clay. There were tears on the kid's sunny face.

"Okay," I said, "let's do it."

Addressing my ball again, I played away.

The 6-iron came out low, as I expected, but I managed to keep my shoulders square and I got through the shot, divot and all. The ball was dead-center headed for the left bunker when once again Bobby Jones raised his arm, and whether it was his phantom intervention or my natural fade, the ball moved enough right that it hit the front bank, kicked right, and ran up onto the green.

I was safely on, though my ball had run up the slope to the right of the flag and I had a long downhill slider for my birdie putt.

My shot hadn't been good enough to earn all the cheers that came again, rolling down the fairway to me. Perhaps the spectators, like me, were just happy I was on in two and still had a chance.

The 18th, over the years, had offered up many memorable winning putts. In '97, Tiger himself had finished off the round with a record tournament. Then there were Hogan's 25-footer in the third round in 1967, Mark O'Meara's 20-footer in 1998 to beat Fred Couples, and Mickelson's in 2010 to win his third Masters.

"Miracles still happen at Augusta," I commented to Roberts. He had come to join me in the middle of the fairway. We were forty yards from Tiger, waiting for him to play his approach.

"You'll make it," Roberts assured me.

"Maybe, with help from you," I said.

"With help from them." Then he smiled at me and added, "Thank you, Tim."

I nodded, suddenly too emotional to speak, and turned to watch Tiger play up. The game was still on. Tiger never gave away a championship.

But as we know, Tiger is only human. He misplayed his approach, hitting too far up the ridge. It had happened to him before, in 2010 when teeing off 9, he had sprayed his drive into the 8 fairway. Now his ball landed and stayed on the top tier of the green, leaving him a downhill putt of thirty-plus feet from the flag. He was outside of my 6-iron approach. I could use his putt to read my own. Finally, Tiger was helping me.

Tiger didn't wait to walk up the rise to the green. He took off, upset with himself for the mishit. I followed in his wake and slowed my pace to let him have his moment with the gallery. They had already been nice enough to me.

Also, I wanted Clay to walk with me. I wanted to share this final climb to the green; I wanted to walk in together. I flung my arm over his shoulder and briefly hugged the kid so the world would know how much he had meant to me. Then I took off my cap and waved, thanking the Masters patrons. They were standing again, cheering our arrival.

Stepping up to my ball, I looked at my putt. I had 15 feet. It was what I had feared most: side hill and downhill. I marked the ball and tossed it to Clay, then stepped over to the fringe and left the stage to Tiger, who was studying his own downhill, sidehill birdie putt. We had both looked like hackers with our approaches. The pressure of the lead, the final hole on Sunday, had played on both our nerves.

Cliff Roberts moved closer to me as we watched Tiger circle around to read the green from all angles.

"He won't make it," Roberts stated confidently. "He'll miss it on the high side; everyone does."

"Tiger Woods is not everyone." I whispered.

"I've been watching pros miss that putt in tournaments since before you were born. Don't worry about Tiger. Concentrate on what you have to do. End this Masters now, on this hole. No sudden death," he ordered, then added nicely, "please."

I could hear the tension in his voice. All his life he had given the orders on this golf course and now he was depending on a stranger.

"Any suggestions?" I asked. Twenty yards away, Tiger was kneeling behind his ball. Stevie Williams had pulled the flagstick and was crouched behind him. They, too, were whispering to each other. Stevie moved away and Tiger addressed the putt.

"Ask Bobby," Roberts said. "Or Locke."

I nodded, but didn't take my eyes off Tiger. I had been watching his routine since the first hole, hoping to discover what made him such a great putter.

Tiger held the putter loosely in his right hand as he settled himself over the ball. With his free left hand, he tugged on his pant leg, freeing it from any tension of material. He set the blade putter carefully behind the ball and looked at the long line of the putt, tracking with his eyes where he wanted the ball to roll.

The afternoon had become amazingly quiet. The gallery filling three sides of the green was silently riveted on Tiger, and when he stroked I could hear the distinctive click of the putter head as it hit the Nike.

It took a long time for the ball to reach the hole, though it increased speed once it caught the slope. From my angle, I saw it would have the distance and the speed, but I couldn't tell if it had the line it needed to catch the hole.

Tiger began to move, following the putt. Out of the corner of my eye, I caught Stevie Williams raising his arms, as if in anticipation of what was to come. He, too, was moving along the far edge of the green, his eyes fixed on the ball. Everyone was barely breathing   .

The Nike slowly turned and turned. The ball tumbled toward the hole, caught the front edge on the low side, spun completely around the hole, paused, and dropped.

I didn't move.

I couldn't move.

The gallery roared, and Tiger danced down the edge of the green as the ball curled into the plastic cup for his final birdie of the day. He had tied me. Now I had to make mine to keep me out of a playoff, because there was no way, I knew, that I could beat Tiger Woods in sudden death.

Tiger stepped to the hole, glanced over to where my marker was to make sure he wasn't stepping into my line, and lifted out his ball to another deafening round from the gallery.

It took me a moment to realize I wasn't just one of the spectators watching Tiger play. I stirred myself and went to where I had marked my ball.

"Take your time," Bobby Jones cautioned. He had left the others on the fringe and walked over to consult and calm me.

I stepped away from the hole. I moved closer to the gallery and saw Kerry. Somehow she had managed to move herself through the patrons to reach the fringe. I could feel her presence.

"The grain breaks toward Rae's Creek," she said, holding me with her gaze, smiling wryly.

I grinned, thinking how she really didn't know what her comment meant. She was always picking up golf jargon from me and my playing buddies and tossing it back at me over dinner conversations, amused by our lingo, using it to tease me about my obsession with the game. But now she was just trying to keep me relaxed.

As if reading my mind, she nodded toward Clay, and added, "He told me."

The pros were smiling, Bobby Jones and Cliff, Jimmy Demaret. Even Hogan. They knew eighteen was too far away from Rae's Creek for it to make any difference in the speed or direction of the grain.

Tiger and Stevie had stepped to the far side of the green. They were waiting for this final putt, my last hurrah at Augusta National. If I missed we would be headed back to the tee at 18 and a play-off.

"Locke says it's a straight putt, Tim." Jones nodded toward Locke, who stepped forward to show me where to aim the ball. I could even see how the ball might hesitate on the ridge, then curl down the slope to the cup. I took my time studying the line, though there wasn't much more I could learn. I just needed to calm my nerves.

"Listen to Bob," Roberts ordered. "He built this golf course. He knows how to putt these greens."

I kept silent, thinking how Bobby Jones and MacKenzie's

masterpiece had been altered over the decades, with all the holes lengthened, the fairways and greens changed and tweaked.

I walked away from the pros, off the green, over to where Kerry was standing behind the green rope. A new murmur swept through the stands guarding the green at the sight of me approaching a patron.

"I'll make it," I told my wife, holding her gaze.

She reached out and touched my arm. I felt her smooth fingertips. Always when we were in need of each other, our first gesture was to touch. Her touch was all that I ever needed to feel secure again, to calm my nerves. I knew what I had to do to save our life together.

"I love you," she whispered, and then a wry smile worked across her face, "But make that putt."

I grinned, suddenly relaxed and stepped away from the fringe, from the closely packed spectators who gazed from Kerry to me and back to Kerry, silent during our whispered exchange.

What we all have to learn in life is that whatever patchwork of triumphs and tragedies happen because of our own family melodrama, or events beyond our making, we didn't get to where we are today all alone. Our lives depend, as Tennessee Williams wrote so long ago, on the kindness of strangers. It was a lesson Charlie Smith hadn't figured out quite yet. It was a lesson a lot of people never understand. But I was lucky. I realized I had strangers who had gotten me to the final green of Augusta National on the final day of the Masters. I was holding in my hands the old hickory club of the greatest putter who ever lived. I could pay him back for his kindness. I could pay back all the old pros who played the game better than any of us by winning at Augusta for them, for Cliff Roberts, and for my wife. And with that resolve firmly in my mind, I stroked the ball.

Time turns to slow motion at such moments, and as my ball

took its agonizing journey across the undulating green I followed its deliberate roll, marveling at each rotation.

And when it tumbled into the white cup the deafening roar of the gallery seemed to come to me from far away, come back through all the decades the game has been played. I spun around to find Kerry and saw Tiger striding across the green toward me. His hat was off, his hand outstretched. He was shaking his head at my unbelievable win.

I looked past Tiger and saw Clay lift the ball from the cup and hang onto the flag for me to take with me home to Illinois and then Kerry slip under the rope and start to run across the green, her arms already extended to wrap me in her embrace. I smiled and starting moving toward her.

Beyond Kerry, down the long fairway of the final hole I saw them—the legends, walking away from 18 green, walking toward the tall pines. They had just reached the forest of redbuds when Cliff Roberts stopped and turned and waved goodbye. He was smiling. An amateur had won at Augusta National. Bobby Jones's dream was realized. And Charles DeClifford Roberts Jr., the maestro of the Masters, finally freed from his earthly prison, disappeared one last time into the dogwoods.

A former caddie, John Coyne is the best-selling author of more than twenty-five books of fiction and nonfiction. A life-long lover of golf, Coyne has edited and written a number of books on golf, the most recent of which are his 'caddie' novels: *The Caddie Who Knew Ben Hogan* and *The Caddie Who Played With Hickory*. He lives with his wife, a magazine editor, in Pelham Manor, New York. Please visit his Web site at www.johncoynebooks.com.

CPSIA information can be obtained at www.ICGtesting.com
Printed in the USA
LVOW110011121012

302559LV00001B/55/P